W9-BZK-576

SISTER INDIA

ALSO BY PEGGY PAYNE

Revelation

The Healing Power of Doing Good
(with Allan Luks)

SISTER INDIA

PEGGY PAYNE

RIVERHEAD BOOKS
A member of Penguin Putnam Inc.
New York
2001

This book is a work of fiction. Names, characters, places, and incidents either are the product of the author's imagination or are used fictitiously, and any resemblance to actual persons living or dead, business establishments, events, or locales is entirely coincidental.

RIVERHEAD BOOKS
a member of
Penguin Putnam Inc.
375 Hudson Street
New York, NY 10014

Published simultaneously in Canada

Library of Congress Cataloging-in-Publication Data
Payne, Peggy.
Sister India /Peggy Payne.
p. cm.
ISBN 1-57322-176-7
1. Eccentrics and eccentricities—Fiction. 2. Americans—India—Fiction. 3. Vårånasi (India)—Fiction. 4. Overweight women—Fiction. 5. Boardinghouses—Fiction. I. Title.

PS3566.A954 S57 2001 00-062557
813'.54—dc21

Printed in the United States of America

1 3 5 7 9 10 8 6 4 2

This book is printed on acid-free paper. ♾

Book design by Michelle McMillian

ACKNOWLEDGMENTS

For the Indo-American Fellowship which allowed me to spend a winter in Varanasi, I would like to thank the Indo-U.S. Subcommission on Education and Culture, the Council for the International Exchange of Scholars, the American Institute of Indian Studies, Smithsonian Institution, and the Department of English of Banaras Hindu University.

To my dream-come-true agent Elaine Markson, I am grateful for making wonderful things happen . . . and so quickly. My editor and friend Wendy Carlton has devoted enormous skill and insight to bringing *Sister India* out into the world; and, bless her heart, she seems as excited about the book as I am. Thank you.

For their superb literary criticism, I am ever grateful to Laurel Goldman's Thursday afternoon writing group, including Linda Orr, Peter Filene, Angela Davis-Gardner, Dorrie Casey, and Pete Hendricks.

I am grateful for years of cafeteria lunches and literary counsel to Carrie Knowles. For the happiness that makes it possible for me to explore darkness, I thank my husband (and in-house psychological consultant), Bob Dick.

For critical feedback, recommendations, or other resources, thanks to Ardis Hatch, Ruth Sheehan, Lee Smith, Margaret Payne, Judy Brill, Georgann Eubanks, Clyde Edgerton, Larry Rudner, Dr. Nicholas Stratas, Dan Wakefield, Jeff Leiter, Leah Renold, Jeanne Fitzsimmons, Mildred Modlin, Dick Hester, Billy Moore, Brenda Summers, C. Michael Curtis, Mary Metz, Tim McLaurin, Bernie Asbell, Chap Johnston, Ellyn Bache, Kay Summerlin, Jack McDaniel, David Morgan, Lynne Tanner, Sharon Overton, Carolyn Bennett Patterson, Seth Gelblum, Randee Russell, Sattee Khanna, Elizabeth Cox, L. S. Suri, Sara Ahmed, Bill Finger, Rosemary James, Anne Fabbri, Diane Brandon, R. C. Smith, Gail Geiger, Betsi Koszalka, Wael Natour, and Nancy Olsen, as well as the work of Diana Eck, Gopesh Kumar Ojha, Swami Prabhavananda, Christopher Isherwood, and others.

I thank those I met in Varanasi for welcoming me: Jagdish Yadav, M. A. Dhaky, T. K. Basu, Bettina Baumer, Holmi Al-Ahmad, Arati Sen Roy, Sashi at Trimurti Guest House, Prakash Shankar, Shiv Kumar, Pratap Pal, B. C. Tiwari; Professors S. R. Jalote, Hersh Sarupa, Pandeya, R. R. Mehrotra, M. K. Choudhury, Mohan Thampi, D. K. Gupta, Suresh Vasant, and Sharma; and a most special thank you to Mr. and Mrs. R. P. Singh and family, and to Sakhai Prasad.

Finally, I offer my gratitude to editorial assistant Venetia van Kuffeler, to Celina Spiegel, to cover designer Lisa Amoroso, cover photographer Wendy Carlton, interior designer Michelle McMillian, copy editor Kim Seidman, foreign rights manager Cathy Fox, publicist Jennifer Swihart, Bill Peabody and the rest of the production department at Putnam, and Dick Heffernan and the sales staff. Thank you all. *Dhanyavad.*

SISTER INDIA

CHAPTER ONE

I AM the keeper of a small guest house in the holiest city in India. For more than twenty years—all my adult life—I have lived here: my great weight sunk, torpid in the heat, into this sagged chair on my rooftop patio, or presiding downstairs at the table that guards the entryway—a once-American woman taking down the passport number of each traveler, managing this inn for the Mohan Joshi family.

The newly arrived always stare: at my bloated flesh bathing in sweat, my fair coloring marked by freckles. I am not what one expects to find hidden away in Varanasi.

This is my home, though, the Saraswati, eleven rooms and a little restaurant, a view of the river, which at this moment burns with early morning light. From my roof, I watch it go by: the Ganges—Ganga, it is called in Hindi by those who revere the river goddess.

I gave myself a Hindi name long ago, just weeks after my arrival here. I am Natraja. It has come to suit me well. I answer to it in my dreams; never mind that I was born Estelle, forty-odd years ago. Such an old-fashioned North Carolina farm wife name did not fit me.

As Natraja, I have gained a modest fame. *The Lonely*

Planet travel guide each year advises the adventurous to come to my table: "Mother Natraja at the Saraswati is worth a side trip. A one-woman blend of East and West."

What the guidebook does not mention is that I weigh perhaps 400 pounds, twenty-five or so stone. I have more flesh than Ganesha, the elephant-faced god. Yet I'm told that once on my feet, I move like an Indian, sinuous and flowing. I've darkened some from the sun, but my hair is still ashy-blond, long and straggly, with threads of gray, and my eyes are light brown to the point of gold. Having these eyes, this huge body, helps me: people keep their distance. In a place just next to the Ganges, close to the pyres of burning bodies, newcomers especially are careful of anything that might unsettle them more.

Even so, the tourists ask me their questions. I rarely tell them anything. They can fend for themselves.

What they want to know I tell again and again to the waters that flow below this perch, a new audience with every moment, or to Shiva, with his many aspects and faces. In a sense, I have named myself for this most seductive deadly god: Natraja is Shiva's dance, the dance of the one who creates and destroys. The river itself springs from his brow, carrying both waters of healing and ashes of the dead.

From where I sit, my left leg gone prickly from the edge of the chair, I can easily see one of the phallic shrines to Shiva, the *linga*. It is below, there, just at the edge of the water, the stone image of a penis, waist-high, nearly, and thick as an oak, a smooth pillar giving off a dull glow where it is touched by sun, garlands of orange marigolds looped at its base. A worshiper adds a fresh offering now—he hunches like a gardener tending a shrub, arranging the flowers, pouring river water from a brass kettle over the rounded head.

The base of the shrine is a vulva, but people rarely notice the female organs, no more than grooves, which serve as a drain for the pourings of water. On some *linga*, a serpent swims in the female canal; on others, it may coil upward, winding itself about the phallus, or not appear at all. My shrine is too far away for me to see its details. But then, I require no reminder of the serpent within.

I see all I need to see from this filthy rope-weave chair. I have planted myself at the city's center. Of the million pilgrims who come to Varanasi each year, many will stop first at this bit of shore. My house sits yards from Dashashvamedh, the main bathing *ghat.* The city's waterfront stretches out on either side, a long curve of riverbend made into a series of waterfront *ghats*, each a tall flight of steep concrete stairs climbing several stories from the river to the level of the city's winding lanes. The bank is a huge set of bleachers facing the flow of Ganga, mobbed with bathers. I supervise them from my roof.

At the other side of my house, though I never look that way, is the city's complicated core: the *galis*, a great labyrinth of lanes too narrow for even a rickshaw to enter. This maze guards my house—like a thorny hedge, or the moat around a castle.

I live my life here, sitting and watching, the sweat soaking my sari and strands of my hair. With Ramesh to do our shopping—and surely he is the one to know what he needs for his kitchen—a year and more can pass without my stepping beyond the scarred table downstairs by the entrance.

I have no reason to leave the house, though once or twice in these years, Ramesh has led me down the *gali* for a glimpse of the market. But I will never reenter the world. My conscience does not allow it. Those who come to me do so of their own will. And they bring me more news from outside than I wish to hear.

Fortunately, I have learned many ways to end a conversation. Should I simply start to rise from my chair in the dining room, the guests at my table will look away, embarrassed at my panting effort. I come up here, latch the door behind me.

It is different, of course, with Ramesh—I watch him as I sit here each morning.

He stands in my sight, waist-deep in the river, at a distance of perhaps a dozen lengths of unwound saris. From here he is clearly visible, though the wet flesh of other bathers presses so close around him that the water does not shine between one person and the next. And I know him from the motion of his arms and head—he cups river water in his big wide-fingered hands, lets it stream down his face. I imagine it lukewarm, filmed with soap and oil like dishwater left standing. I feel it in my own hands, water that both soils and cleans. I feel it running down my face. I recognize his way of holding his shoulders, standing so erect that his shoulder blades nearly meet in the middle of his narrow back. I study him out of habit as much as anything; a mind cannot remain empty, or unwelcome thought will flood in.

For the devout, this is the hour of the bath. The sun is just up. Prayer and singing are over. Ramesh scrubs up under one arm; he bends his knees to let the water rinse through his underwrappings. He and the others are simply washing now, ridding themselves of their dirt and their sins. What crimes could he believe he has committed since this time yesterday, my irascible old companion, fellow monastic? He and I have lived beside each other in this house so long, he sleeping on his servant's cot at the wall of the dining room, I in my cell of a room.

There is a rattling behind me—who is it? But the door to the stairwell is shut. No one here. Perhaps my eyes closed for a moment and I dreamed it. Though if I dozed, it was not for long; or else the sun is slow in its journey up today. There is Ramesh still at the water, brushing his teeth with a neem twig, finishing his toilette.

My eyes return to a waking focus.

Then from below, a thumping, something being dragged. It's a little peculiar, though not of sufficient interest to move me from my chair. Travelers do arrive sometimes with great trunks, bringing with them all they own and enough pills to set up a hospital.

Most of that sort would never reach me, stopping, no doubt, when they take one look at the path that leads toward my house.

The *galis*, even more than the cremation grounds or the river itself, unnerve a foreigner. They have a hellish feel. Not enough light filters down between the buildings; it's too dark at noon to take a picture. Newcomers think they have entered the underworld.

I laugh at the uneasiness of my guests, coming in at dusk their first day, white and shaken in a way that heat and dehydration don't account for. They've read on the train: this is the Hindu holy city, the place to die, to have the body burned and offered to Ganga, the place to bathe and be purified. Yet they don't know how it feels to walk into a lane only two sets of shoulders wide and look behind them to discover the exit is no longer in sight. A fear rises, of being buried alive. But it's the only way to reach this spot, either by river or through these *galis*.

That sound again . . .

Odd.

Now it's like the wind moaning almost, but surely not in this stagnant heat.

It is a priest, no doubt, blowing a long note on his conch shell somewhere close by. Breath in a conch shell is an inhuman cry.

But Ramesh has stopped his washing. He stares toward a spot at the base of the building.

Pushing upward, I rock forward onto my feet.

Ramesh and so many around him, they are turned this way—something is wrong.

Close to the guard wall with my unsteady weight, I look over to the *gali* floor below, hear a scream.

The white-clad backs of two men—no, three—running head-down for their lives. They disappear into the alley beyond the next building.

Below, a man lies fallen to the paving—his legs struggle, feet digging at the stone. His face, in the building's shadow, is cut off from view. . . .

Where is Ramesh?

There—coming out of the water. Behind him in the water, parents huddle together with their children, faces averted so as not to have seen. Ramesh is hurrying up the steps though, wrapping his *dhoti* over his wet underbinding as he goes.

I wave at him to stop. He must stay where he is and not look.

He continues to climb, scowl on his face, lips pressed down hard. He comes up and up the steep steps, looking toward that same spot.

"Ramesh," I call out.

He glances once my way but keeps climbing. I know he has seen me. "Ramesh!" I scream. My voice has gone shrill: "Go back!"

But he does not.

I feel myself swaying. I must get into the house. The ends of my fingers hunger for the cool walls.

Lurching toward the door, I am seasick—where is the door latch? Inside, all will be as usual; I'll find him downstairs in the kitchen.

CHAPTER TWO

DAZED FROM the heat, groggy after her night on the train, Jill looked across the crowded market in the direction the rickshaw driver had nodded. She squinted in the bright sun, her eyes roaming the far wall of squat gray buildings. There was no road there.

Had she told the guy wrong? This looked like a farmers' market, women in faded saris sitting on their scraps of burlap, selling produce—those huge things had to be squash or some kind of gourd. But there was no time to look—not until she'd found her hotel and checked in, then she'd be free to relax.

The driver was patiently, condescendingly waiting. She looked again for anything that resembled a street corner. A bead of sweat ran down her chest. It was barely seven A.M. She wasn't certain she'd put on her sunblock. It would be so easy to get badly burned and wind up wasting her valuable time off. She felt again for the sack that hung under her shirt: passport, travelers checks. "Saraswati," she repeated to the driver. What had she done with the address? She crammed her hand into her pants pocket, searching for that piece of paper. Probably it was with her files and product samples, in storage at the hotel in Delhi.

In front of her, the man pointed again toward the far

wall of buildings, waggling his head and grinning. His teeth were stained red from the wad of betel nut bulging in his cheek. "Thirty rupee," he said, eyes shining as he gazed at her blond hair, short as a boy's, and her loose-weave safari pants.

Now he was laughing, tossing his head in delight at the sight of her running shoes, cut high on the sides for added support; her company had just launched this model with a major campaign. The driver pointed her out to a man standing nearby, who eagerly alerted a friend of his to look too. Well, they could just get used to Trakker running shoes; with all the work she had done in the last few days they were going to be seeing them all over India.

"Thirty rupee," he repeated. "Hotel is there."

She counted out the bills, adding a substantial tip. He was probably living on less than she spent on a haircut, pedaling the weight of herself and his rickshaw wearing only rubber flip-flops. Some men they'd passed had been pedaling barefoot.

"Madame." Jill was startled. Seated almost at her feet, a gaunt old woman was staring up at her from beside a mound of cauliflowers. "It is there," the woman said, with a tilt of her head toward the same buildings.

Jill looked again at that tight-packed row. From the eaves of one hung a hand-painted sign: "Communist Party of India (Marxist)." Big green wild parrots came and went from the rooftops, flapping and squawking. She still didn't see any street. The driver spurted a stream of scarlet juice onto the broken pavement, and smiled sweetly. "You are married?" he said. "Where is your husband?"

"Yes," she said, though at thirty-two she had never even lived with anybody. She gave him ten more rupees, and he swung back onto the bike and was gone. New Delhi, with its taxis and office buildings, suddenly seemed almost easy.

On the far side of the market, carrying her suitcase—the wheels squeaked too much, she didn't want to draw more attention—she came to a stop at the row of vendors along the front of the buildings. A man sat cross-legged on the floor of a little open-front stall stacked high with shiny aluminum pots. "Saraswati?" she said, assuming he spoke no English.

He waved flies away from a bowl of yellowish mush that sat at his knee. "It is only just around this corner," he said. "Follow to the side and you will reach."

She stepped to the edge of the stall and looked. There, between two buildings, was a space perhaps four feet from wall to wall, the buildings rising straight up high on either side. This was a street? It was about as wide as a double bed.

Even the buildings looked wrong: heavy grim-looking blocks with a balcony here, a turret there. In this holy city, she'd expected classical Hindu design, like Gothic, but softer and more fanciful.

The alley was hardly more than a crevice—it was unthinkable to walk in there. Her mind felt dull with fatigue.

But she saw now that people came in and out of the opening: a man with a tray of glass bangles, a boy pushing a little cart. Tall enough to look over their heads, she could see to where the passageway bent out of sight. She thought of the narrow lair she'd seen once when she was diving, of a giant moray, its head and a bit of body visible; the roar of her air had quickened. . . .

A hand grazed hers on the handle of her suitcase. She jerked the bag away. "I take," said a man who had materialized out of the crowd. He waited for her to understand: he wanted to carry it for her.

She shook her head, keeping a tight grip on the handle.

The cookware man had stepped to the corner of his stall, motioning her abruptly to go, go. This was the place.

She wiped at the sweat where her hair was pasted to her neck. The vendor lingered to see what she was going to do. She headed into the narrow lane.

The light was dim. What sunlight there was stopped high overhead, falling only halfway down one side, the bright open air taunting from four stories above. In this tight corridor paved with big slick stones, the heavy air and even the walls felt damp. People passing single-file close at her side seemed to glide at a different, slower pace, which only made her want to go faster. Two men in loose white *kurta* pajamas eyed her from the shadows of a doorway alcove, a steady, neutral gaze that stayed fixed on her as she passed.

She looked back, but the curve of the lane had already hidden the entrance from sight. Stepping over a wet heap of cow dung, she pressed on.

The lane made another bend. Then a fork, one passageway branching off to the left. A man in a loincloth crouched by a faucet, washing his clothes, his hair piled high on his head in a coil. She kept moving, hoisting her suitcase along with her knee; she imagined cool water from that faucet drenching her hair and clothes.

She probably had come three quarters of a mile, but it was slow going. It was good she had left most of the weight—suits, the blow-dryer—back in New Delhi. A little girl appeared in the lane ahead carrying a stained cloth gathered by the corners, full of a sodden weight. Jill had heard they burned the cow patties for cooking fuel. She'd had no time to read up on this place beyond that it was a holy city, and that was all she'd needed to hear: a restful sanctuary to settle her mind. The child came closer, about seven years old, wearing an ancient pink party dress like American children in the fifties. She passed, silent, at Jill's elbow, a ghostly little creature. Maybe she'd gotten the name of the place wrong: the client who'd recommended it had said it was a great location. The guidebook where she gotten the address had said it was for the adventure-lover. No one in sight now in either direction. If she had to, she thought, she could climb one of these walls. There were plenty of holds.

Up ahead—was that a sign hanging out over the lane? Please let this be it. A few more laborious steps, and she could read it: SARASWATI GUEST HOUSE—and there, beside the sign, was a curtained doorway.

In another moment, she had pushed aside the canvas flaps, entering a hallway lit with one bare overhead bulb. She slowly put down her bag.

She pressed the cramped fingers of her carrying hand flat against the wall at her side. She'd made it. Ahead of her were the three—almost four—long-awaited days of no worries, no responsibility. The smooth concrete felt cool; she could lean her hot face against it. She was exhausted. She'd hardly slept on the overnight train. On the floor, beneath the snoring businessman in the lower bunk, two boxes had knocked against each other all night in an uneven rattle. She stretched her other hand against the smooth surface, searching for its faint declivities with the tips of her fingers.

"Yes?" The voice came from behind her.

Jill whirled around.

Someone was sitting motionless, straight across from her, a woman who was immense, grotesque. . . .

"I didn't see you," Jill said; she could feel the adrenaline pumping in her chest and neck.

The woman's eyes were two lighted slits glaring out of a mound of fat that seemed to spread out into no particular shape. Her puffy hands lay on the ledger book on the table in front of her.

The bright eye slits were watching.

"You are wanting a room?" the woman said. Her accent was peculiar, half Indian, with a quality both familiar and unidentifiable. The mixture was disturbing.

"I have a reservation," Jill told her. This place—well, she could at least park her suitcase here long enough to search out a regular hotel. "It's under Thornton."

But the woman had stopped paying attention. She was staring at the doorway, flushed dark red from the top of her sari blouse to her filthy hair. Jill followed her eyes to the entrance as the woman began to shriek in Hindi.

Coming in the doorway, the flap swinging behind him, was an Indian man, dark, shirtless, not young, with white cloth tied like a towel around him. He looked damp, as if he'd just stepped from a shower. He gave the woman a moment of scrutiny and muttered a few gruff words, waving a dismissive hand. Then he disappeared through an archway into the interior.

The fat woman let loose another flood of Hindi, shouting after him. There was a wild note in her voice, like somebody calling out in her sleep.

Jill backed away from the table. Did this have anything to do with her arrival? Had she done something to set it off?

"Passport," the woman said, the terse word of English aimed at her, Jill. Before Jill could speak or move, the woman's eyes grew hotter: "Do not look at me that way."

Jill had tried not to stare, but there at the bare waist of the woman's sari was all that hanging flesh, layers of fat that were mottled and dingy-looking. "Sorry," Jill said. "I—"

"You saw I could do nothing." She must be talking about the man who'd come in; what else could it be?

Jill steadied herself on her feet, working at keeping her face calm and ordinary. She thought of her red Geo, snug and familiar, parked in the long-term lot at the Atlanta airport; she could feel the precise curve of the steering wheel in her hands.

Not a sound came from the dark corridor or the rest of the house.

"I told him not to look. I cannot be held responsible." Her voice rose as she opened the ledger. "Sign in this place." Jill signed. She'd find another hotel this afternoon.

A boy had slipped behind her to take her bag. She wasn't sure how he'd been summoned.

She followed his bare legs up a flight of stairs, a steep, narrow corkscrew they ascended holding on to a rope along the wall. Her bag laid across his shoulders, the boy led her down a dark hall, then gave her a key as long as her hand.

She let herself in the door. In the slivers of light from the louvered window, she could see a rope cot, concrete walls, wooden pegs for hanging clothes. Locking the door behind her, she shoved her suitcase against it and fell onto the cot. The ceiling was gray like the underside of a parking deck, the room so barren her thoughts could echo in here forever. She lay wide-eyed, one foot jiggling against the bed frame, trying with images of peaceful places to make her mind rest.

CHAPTER THREE

AT LUNCH, as usual, I sit with my guests, the two Israeli boys, the Australian couple, the girl Jill; all the others are out prowling the city. Over the last hour I have drifted into a state of watchfulness. I am like a crocodile sensing threat, sunk into a riverbank, betraying itself only by the gloss of its yellow eyes. Upstairs in the hallway, hours ago, Ramesh was weeping as he told me of the skirmish outside.

But I know the trick of staying calm: observe and catalogue the minutiae of the day; no memories, no fantasies or speculation.

When he began to cry, we stepped, the two of us, into a just-vacated guest room, closing the door against intrusion. Rumpled linens lay in a ball on the *charpoy*. "Outside," he said, "just now, a Muslim has stumbled against a vendor's tray, shattering the figurines of Lakshmi. Two others standing near took hold of him and beat him. The last blow—I saw this myself, *memsahib*—it crushed his chest. They told him he had dishonored the Hindu, that he had assaulted the mother of the world."

Ramesh stared across the empty guest room, the creases of his face full of his tears. Out the window, we both could see the smooth surface of the river's center, though not the near shore.

"They ran," he said, "the two thugs—hired, I know boys of that type—they left him gulping for air. And that young policeman, Jawahar, rested himself in a doorway just down the *gali,* looking me in the face and smirking like a bridegroom. I knelt with some others beside the man, a poor silk weaver, I could see from his hands. One thought to try to blow air into his lungs, but men of his community seized him; we were shoved away."

Ramesh seemed not to know he had swayed on his feet until the hard corner of his shoulder grazed my arm.

"He will not survive the hour," Ramesh said.

In this ground-floor cellar of a dining room, we sit perhaps twenty feet from where it happened, from the spot where Ramesh put himself in sight of those murderers.

"Bahut achaa." Dov, at my table, one of the two Israelis, is speaking to me. He grins, trying out his Hindi. Bright-faced, eager—he dares to laugh when Ramesh, coming and going from the kitchen, grieves at the horror on his sacred shore. The Israeli boy needs a slap across his face. He is handsome, though, his dark lips full, and only being playful.

"Yes," I reach for a platter. "*Bahut achaa.* It is indeed very good. Ramesh is the finest chef in the state of Uttar Pradesh." Ramesh, standing near, does not change expression.

These *roti* are like pancakes, almost—I have never thought of it before—stacked and still hot. I take one, first pressing on the butter with the curve of my teaspoon, then sugar, a generous layer. The pancake rolled, it fills my mouth, a pacifying sweetness. I would bow to the goddess of sugar in gratitude. It is a wonder I have any teeth. Dov and his friend are speaking softly, hurriedly, in Hebrew, no doubt planning their afternoon. At home in Israel they are probably accustomed to news of fighting, Israeli versus Muslim Palestinian. Yet, like me, they would not think of it happening here. My hands have begun preparing another bread. There is a narcotic rhythm to the motion.

India has been peaceful, relatively. In all the world, a holy city on a holy river should be safe ground. The Muslim invaders in this valley were defeated before America had even begun. How long does it take for rage to die?

Ramesh's bare feet whisper against the concrete as he goes again to the kitchen. He must not go out for his river bath tomorrow. Surely he would not consider it. I don't have to worry. I will die long before him, in my bed after dark, eating the sweets Varanasi is famous for—rich *ladoo,* nut paste *burfi,* flower-scented pistachio rolls, *gulab jamun*, and some nights even *rasmalai* mounded and soft in its milky sauce. I lick the paper bottom of each carton until it is pulp and my face is sticky with food.

I came here imagining a water garden, people of a thousand different sects living in quiet harmony, with their doll-like god-figures blessing every act of life. It was a child's dream of Eden. It is clear since this morning how I have lied to myself, for years taking the afternoon papers—which Ramesh has first studied like Torah—only for gathering my peanut hulls and empty sweet boxes. I have known of trouble not so far from here and managed to ignore it. No better than the police boy, I have sat wrapped in my thoughts.

Ramesh places more bowls of soupy, steaming vegetables before the young Australian couple, Eric and Laura, who are speaking privately to each other. Couples so wound together risk missing what goes on around them. These two would not know if a bomb went off.

People see them, though. Tourists in India are always startled if they happen to discover how their movements have been followed. How a stranger who sees you on the street can say what you wore as you passed three days ago at eleven o'clock in the morning. We live on top of each other here. It was like that in North Carolina, too, in Neavis; men around the gas station and the mothers of girls my age tracked me with their eyes, faces flushed with curiosity and blame. But they knew more than I did. All I had was what I overheard of their whispers.

Here there are no secrets; everything that happens becomes known. The knowledge seeps, house to house, the very smell and feel of an event traveling from doorway to balcony: it is as if each were there to touch where the man spit his blood onto the paving stones of Khula Gali within sight of the morning bathers.

Dov reaches for the cauliflower. "How have you come to this place?" he says, glancing toward me. "Why did you choose to live in Varanasi?" The American girl, Jill, looks up from her food. She is a pretty one, those eyes wide-set like Jackie Kennedy's, the lithe body of a swimmer—yet she moves like a mechanical toy.

The table has grown quiet; they latch their eyes on to me, even the couple. "Of course, you know I am asked this question seven times a week." Sipping my tea, I fan myself with a folded sheet from the newspaper. The to and fro of the hot breeze helps me keep my thoughts from stirring.

"What is the lie you tell seven times a week?" Dov says in his heavily accented English, laughing again, teeth brilliant against his toasty-brown skin. "Or do you tell a different one every day?"

"I came here from the U.S. with nothing more on my mind than the usual things, to see the spiritual side of life. I was near her age"—I nod toward Jill, who avoids my eyes—"or even a bit younger." She couldn't be more than twenty-two, her face like a wary child's. "And from the same part of the world."

The night I finally left, I was twenty and slender, accustomed to drawing glances even from people who knew nothing of me.

"Did you see it, the spiritual aspect?" says Dov's friend, a serious-looking boy.

"Yes, of course." Jill furtively takes note of me. She does not like what she has seen so far.

"Are you a Hindu, then?" says Laura, Eric's wife.

"As much as I can be. I wasn't born Hindu, as one must be. But

I have gone into the temple of Annapurna, where those who are not Hindu are never allowed, and I am accepted there. It is Annapurna, as you know, who takes care of Shiva and feeds him. I am certain you have all studied your Hindu pantheon before you ventured to come here." Ramesh is, of course, Hindu, like most, but today I cannot speak of this, not when I know that retaliation, Muslim against Hindu, will come somewhere near in a few days.

Eric picks at his food, eating only the rice. Jill, intent as a surgeon, is tearing a *roti* into halves and then quarters. They are new in the country, and nervous, though they have no idea yet what has happened outside our door.

"I will tell you a story," I say. "About my early days here."

Ramesh knows from my tone that I avoid the matter at hand. Why should I speak of it? There is no reason to frighten the tourists. It is a Hindu who will be the target in the coming days. Ramesh is the one who needs a bodyguard, though he doesn't believe it. He has the spirit of a bull, always knowing, with his twenty years beyond my forty-two, what is right and proper.

"When I came here"—I force the words out—"I lived in a room I rented from the Mohan Joshi family in a big house near Man Mandir Ghat, the family for whom I manage this guest house." The rote telling of the tale begins to take me over. "There was a young uncle in that family who became enamoured of me. Try to imagine me as I was once, not so different from yourselves. The young uncle—I always think of him that way, though he is closer to an old man now—he himself made a small doll of me from straw reeds, a stick figure that looked like some talisman for fertility. He dressed it in a bit of red silk, a sari that the doll wore perfectly because of the carefulness of his hands. He had made my long blond hair with gold silk threads.

"He showed me this figure. I admired it. Then he told me what he was going to do, so that I could look down from a high window in the big family house. On a full-moon night, he descended alone to the wet bottom step of the river *ghat* and splashed the doll with handfuls of water. I could only see well when he held the figure up—not toward the moon, though it might have seemed that way, but toward the downstream flow of the Ganges as it pours toward the Bay of Bengal.

"It happened that someone blew a blast on a conch shell at just that moment. Have you heard that sound?"

They all shook their heads. "Hear it before you leave this city. It is like the howling of a wild dog.

"That night from my window, I heard that wail and saw the silhouette of the man and the doll in the moonlight at the edge of the water. I tell you, there was a second when I could see the shine of the silk hair."

They are rapt in their attention.

"On the morning of the next day, I stopped when I saw him head into the rooms in the house where the family sold cloth."

All have paused in their eating. They think they are about to find something out. Putting down my cup, I stretch my arms out on either side so that I can feel the fat that hangs on my arm bones swinging. "He told me he had offered a prayer that I would become a good Hindu wife."

I know what it means to be such a wife. I can see Mama, standing there at the stove making supper, the air damp, full of food steam. I play near her on the floor. Her white legs, feet in pink sneakers with no laces. The pan lid clangs down on the rice. I reach to place a fingertip on an empty shoelace hole. "Move," she says. "I don't want you to get splattered with this hot grease." Vic is awake in the next room, putting on his work clothes laid out on the chair. He'll eat fast—fried sausage patties, tomato slices sprinkled with sugar—and all the while his eyes will wander around the room. He sits stiff—my stepfather—sops his bread in gravy, doesn't say a word until "Thank you, ma'am," when he finishes and puts his napkin beside his plate. In his pants pocket, he'll carry to work a starched white hanky I helped fold. Mama sits at the table, smoking a Lucky Strike, a little hint of a smile on her face all the time she looks at him. She and I will eat later, after he's at the mill.

My guests are silent, and all have the same expression: bland, expectant. I push to my feet, steady myself at the edge of the table. It is three steps to the mouth of the stair. All eyes follow me as if I were a performing elephant.

"I don't have to tell you anything more," I say. I am sick of their looking to me. I am not responsible; trouble has followed me. I look them one and another in the eye: there's nothing I can do. "I don't have to sit here," I say.

In the stairwell, I am hidden, hoisting myself upward in the narrow spiral. They think I can't do this. But I do it every day, holding on to this rope as thick as a fist. Two steps at a time—the wall sends my hot odor back against my face. I must get to the roof or I will scream for air.

CHAPTER FOUR

THE STRAP of her shoulder bag diagonal across her chest, her documents zipped into their various sacks, Jill slowed at the doorway into the foyer. The woman had already returned to her post, sitting just ahead at the table by the door. Jill hesitated, then strode ahead. "Hi," she said, too brightly. "Just going out exploring."

Natraja let the sharp end of her pencil drop against the table; the tiny tapping hammered fast, then dwindled. She made a shrugging motion that might have been a nod. In two long steps, Jill crossed the space in front of the table, reached to push aside the canvas flap that let in a sliver of weak *gali* light.

From behind her, Natraja's hard-edged voice: "You must go to Manikarnika." She talked in the carrying tone that marked the kids in high school drama club. She pointed her pencil in the direction Jill had come this morning. "The burning *ghat*. All the tourists go there. Dusk is the best time to see the fires."

"Thanks." Jill knew that, had just read it in the guidebook. Sunrise on the river—which she would do tomorrow—and burning bodies were the main sights to see. She glanced again at Natraja: vacant eyes. The woman obviously had problems, and it wasn't because of anything she or Dov had said. She wished the older guy could speak English. Outside, away from that woman, the *gali* winding ahead of her felt now like safe, familiar ground.

She'd walked for two hours, pushing through the crowds at the walls of the buildings. The traffic of rickshaws in these open streets was like a fast river through a canyon, wheels flashing by at the speed of a chariot race. She was certain every minute a rickshaw was going to run over her feet.

She pushed the wet hair off her forehead, imagined sinking down into a swimming pool. God, it was hot. She'd never felt such wet heat, even though she'd lived in Georgia her whole life.

In front of her: a tea stall, three tables arranged around an open doorway. A small boy knelt on the pavement beside a burner, frying bread. He tipped the wok full of simmering oil toward himself. He was on the verge of spilling it. She looked away, not wanting to catch his eye and distract him. She pictured the face of the man she'd stared at in the mall when she was a kid, maybe six, tagging along with her mother. His hair was red, and his face, too, swollen with acne. Whisked along in the opposite direction, she'd turned to stare as long as possible, and he'd looked back at her until he'd tripped, pitching forward—she'd seen it over and over in her mind, thousands of times. She didn't know if he got up, if he was okay. Her mom had even taken her back the next day to show her that no one was lying there. By the time she was ten or so, she'd mostly outgrown those episodes.

She dropped into a chair at one of the tables, glad for a chance to sit. Wasps buzzed around the little glass-front case of sticky candies and cakes. She needed liquid, anything cold and bottled. She was getting the woozy-headed feel of dehydration. The boy had cast an eye in her direction, noted her foreign-ness. He seemed to be in charge of the whole place, a child who looked eight but probably was twelve. She blotted the sweat on her face and neck with a paper napkin.

She'd decided against picking up and moving to another hotel, now that she'd seen what the city was like: just trying to cross a street was tricky—torrents of rickshaw traffic, and they didn't have stoplights. She needed water. What was the word for drink? There seemed to be no dictionaries in existence that spelled out Hindi words in the English alphabet, and even the proper nouns—she'd heard several names just for this city, Benares, Banaras, Varanasi, Kashi. . . .

From behind her came the sound of a beat, barely audible. In the high, swarming-crowd sound, with all its random shouts, she could hear a thread of singsong rhythm.

It was coming her way, growing more distinct: male voices, the same few words over and over. She looked around to see if others were noticing.

An old man leaning against the wall squinted at her; he was smoking one of the tiny cigarettes that looked like a joint. "Dead body," he said.

He nodded in the direction of the chant. "For burning. Many dead bodies every day."

It was coming closer: "*Ra-ma na-ma*," and a second line, hard to hear.

She got to her feet. She could see a bright shape traveling toward her, held high, the crowd opening a small space for its passage. Each beat of the chant rang out clear now: "*Ra-ma na-ma/Sat-ya hai.*"

Then it was in front of her, inches from her face, a human body bound in thin orange silk on a bamboo pallet. The corpse rode close to her eye level, the four carriers, teenage boys, weaving and parting a way through the traffic.

As they moved past, she saw how the head was tied round and round with packing twine, unmoving as the body rode with the rhythm of the boys' gait.

The chant, insistent, high-pitched, floated to her. She followed with her eyes; the orange, catching the light, looked like a sheet of flame. The boys cruised as a single unit through the traffic of dark heads. Forgetting her thirst, she set out after them.

They traveled fast. She darted left, then right, dodging pedestrians. She lost sight of them.

She got another glimpse: the silk shape tilting as it entered the mouth of a *gali*.

Of course—the maze of lanes lay between this main road and the river.

Only seconds later, the carriers' voices were almost smothered. A corpse in that narrow tunnel . . . She cringed at the thought.

She followed as far as the entrance to the *gali.* The beat of the chant thrummed, still faintly audible. She could follow from a distance. She stepped in. In the diluted light between the buildings, the dusk was almost night; lanes winding off in three directions; people slipping past.

She darted around the boy pushing a bike, the man carrying open bowls of white cream. The voices, the rhythm of that sound kept her walking. She was saying it with them in her head. *Ra-ma na-ma . . .* They were in sight again, just up ahead, pressing through the winding corridor that seemed to grow darker by the second.

A light brush of flesh against her arm, and she jerked away. It was only a kid, bare feet, bare chest, a boy running along beside her. His hand, damp and little, attached itself again to her arm.

"Hello," he said. "Hello. Come."

He was running, half skipping, holding her hand now, pulling her along. "Hello, hello." He looked up at her, smiling, as they ran.

Running with him, she felt as if she were being carried, everything flitting past, the faces, the openings of other *galis.* A man grabbed at the boy, swatted him across the head, yelled at him in Hindi, but they dodged him and kept going.

They passed shadowy doorways, now and then a barely visible face in the recess: a man with sunken eyes crouched against a wall.

"Baksheesh," he said. "Two rupee." His eyes were fixed on Jill. He squatted as if he were shitting.

Up ahead, the light looked faintly brighter.

A thin line of sky.

Then the *gali* opened and they were out. They were on the river.

She was standing in open air. Suddenly her legs were trembling; she was so relieved to be out of there.

In front of her, the water glinted gold from the sunset, out of sight on the other side of the city. Closer, along the steps, people went about their business in normal five-o'clock-in-the-afternoon light. She could stop a moment and pull herself together.

Before her, wide and shining, blessedly open to the sky, was the River Ganges.

The four men with the body had disappeared down the steps to the water's edge below, hidden from view up here where she stood. Their chant had stopped, releasing her.

Out on the water, a long rowboat crowded with tourists sat thirty feet from shore. Their cameras were firing; people scrambled over each other with long lenses, ignoring the boatman's pleas to stop taking pictures. She couldn't see what it was they were photographing, though she knew what it must be. This was the main burning *ghat*, below at the water's edge.

She hesitated to step forward and look, gazing instead out across the river at the empty white beach on the other side. She'd have thought the air would be smoky, but there was only a faint haze, a blurring of the view over the place below where she supposed the funeral pyres were. They sent up a smell; no, it was more of a feel, of grease in the air, like the exhaust from a restaurant. Her mind rolled at the thought. She needed water.

"Come, come." The little boy tugged at her arm again. He was a sweet boy, with an appealing face. She couldn't remember seeing kids look quite so wide-eyed at home. She wanted to look at him and nothing else.

She let him lead her forward onto the stone parapet that curved out toward the water. Below, in a semicircle of shoreline, a little man-made bay, half a dozen fires were burning, wood stacked high on each. She cast one glance wide across the whole swarming scene.

Tending the fires, scurrying from one pyre to the next, were near-naked men in loincloths, their heads wrapped in rags. Boatloads of firewood floated nearby in the water, piles of wood lay stacked against the walls of the shore.

In the edge of the river was the body she and the boy had followed, men stooping now to lift it out. She steadied herself, both hands on the low concrete wall in front of her. Wrapped tight in that orange silk, laid out on the steps, the body was soaked, dripping with Ganges water. She could see the particular shape of the feet where the silk had slipped loose; they were held close together in a single mesh stocking.

It was a woman's body, shorter than her own, and thicker. She imagined being carried out into the open like this, through the crowds, not even a coffin. . . . Had the woman known her death was approaching?

Another body was being carried to a pyre. They were baring the face; the mouth gaped. Jill felt herself draw back.

Below, a man stepped forward toward that bare face, that mouth, bending over in a *namaskar* bow of respect, saying his farewell, as the body lay on the logs. Another person stepped forward, and another. She pulled at the ties of her shoulder bag, picking at the knot. She should have gotten sleep before coming here, she felt empty, agitated. She looked around for other tourists, to see how they were taking this, but all the faces were Indian people who had reason to be here.

In Atlanta near her office building was a huge funeral home, and a block away in an unmarked low brick building was the crematorium. At least she had heard it was that. Dying wasn't something she worried about; she just wanted to get through the day without causing any disasters—leaving the space heater on in her bathroom and burning down her apartment building, or making a mistake with numbers that would ruin the company, make people lose their jobs.

She could feel the heat of the nearest fires on her face. Down where the men were shoveling up ash, the firelight flickering on their sweat-soaked necks and shoulders, the temperature must be deadly. The smell of grease would soak into your very pores.

Yet the impact of it all seemed to skirt just past her. What she was seeing now would hit her, in jagged little flashbacks weeks from now when she was back in the office, trying to meet a deadline.

"Madame, you must leave."

A man had stepped down onto this stone outcrop behind her. "Go now," he said. "Look one minute, two minute." Good God, what had she done? "Tourists are not allowed to look long. Please respect."

His posture had a stiff dignity, the expression in his eyes affronted. She hurried back to the spot behind the burning *ghat* near the *gali*. The little boy, whom she'd forgotten, was following close beside her.

From here the fires were hidden; all she could see was riverbank, the boats, and water, people going about their business. She glanced at passing faces; they'd probably seen what she'd done. Was this an okay place to stand? The child was staring out at the boats, bouncing a little to an uneven beat.

An older boy, a teenager, sidled up beside her. "You have seen the burning?" he said. "It takes three hours to burn one body. Firewood is very expensive." His face was movie-star handsome, his prettiness shocking after the face of the corpse.

"Come to my family's silk shop." There was a purposely playful air about him, a teasing smile. Maybe he was older than she'd first thought. . . . "It is near," he said. "Very beautiful rich silks, only look, no buy." The way he gestured with his forehead, he seemed aware of his long eyelashes. She didn't want to think about his eyelashes. "Sit for one moment," he said. "Take a nice cup of my family's tea."

Tea—she imagined the feel of liquid in her mouth.

"Thanks." She was surprised to hear her own voice. "But I have to go." It had been hours, she realized, since she had spoken.

He nodded to the child standing close to her leg. "He is not right," he said, touching his own forehead. "He is simple."

She glanced at the little boy; he was smiling, his gaze mild, undiscriminating. There was no sign on his face of thought in progress, of knowing how he'd gotten here or how to get back home. He was retarded, and she hadn't seen it.

She looked up at the sky, craving the space. What else had she not noticed? Overhead, parrots flew in long swoops from the walls, squawking. The heat must have addled her brain.

It was certainly night in the *gali,* though still sunset here. She remembered too late what she'd read: there were no roads to the burning *ghat*. The *galis* would be the only way to get to that main artery of rickshaw traffic.

Had the boy wandered away from his parents?

"What is your name?" she called out.

He and the teenage boy were punching and shoving each other now, laughing. The older one clearly knew him. The child obviously knew how to find his way around. If she took him to the police, that might get him into trouble.

She headed into the *gali* quickly, before second thoughts could overtake her.

CHAPTER FIVE

CROUCHED AT the kitchen drain, Ramesh inspected the lingering stain on the brass pot he'd just scoured with sand. He caught sight of his distorted image dark on the polished metal. He was near to being old: no one would have expected him to leap in and save the poor man. The pleats of his face showed his age; his body knew it was old each time he rose from this floor. Though he was not yet willing for his own release. His newest grandchild, Sunitra Caitlin, lived far away in America. He had never seen her, and it would be three years or more before the family would come home, surely with another as well by then.

He couldn't help thinking about it: the meager chance that he might have rescued the man. If he had climbed faster up the steps of the *ghat,* he could have arrived in time to ward off the final blow. Odds were, though, he only would have given the man longer to suffer and been beaten himself. And any blow Ramesh had managed to land would have been on a fellow Hindu; this troubled him, too.

He was not the warrior Arjuna these days, nor had he ever been, though the gods had given him many strengths that served him well in the life he lived. In most circumstances, he knew what was right; surely that virtue was the equal of any.

Tonight as the dishes dried, he would take the *Gita* from his bureau drawer. He would read about the choice forced on the great guardian Arjuna, when the noble one lets himself fall against the seat of his chariot, overcome with sorrow at the decision he must make: either to abandon his sworn duty or to go into battle against his kinsmen. He had by heart some of Arjuna's anguish: *My mind gropes in darkness. I cannot see where my duty lies. Krishna, I beg you . . .*

It was not, of course, those Hindu boys who hated the Muslim. It was political men, brigands among them who could seize some power for themselves with the outbreak of trouble and so gave word for the trouble to occur. Those men could now say to the most poor and ignorant Hindus: you see, it is the Muslim in lace cap emerged from his dingy neighborhood where the lanes smell of animal flesh and hide, it is he who disrespects you and brings you all your suffering. Elect us and we will protect you.

Living here in the *galis,* far from streets wide enough for a car, at least he didn't have to hear the loudspeakers that would squall these messages at the crowds.

His own responsibilities were clear in his mind, thanks to Ganga, who had listened to his sixty-odd years of prayer. He ticked off his proper duties, muttering as if reciting scripture: "I knelt at the side of the dying Muslim. In future, I will say no identifying word of the Hindu boys who shed the blood, no doubt for rupees to buy a sack of lentils for their mothers. I am wasting no gesture of respect on the officer Jawahar, a man charged with maintaining peace who stood idly by. Such louts should be sacked, sent to remand home like any other young hoodlum.

"The greatest thing—O Krishna, who counseled Arjuna." He felt the giddy surge of hope and gratitude that buoyed his daily petitions. "Hear me, Shiva and Ganga; I will pray as I have since a small boy with mother and father: whatever cries of fear Madame

Natraja might unleash, I will immerse myself each day at dawn, praying for the sanctity of the river, for peace along this shore."

He felt the tightness in his chest start to ease.

He wiped his face with the knob of his wrist. Finished, he leaned to set in place on the shelf the brass pot that held river water to bless his kitchen prayers.

With creaking knees, he pushed himself to standing, blew his nose on the cloth he kept tucked in his waist. At the sight of the clock, he hooted; it was a full quarter hour past when he should have boiled water for the rice, and there would be eight—no, nine—clattering in soon to sit at his dinner table.

CHAPTER SIX

LAMPS HAD come on in the little stalls that sat in cavelike openings off the lane. Coming to a fork, Jill couldn't remember which way she had come: neither looked familiar.

A woman approached, the hem of her sari pulled up like a scarf, shadowing her eyes. "Main road?" Jill said. The woman raised a hand and, staring at Jill's face, pointed over her shoulder. Jill took off at a run, her rubber-cleated shoes squeaking against the damp stones.

At each divide, she asked, "Main road?" and someone pointed. The route wound and turned and turned until she began to feel that surely she was traveling in the wrong direction, back toward the river. And then, with the same abruptness as before, she emerged, out onto the open-air street. The traffic—she was grateful to see it—milled past in front of her; from close by and from a distance down the street came the constant ringing of bicycle bells. She felt herself calming. Anybody who'd been cave diving ought not be afraid of tight places in the dark.

"Rickshaw, madame?" The voice was at her shoulder, a hunched man with one deformed arm.

She hopped up into the seat behind him. Half a dozen other rickshaw drivers had caught sight of her, calling out.

"Madame, he is old. Very slow."

"Madame, here, look—"

"Where are you going, madame?"

"Dashashvamedh," she said to her hunched driver, who was pulling them out into the flow of bicycle traffic. "Saraswati Guest House."

She leaned against the low back of the rickshaw seat, did a shoulder stretch. In no time, she'd be eating supper in the little dining room. She wished she could ask the cook, Ramesh, about the retarded boy, if he knew him and whether it was safe for her to have left him back there.

Up ahead of her, the street stretched wide and straight, jammed with people for as far as she could see. The dusk was yellowish, dusty-looking, hanging over the moving crowd.

She pictured night settling out on the riverbank. By now, they would be burning that woman's body, her skin bubbling and splitting. She felt for her neck pouch, the hard corner of her passport, then straightened and resettled the cord around her neck.

The man on the bike seat in front of her was pedaling hard. Ribs showed through his thin shirt; he leaned forward into the push to get up a hill.

Scenery was passing on either side. She didn't want to miss anything. To her left, the buildings—offices?—were three-story boxes, brownish-green, like water in a murky fish tank. And here was a peculiar sight: a man wearing only a shiny red loincloth stood, beating a tambourine and calling out like a street-corner preacher. She twisted to look. He was burly, well-muscled, not so bone-thin as the rickshaw drivers, and standing on a red cloth. The rickshaw swung sharply to avoid a cow; Jill grabbed for the handrail. Everywhere the sullen-eyed cows, surrounded by flies . . . At the street crossing, a handful of people stood in the jostling traffic, praying before a little metal figure that gleamed like aluminum foil.

From above the crowd, a loud whap! At the edge of a roof across the street, two goats were fighting, their curved horns clattering. They were about to topple, she was sure, fall forty feet into this traffic. Jill shut her eyes; the hot, gritty breeze poured past her face. She was tired.

One afternoon wandering in this city felt like months. Atlanta was so distant it didn't seem real. The coffee shop on the ground floor in her office building, her bike chained to the rail of her balcony—they were like fleeting images of places she passed once in a taxi.

The rickshaw was slowing.

It came to a stop.

Jill hoisted herself up to look over the driver's head.

In front of them, the traffic was pulled to a halt, the street a solid pack of bicycle rickshaws, humming motor scooters, and the yellow awnings of three-wheeled auto rickshaws. She couldn't see what was going on. Her man rested on his bike seat, wiping the sweat off his neck.

They waited.

The traffic inched forward—a foot, two feet—stalled again.

In the next rickshaw were six people piled onto the seat less than a yard across. An older man held three big children on his lap; a boy clung to the rickshaw on each side.

The massed congestion crawled forward again. They were almost into the intersection. There must be a thousand rickshaws within her sight.

She heard shouting, but she couldn't tell where it was coming from. Then coming into view: a knot of men, maybe a hundred, stood in a cleared spot in the intersection, fists raised, punching the air in time with their shouts.

"What is it?" she called to the driver.

"Politics mischief."

She wasn't sure if he was angry or frightened.

Some of them had red strips of cloth tied around their hair. She saw white teeth, bright against dark skin in the dim light. In the wild motion of arms upraised, she caught glimpses of one excited face and another. Now she wanted to stop, but there was no stopping: the packed mass of vehicles was taking her around the traffic circle toward the demonstrators. The man in the next rickshaw was on his feet now, yelling toward them.

She twisted to look for a policeman—the white-helmeted cop stood on the raised traffic platform doing nothing but blowing his shrill whistle. Couldn't he see there was going to be a riot?

Then she saw the body. On the pavement just ahead of the front wheel, not ten feet away. A man dragged each leg, pulling it toward the shouting crowd, the arms flung upward, the head lolled.

A flame licked out of one shoulder. It was on fire.

Then it was in the air, above the crowd: a fireball, coming down, going up.

An arm flew apart like a doll arm falling off, losing its stuffing.

Straw— God, it was only straw, the whole thing. They were burning a dummy, big as life.

"Go!" she screamed at her driver and the drivers up ahead. The men yelled louder as pieces of the figure fell in flames to the pavement.

Jerking forward with the weight of her body, she tried to make the rickshaw roll. Helmets of police bobbed now, along the distant edge of the crowd; they shone white among the waving arms. A bamboo billy stick flashed.

"Go! Please!" Her pulse beat in both her ears.

The driver motioned helplessly with his crooked arm to the sea of vehicles around them, a hint of reproof in his glance at her as he shook his head.

CHAPTER SEVEN

TONIGHT, THE sky is black, not a pinpoint of light. The girl Jill has returned this evening with tales of an effigy burning that has stopped the center of the city. The old violence between Hindu and Muslim, so long at rest, is out walking.

And yet the river air on my arms, on my neck, is soft.

Ramesh is inside, asleep, downstairs on his cot. I begged him to let me fetch a tub of river water for his morning bath. I offered him this roof for his private temple: to bathe in sight of the river as the sun rose. He would not hear me out.

I could hold him prisoner, bar the door tomorrow until the sun is well above the horizon and the sacred moment is past. But then there would be the next day.

Or as light breaks, I might take myself to the river with him to stand at his side as he washes. He so often urges me to go with him there, believing I will find comfort. But then later I would need to troop after him as he shops. And some days he does not tell me where he goes; it's his own affair. He is a man, I know this; I saw how he masked his expression when the Swedish girl asked his help with her sari.

Escorting him to the river would be futile, like trying to seize the water itself. What I know is that I would bring trouble on him, somehow, if I went. This is what I must hold before me, this and no other thought.

Just now the morning seems distant, though, as if it may or may not come. Down below, the dark water washes along the edge of the paving. I hear it, and the night grows almost cool, blending the city's supper smells and the dampening of the day's dust. I have so trained myself to lie low. I can almost believe that if I do not stir from this chair, all will remain as it has been. The violence will hold in abeyance, Muslims worshiping in their austere manner, Hindus with their parades and shrines. I will simply sit here for eternity in this soft air.

Slow—reach down with one foot into the dark *gali,* hold to the doorjamb.

Air wheezes in and out of me, the sound of it filling my ears. It must be near five, the darkness total: I cannot say if my eyes are open or shut. This single step down from my doorway takes more strength than climbing the spiral stair inside all day long.

It is done—I must pause, hand against this damp wall I cannot see, and get my balance. It has been two years at least since I stepped out the door.

In the night, though, such dread began to grow in me. I must find counsel. The astrologer Gomati I know has knowledge.

I will go and come back to the house before light has fully risen. No harm will come of it.

The dirt from this clammy wall does not easily brush off.

Inside my house, the walls are clean; Ramesh has help come in to take care of that. Passing through the dining room, I could see the white of his bedsheet faintly stirring with his breath, perhaps a quarter hour before he will rise.

Groping forward, I see nothing. This whole night as I sat on the roof, it was never so dark.

I won't sit up there this morning and watch as he wades out into the river, when Muslim vengeance can come to our door at any moment; and I know him, Ramesh, how he rushes to the center of every trouble.

My hip joints ache in the damp. There is emptiness to my right at the level of my arm: this must be the opening of the first branching lane. So slow in my steps—at least no one watches. I am stiff from my night in the air, not once closing my eyes. Staring for so many hours—I have not passed such a night since years ago. Gomati can say if he sees the trouble to be finished; that much will reassure me, and I haven't the courage to know anything more than this.

Along the wall here runs a window ledge, let my hand follow it—something wet, dung of a bird, or cow slobber. Wipe it onto the concrete, or carry it on my hand, a warning to all? Soon the path ahead of me will show. It cannot be long 'til light—by that time I will almost be there.

The light in this catacomb is faint now; twice I have had to stop to rest my weight against a ledge, but pushed off again quickly. Walking—the work of it—steadies me.

Out on the river, the sun is above the horizon. The awnings along this corridor that hide the narrow stripe of sky show the pale glow of the light they block. It has taken longer than I thought.

My astrologer friend will be inside his house, attending to his breakfast. The room where he works opens onto Lal Peda Gali, which I am guessing is only a short distance ahead.

Or he may be asleep still. He is no river bather; he puts his faith in the stars. Indeed he should—they have brought him a good living. Gomati has accused me before of disrespect for his profession. But whatever his tricks, he knows more than he has reason. In recent years, he has sent his wisdom by messenger, a boy arriving at the house on my birthday with Gomati's handwritten concerns for my future and a bill for services.

The straps of my sandals have sawed at my feet: I had forgotten the unevenness of the *gali* floor. Gomati will at least give me a place to sit. It will be as if I am in my house.

Up ahead, I see his room, a little cave opening in the wall a meter off the floor of the lane. He is not yet at his station.

I must hoist myself up onto this stage on my own.

Studying again the height of the wall, I see it is not possible. He'll have to come down into the lane and speak with me here. In the distance, a shout rises in the clanging of temple bells from down near the river. Closer at my head, someone scrapes a fork across a fry pan behind a nearby window, the smell of spiced potatoes floating out. Ramesh stands in our kitchen at this moment, freshly bathed, his hands fast-moving over tea and breakfasts.

"Gomati," I call out, reckless. I don't care who I might wake. The sun is up. He must help.

"Madame Natraja." His voice comes, mild and level, from the rear of the little room. He sits up from where he slept, hidden among pillows and stacks of books. Breathing heavily, grabbing at the folds of my sari, I straighten myself.

"So," he says, "you are liking to come to me today." Near the far wall, he has been lying on his side on a mattress that covers the floor of the room. He arranges himself slowly in sitting position.

"I am out for a walk," I say when I can speak again. "Running from my troubles." For a ten-minute wash in the river, Ramesh would risk his life.

"It is long since I have seen you," Gomati says. "Come into my office and put yourself at ease."

"How can I? You must bring me a chair and I will sit down here before you as if I were given an audience with a king."

He laughs. The last time he has seen me I was merely very fat.

Those who are fit and limber may step up into his room; I remember doing it easily myself. Now I hoist the folds of my buttocks onto this ledge; with arms and haunches, I haul my weight backward. There—my scraped and blistered feet leave the ground. I am up. I curse him for the lordly way I feel his eyes watching.

"I arrive without warning." I wipe my forehead with the tail of my sari. With the task at hand, I am myself again. A fan blows in the corner. Gomati is rich—this room has a door that leads to the rest of his family's house. He is big-bellied from his rich life and his lying here all day. Like me, he does not go out so often. He props himself against a cushion at the wall, pushes a big pink plastic comb from the top of his book of star charts on the little table. Gomati is proud of his thicket of beard.

He has begun flipping through his ledger of charts to find me. "You are having some special question to put before Gomati?" The two of us sit facing each other on the mattress. I see again what a coaxing smile he has.

"Tell me what you see."

He takes my hand—how long has it been since anyone has done such a thing? I think he was the last. He holds it palm up in both his own small soft hands. He waggles one of my fingers, checking the looseness of its joints. His eyes glaze, and he begins to rock from his hips as he cradles my hand.

"You are soon having strong dental problems," he says. "Some difficulty in this area."

He tries my patience sometimes.

"Your tranquillity"—his voice quavering upward in his professional singsong—"it is not good. You are both water and fire; there is always the conflict in your nature. That is there, this conflict. I have been telling you."

"Always you are telling me the same thing." Two men have now stopped in the *gali,* watching, not troubling to contain their amusement at the sight of me. In only these few moments, I am beginning to gather a crowd. Creeping closer, edging into the room with us, are three children, elbows already up onto the mattress; faces, shoulders, bare chests coming up into view, though I never see them stir. Each time I cast a sharp eye toward them, they are motionless, three small, dark-eyed faces, the girl with a wild mat of hair. The men, now joined by friends, are falling against each other in fits of laughter.

Gomati ignores all, continues his rocking, watching me, his chin lifted.

He hesitates. In his gaze, I see a hint of something I do not like. Tightening his grip on my hand, he leans toward me. "I must tell you. In this autumn month we call Kartika, in this time, the planets bring a new position. A change." He has stopped his rocking, his eyes locked on mine. "This period makes great difficulty. The danger," he says, "is also present."

He pulls at my arm by the hand he holds. I yank it away.

"Do not play games with me, Gomati."

"Only I am telling you: before the full moon of Kartika, a guest will disrupt the peace of your house."

None will disrupt me. I will not allow it.

"What of Ramesh, Gomati?"

"You will tell me."

How could I? What do I know of the man who lives so close to my side? He gives me only his Hindu bible verses and nags about my health and diet. Already he lived at the house when I arrived, newly fattened, to replace the old innkeeper so suddenly fallen ill. He—Ramesh—offered me from the first a starchy friendship, from the formal distance of his station.

"Gomati, I won't settle for this."

"Madame, I know only the ancient sky." His gaze is opaque, his plump lips pursed.

"So." He unfolds his legs, speaking again in his normal voice with a brisk businesslike air. "I have told you the truth. It is two hundred rupees."

The three children are sitting in the room with us, the boy nearest with the bare soles of his feet stuck out in front of him. "Madame," he whispers, "madame, please, one rupee." Then the other children are calling: "Madame, madame, madame." Beyond them, the audience in the *gali,* people line the opposite wall, some sipping on little clay cups of hot milk tea. I see them etched so sharply in the gray-green light, a mob gathered before a spectacle. Did people watch as the man was beaten in the *gali*? The faces stare at me, eyes dull with waiting. The danger could come from any direction.

Tossing my money purse at Gomati, I push myself up.

Smiles hovering at their lips, the men watch as I struggle to get my feet under me. The wind of the fan plays with the hem of my sari, coming and going across my legs. Eyes roam over each swollen layer of my flesh. They relish their disgust.

Blind, I reach a hand out for Gomati's aid. In one knee-jolting step, I am standing down among them, maneuvering myself onto the path to my house. They are so small, these men, thin and underfed. In the moment before they draw away from me, I feel their heat and air whisper against my upper arms and shoulders. Their faces float—teasing eyes, mouths—the crush of them around me traps my smell. They dare not stay close. They fear me, of course. I am monstrous beyond any Hindu demon, well able to manage my guests.

CHAPTER EIGHT

THE SUN blazed on the stairstep-riverbank. T. J. Clayton shifted his clipboard where he had it propped against his leg. It was ferociously hot for this early in the day; nothing in north Florida to compare to this. The bare strip of mud bank under the pumping station was dry and fissured except for one little ditch where a narrow stream of water was heading crookedly toward the river.

A few steps down, Dr. Rai was supervising a couple of his grad students, who dipped test tubes into the river. The water was turbid, full of grit and trash. What he could see in it set his teeth on edge, and that didn't even take into consideration the fecal coliform count.

He let his gaze travel along the shoreline, crowded with people bathing, with goats and water buffalo, all the old maharajahs' palaces up along the top of the steps. In spite of the water quality and the dung-smeared shabbiness of the old buildings, this bend of river was a sublime sight to behold.

His host, Dr. Rai, climbed toward him up the bank, a thin guy with a lot of matinée-idol gray hair. The man had been expecting a Ph.D. scientist like himself, not a bureaucrat, that was clear. He was just a county-government middle manager with a grant. He suspected the foundation had funded him to fulfill some quota: he was probably their token rustic, or perhaps actually their once-a-decade investment in something urgent and practical. His mission was to find a way to stop people from dumping garbage into the backyard stream he'd fished his whole life. But so far it didn't look as if the Indians had even a start on an answer. They'd been working on it long enough, though, with their Ganga action plans, at least to be able talk about what hadn't worked and why.

Rai was shaking his head. "The students have no discipline." T. J. looked at the three young men huddled on the wet bottom step marking test tubes and packing them up in a nice little wooden case. "They have no dedication to the inquiry," Rai went on. "I find, as a general rule, that the adults who volunteer their time on the cleanup project are far more careful in their efforts." He focused a penetrating gaze on T. J. "With the youth, it is much the same now in your own country, I am told."

"It's terrible. My fifth-grader couldn't tell you the names of five presidents."

A deeper frown crossed Rai's face. No doubt he'd wanted to hear something more weighty and global. Dr. Rai was not what you would call easygoing, hauling him out here just after dawn. A sophisticate like Rai ought to know about jet lag and how it could cloud your brain.

He was determined not to stay at Rai's house any longer than necessary. He wasn't even sure why he'd been paired with him. Rai was working with an engineer at Berkeley and some others on algae ponds for water treatment, whereas T. J.'s own interest was in the public relations campaign.

He wanted to know how they'd persuaded a fair number of Hindus to use the electric crematorium instead of the pyres that would leave body fragments unburned to rot in the river. And for his part, he was prepared to talk about farm runoff and the incentives they'd used with landowners along the Nagacochee, if anyone wanted to know.

"Come," Rai said. "Mrs. Rai will have breakfast ready."

T. J. cast a parting glance at the wide expanse of khaki-colored water. A quarter mile out, a fish rolled, so close to the mud color of the river it was as if the water had bulged upward for ten seconds. It was big, six or eight feet, and as wide-bodied as a manatee. Probably a river porpoise. He'd never seen one, but he didn't feel like asking Rai about it. His eyes scanned the surface for one more moment: this was the Ganges. He'd come here again by himself to give it the kind of admiring a body of water deserved.

Rai's car—a Maruti—was waiting on the nearest street, the crowds flowing around it like high tide around an island. It was a dignified little vehicle, with the upright posture of an old Mercedes or Citroën. The seats were plumped up higher than on American cars, the upholstery had a deeper pile. He rubbed a hand over it; this was what his grandmother would have called "sumptuous," except that it was like crawling into a microwave. You could cook in here in a minute or two. Rai, in no apparent hurry, was paying the ragged boy who'd kept an eye on the car. The wet students with their case of samples had vanished into the crowd.

Rai steered calmly through what seemed like a solid mass of people that parted again and again at the last possible second to allow the car through. T. J. felt his foot jerk toward an imaginary brake: they were constantly on the verge of plowing into somebody.

At home he insisted on driving; he liked to have his hands on the wheel. Jane had apparently realized, finally, that he was the better driver and given up arguing with him about it.

At the house, Rai got out and unlocked the chain on a big metal gate, pulled the car into his enclave. The place was nice; coming in the night before, he could not get a good look. It had been too dark. The garden between the wall and the house was a swarm of vines and flowers. That real deep orange looked like *prunifolia* azalea, but he'd thought that grew only in Florida and Georgia.

Inside the house, the concrete walls were smooth and cool-looking. This was the way he envisioned the interior of a monastery—spacious and simple, no clutter.

"Hello, you are ready for some breakfast, I hope?" Mrs. Rai stood before him in the doorway in a gold sari. The silk and her skin seemed luminous, her glossy hair worn up, and a *bindi* between her eyebrows.

"Breakfast sounds great," he said.

"We are vegetarian, I'm sure my husband has told you. I hope you will be happy."

"I'm sure I'll be very happy."

"Please come in and sit down." She motioned him to a chair in the living room. "Our home is your home. We are glad you are here." Then she disappeared down the hall where her husband had gone. Handsome woman.

He rested his head against the wall behind his chair. At home it would be about midnight. Jane would be out in the hammock on the porch, where—though neither of them had mentioned it—she'd slept most of the time lately. He didn't like to think about what a month away was going to do. But the grants people were operating on their own schedule, not his. So was Jane. And Dr. Rai.

He heard a rustling and lifted his head. A little girl likely no more than about eight years old was standing in the doorway with a tray. She came and set the whole platter down before him on the coffee table.

"This isn't all for me," he said to her. He feared it was: a stack of round breads, lots of relishes, which were no doubt hot enough to smoke his eyeballs. She smiled and pulled at the hem of her shirt. Pretty little thing, tiny hoops in her ears and dusty bare feet—she looked to be a couple of years younger than his Sally.

"You speak English?"

She continued to look at him, smiling.

No English, or maybe she was just shy; he wished he had some toy he could give her. He missed his girls already.

One of the wildlife patrol guys had asked him recently if he was going to try again for a boy. What in hell would he want with a boy? The amazing thing was that he could be the daddy to anything as sublimely perfect as Sally and Elizabeth. He could sit for half an hour and watch Elizabeth play in her sandbox, burying pop-beads and trinkets and digging them up again. She was so much like Jane, dark hair that showed red in the light, both so intent on any little thing they were doing.

The Indian girl was still looking at him.

He was tempted to offer her one of the round breads, but that would probably bring on a diplomatic crisis.

Mrs. Rai glided into the room. He stood up. She motioned him down.

"I apologize for not serving you myself," she said. "But Amrita is with us since her birth, like a member of our family. Dr. Rai will rejoin us shortly. He has something he must attend to." She was gone again, the child tagging behind her.

Was he supposed to begin eating? Manners had not been a big issue in Da Nang, which was the only other place he'd been outside the country, except for the Bahamas.

The prickly smell of spiced food came up at him in a wave. He hated not being on sure ground.

Dr. Rai returned then and settled his bony frame into the armchair across the room.

"I had a communication by the e-mail from one of my colleagues in Germany," he said. "The man is at an impasse and wishes me to share his despair. Some numbers in which we had placed much hope have failed to crunch, as you so vividly say in America."

"Sorry to hear that."

Mrs. Rai came in with her husband's platter, set him up for business, and took a seat near him with her own meal. She and Rai began eating with their fingers—he looked from one to the other—using the pancake breads to gather up bites of casserole without getting the first drop of juice on themselves. T. J. took up a floppy bread, arranged it in his hand like a washrag.

"Your own work," Rai said. "It is not such an easy thing to undertake, getting people to clean up their river. But certainly the situation must be drastically different from ours here."

"That's exactly what I'm here to take a look at—precisely—to see just how your pollution-control program is handled from a grassroots standpoint, compare notes with what's being done in a couple of the instate river municipalities at home." He cringed at the government jargon coming out of his mouth.

"Here in Varanasi," Rai said, "we have a complicating matter which you presumably do not face in your town. Hinduism, as you know, considers this river divine. It can be very difficult to persuade the devout that a divine being needs taking care of. These people instead expect that the deities will take care of them."

"My husband does not place much hope in god or man," said Mrs. Rai, pouring Rai more tea. She met T. J.'s eyes for a longer-than-you-might-expect moment of amusement. She was probably fifty, five or so years older than himself, about ten younger than her husband. She had presence. He had a quick image of her at home in Satterfield, running for mayor or for Congress. He'd tell her to keep it all: the sari, the red dot, that worldly glance that made you think of cigarette smoke and older actresses like Lauren Bacall, if Bacall were darker, of course.

"I'm not a great one for sitting around hoping, either," T. J. said. "It's going to take a lot more than that. Our water quality is deteriorating by leaps and bounds."

Mrs. Rai flashed her dark eyes toward him as if he'd said something marvelous.

"Leaps and bounds," Rai murmured, gazing toward the top shelves of his bookcases, pressing down his hair with one graceful hand. Dr. Rai did not find him marvelous.

"I'll be wanting to find a place to stay, of course," he said to Rai, "and I was wondering what you recommend."

"Our home is yours, Dr. Clayton. There is no need to go elsewhere. Though I do understand that usually the visiting scholar wants to find some spot that is peculiarly his own. Are you thinking that you'd prefer a hotel or a flat? If you take a flat, you'll wish to hire a servant or two, and we can certainly help you there."

"A hotel, I think. Something small, close to the river."

"You'll take him to see our friend Mrs. Natraja?" Mrs. Rai said, smiling, lifting her eyebrows. Her eyes were bedazzling.

"I am thinking," Rai said slowly. "It is the center of the city there, at the Saraswati."

Mrs. Rai frowned. "That is true."

"A political rally there this week"—he turned to T. J.—"has caused some concern. It follows on an incident of possibly sectarian violence. But then, as my wife has mentioned, I am something of a pessimist and I may well exaggerate the seriousness of these matters. I know that Mrs. Natraja will take good care of you."

T. J. looked over at Mrs. Rai. Like a ballroom dancer, she'd followed Rai's lead. "You will come and visit us," she said. "My husband is right. Madame Natraja will make sure that you have every safety and comfort."

CHAPTER NINE

THE LEDGER page grows damp under the weight of my forearm. He stands—this new one Rai has brought—waiting for me to hand over the book for his signature; he is sway-backed, belly pushed forward like every white man ever born in Hawley County. In Neavis, boys of eight years old knew how to stand like that.

Rai must take him away.

"I don't quite place your accent," he is saying as he grabs up a pen and reaches across. He smells of Bay Rum, the bottle wrapped in basket weave; boys in high school wore it. I have let him yank the book away from me; he is flipping open the cover of his passport. "Where are you from?" he says.

"North Carolina." He has me transfixed, like a diamond-headed cottonmouth, its tongue shimmying, the stalk of neck lifted and swaying.

He smiles to himself, copying numbers into my ledger. Ramesh's voice carries from the kitchen, talking politics with Rai.

"Now, where in North Carolina?" He would use the same ingratiating tone if he were here to kill me.

"Little town in the eastern part of the state," I hear

myself falling into that old manner of speech. Why do I even answer him? "You wouldn't have heard of it."

"Probably a lot like Satterfield. In the Florida panhandle."

Neavis had a population of 3,000, though people like us out on the highway weren't counted.

"I'm here doing some research," he says, a strut to his voice.

I hate his type. "It is common," I say, "that we have visiting lecturers here."

He laughs. "Any of them staying here now?"

Gomati might say this is the dangerous one. If so, he has already done all the harm he is going to. I have recovered myself; there will be no more reminiscing.

"I'll put you in number two," I say, pushing myself up from my creaking chair. "On the first floor." I will escort him to a room myself.

In the hallway, he follows too close behind me, the straps of his various bags strung over his shoulders. I hear his shortness of breath. Two hours I have been home from seeing Gomati, and now this man arrives.

"How many nights?" I say over my shoulder. Is it possible I forgot to ask?

"A month."

I come to a halt.

Behind me, he has stopped to gawk into the corner room that has been left door ajar. "Most of my guests are here for only a brief stay, two nights, maybe three."

"Well, as I was saying"—mopping the sweat off his ruddy face, eyes roaming a room that is not his to look at—"I do have business here."

Ramesh stands at the counter slicing *karela* for dinner. "I think you are not listening," I say in Hindi.

He shrugs.

"Take me seriously in what I am saying, Ramesh. You need to be careful. This is something I know."

He lets this pass over him. "If you would wet your feet in Ganga each day," he says, "this would help you to calm these fears you have. Tomorrow, bring yourself to the river with me."

"Every day now I will have your going out to fear. Who knows when there will be some retaliation? It could be on the same spot here beside us. You could be coming through Khula Gali to the house."

"Come to the water. Stand at my side and watch over me, you and the shining goddess Ganga."

"You use this time of trouble to try once again to convert me. I cannot go with you. Besides, if you did not go, I would have no reason to fear."

He rinses his knife. He will say nothing to such an admission of feeling; it would not be proper. He has, after all, a wife in the ancestral village of his parents, little more than a day away.

"You would not say this to an Indian woman, telling her to go out in time of trouble."

He laughs. "*Memsahib,* you are not Indian."

Ramesh is wrong. I do not need to go out to the river. From this roof I can feel Ganga as if she rushed around my chest, seeping into the folds of my fat.

Why should I go? Even from here, the day nearly gone, I can hear the river chide me: what use have you made of the safety you have had here? Sliding past, the waters sing to me by name: Estelle, what do you do?

I fill my mouth with sweets, over and over: I eat.

"Estelle, Estelle, Estelle." The sound is like evening temple bells calling.

I wait to hear the river's secret voice, whispering what I cannot imagine. Down below, a boy with a stick calls, *"Hei, hei,"* hurrying his water buffalo and her calf out of the water. The concrete steps of the *ghat* echo the cloppings and snortings.

I sit here day after day, year after year, straining to hear something more than the noises of the day, though I expect I will sit until I turn bluer than the neck of Shiva and not hear a syllable.

What the river does give me are the circles of women singing on the bank at dawn. Ten women or twelve will walk to Ganga together, different groups from different neighborhoods, to make their morning *pujas*. It is a lovely thing to see them circled together on the bank and hear the sound float up.

I envy them. But as Ramesh reminds me—as I myself told the young uncle long ago—I am not an Indian woman. I am hardly a woman at all.

Sometimes, I think how I would like to see my mother. But I content myself with her letters. Of course, I send the money orders to my half sister to be sure Mama has what she needs. What else can I do?

Out on the river, a long overloaded rowboat is passing, a good twenty people sitting along the sides, burlap bundles piled in the middle. The voices of the passengers seem close, the stroke of the long oars so slow, as if the boatman is digging down to the clinging mud of the river bottom. At the bow, water breaks white with each surge forward; the riffle makes me thirsty.

My limbs go to sleep from sitting. I must stir, lift my arms off the sticky wood of my chair, hold them out for a moment, to stretch, to cool. When I raise my arms, I am lifting weights, so much flesh pulls at my bones. It takes strength to be this big.

I have become strong; I can stare at whatever comes my way. Once, years ago, as I was being rowed in a boat down to Assi Ghat, I saw the bloated body of a child float past. When a child dies, the body is not cremated, it is given straight to the river. Facedown, hair waving, a little swollen hand trailing, the shoulder bumped against the oar. I met the boatman's eyes, and we said nothing. I am able to keep my silence.

It is the trouble in the city that threatens us, I know, not the guests, whom I rarely see except at dinner and sometimes not even then.

CHAPTER TEN

MARIE JASPER stood just inside the canvas curtain of the Saraswati, propping herself on her three-pronged cane, touching her cheeks and upper lip with a tissue from her travel pack. "My travel agent wrote ahead," she said to the shocking-looking woman seated at the desk, "but at the time of my departure, we had received no reply."

This must be the "Mother Natraja" the guidebook mentioned. They could have said a lot more than they did.

"I have your letter. Your room is ready. Six nights. River view."

"That's very nice news. I'd hate to have to set off looking for another place. Yours is not so easy to find."

"Nothing here is so easy to find."

This innkeeper seemed to be studying her every wrinkle and gesture. She had mean little eyes in all that fat. How did she bear the heat in such a condition? So far, though, to her credit, the woman had not offered the usual patronizing comments: on the wonder of Mrs. Jasper's coming so far with such infirmities at her stage of life, etc.

But she had to admit, she was tired, ready to take

her pills and lie down. The drive from Bodhgaya had taken three times as long as it looked on the map.

This Mother Natraja still had not troubled herself to produce a room key, or the ledgers for her to sign.

"What has brought you to this city?"

"Pleasure." Surely that was all that was needed—business or pleasure. But the woman continued in her silent staring.

"I'm from Cincinnati. My husband died three years ago—Michael Jasper, the pianist."

She touched the Kleenex to her temple again; she felt impatient. It was the heat and her fatigue. This woman had such a hungry way of staring. "I have some trouble with arthritis," Marie said.

She looked around for Dilip, her guide; she wanted to be done and go to her room. He was out in the lane; she could hear him flirting and cajoling in Hindi, the way he did with her in English. She knew that tone.

Marie started to speak again, then stopped as she glimpsed a fleeting expression on Natraja's face. While she had turned away, Natraja had been looking at her, taking in details with an expression altogether different from the sullen glare that was now firmly back in place. In that glimpse, Marie had seen a childlike look, the set of Natraja's brow and lips softened. No doubt it was a rare occasion when an American the age of her parents registered at this desk; probably it was mostly young backpackers who dragged in.

Natraja busied herself with organizing.

Marie carefully took in the elegant line of the features dimpling the fat face. It was possible she had been a beauty.

Clearly aware of scrutiny, Natraja slammed her pile of documents back into the drawer. "We will complete the paperwork at another time," she said. "Ramesh will show you to the room." She noted Marie's one compact suitcase. "Your own porter will have a cot in the dining room. When you're rested, come up to the roof and take tea."

Tea? She tried to picture the other residents of the house: a rag-tag band of solitary travelers, maybe a few young couples. Of course, she wanted to meet people, but dinner would be soon enough.

Natraja eyed her cane. "Since you've made it this far," she said, "I expect you'll be able to make it up the stairs. Have a good rest and then come. A view of Ganga is good for the joints."

From an old garden chair up on the cracked-and-patched rooftop patio, Marie looked down the river. The whole city was sitting up high along this curve of shore, and down at the far end in the bluish haze, she could see the fine lines and arches of the distant railroad bridge. At the water's edge in front of the house—down a hundred yards or so of steps—three white-*dhoti*ed men were slinging wet fabric against rock, the heavy slap of it repeating against the buildings behind her.

"Do you believe wading in down there will cure me of my ailments?" she said to Natraja. It seemed it would be just the two of them up on this barren concrete square. If the place were hers, she'd have greenery growing along the guard wall, blooming hibiscus, perhaps a couple of banana trees in big tile pots.

She was feeling much better after a little sprucing up. She'd changed into a fresh flowered blouse and unpacked the roll-up hat she'd brought for the murderous sun. It sat down tight on her head, pushing her hair into a wispy fringe: unbecoming, but necessary.

"I couldn't make you any guarantees about a cure," Natraja said. Apparently she was taking the question quite literally. "But there are a lot of people who would."

Natraja was presenting herself in a pleasant enough manner now, chatting on about the Ganges, which was, after all, the reason Marie was here: to sleep in a room that looked out on the holy river. And indeed her room did have two louvered windows, albeit narrow and screenless, that let in voices, bird squawks, even the scrape of oars, as well as two hot shafts of river light.

"You know, if you think there's a chance of a cure," Marie said, "you and Dilip could throw me straight from here into the water and I wouldn't have to fight my way down those steep steps."

Natraja laughed, a surprisingly girlish titter, then quickly recomposed her face. Marie brushed at a smudge on the knee of her Perma-Prest slacks; she'd always had a knack for putting people at ease.

"Many of our guests have claimed to be healed here," Natraja said. "Relieved of their pulled muscles, their depression, their deteriorating vertebrae or skin conditions. They come in at dinner proud and eager to tell their tale of healing, like fishermen showing off the catch of the day."

"I expect you've met a lot of people here. Do you keep up with many?" She took a sip of the tea, almost like cocoa, it was so milky and sweet. The air up here had a smoky cooking smell she couldn't quite identify; maybe it was coming up from the kitchen.

"The guests? No. If I took that on, where would it end?"

Marie let her gaze roam down the long arc of city front, the row of palaces and temples high over the river's edge. To have this to sit and look at every day—Cincinnati was a very pretty city; she thought that again every time she saw Paris. Cincinnati stood up very well, with its steep hills that were getting to be more and more of a problem for her, and its river. But this went beyond beauty. It wasn't a question of beauty, really; the scene offered so much to look at, with all these people living their lives out here in the open, praying, and brushing their teeth, shampooing their hair. She tried to imagine herself soaping up out there in the river. It seemed so cozy and companionable. And of course, she could avoid the difficulty of getting herself in and out of the tub. A big-bellied man in what looked like a primitive droopy version of one of those thong bathing suits was oiling his arms and his stomach so that he shone in the sun. Farther along the shore, a cluster of huge mat umbrellas for the holy men tilted every which way, like a mushroom forest in a Walt Disney movie. If all of this were packed into a painting or a fabric pattern, she'd complain it was too busy. This was the precise opposite of evenings at home in her condo: the blue-white glow of the refrigerator light; she'd lean to take out the Styrofoam doggie bag from dinner at a restaurant the night before, then dump it onto a plate. Usually she'd play the radio, listening to the NPR commentators. Music, since Michael's death, was too painful.

"About this bathing"—she was fascinated by it—"do you take baths in the river yourself?"

Natraja looked out at the water. "Not in many years. I did it once. The river was cleaner in those days, or maybe it wasn't and we gave less thought to such matters then. Now even some of the devout Hindus do not drink the waters. They bathe and they pray, but they are careful."

"Well, one wouldn't have to drink."

"Thinking about it, are you?"

Marie laughed. "What do I have to lose?"

"You could get sick and have to go home. You could get sick and die."

"If I thought like that, I wouldn't be here in the first place."

Natraja fell silent, cradling her teacup in both hands. A gaunt man in saffron swaddling was slowly poling his way along the *ghat* with a staff. He seemed to make infinitesimal progress. "Holy man." Natraja pointed. "More or less."

"I've read about them. I'm a lifelong Lutheran." Natraja made no response. "What about you?"

"Southern Baptist."

"Oh, my. They're having quite the to-do at home among the Southern Baptists. The liberals and the conservatives have had a time."

"I can imagine."

"It's been in the Cincinnati paper. The conservatives want to believe every last word of the Bible as the factual truth and insist everyone else do the same."

"Sounds like you keep up with the news."

"I keep up with everything."

"This is a time of religious holidays here; you might find it interesting. We have just had Diwali, and the Kartika Purnima, the full moon celebration, will be coming soon."

A streak of green zipped across the guard wall—gone before she'd had time to jump. She fumbled for her cane. "What was that?"

"Wall lizard. They don't bother anything, they stay where they belong up on the walls."

"I don't know that I like lizards."

"You get used to them. Have one of these." She pointed to a particularly gooey candy in the box that sat between them.

Marie took a bite of a honey-soaked morsel, wiped her fingers. It was obvious what had made Natraja fat. A few of these every day could bring on diabetes in a week. They were excellent.

"I have thought of putting up a sign to warn people to expect the lizards, not to rouse the whole house in the middle of the night because they have seen a small creature dart across their window. But I don't do it. Why should I stand in the way of the traveler's experience?" She let out an unattractive snort. "There is a guest house here that posts a sign: 'Beware for Monkey on the roof.'"

Marie helped herself to another sweet. "Does your Ramesh make these?"

"No, no, the universe provides. There are sweet shops all over the city. Everyone has their favorite. You'll see them when you go out tomorrow."

"Tomorrow is when I would like to go ahead and have my dip in the river."

Natraja stared at her, the candy stopped at her lips.

"You're going to do it?"

"Yes, and I think it would be nice if you would come."

"If I would come," Natraja repeated, pressing the rest of the cakey sweet into her mouth.

"I want you to tell me exactly how it works. Is there a special way to go about it?"

Natraja's attention seemed to have drifted to a spot somewhere out across the river; her jaw worked slowly. "Sunrise is the prescribed time." Her eyes, when she roused, were dull. "More than that, I cannot say. Prayer and magic don't interest me."

CHAPTER ELEVEN

MY DINNER guests still in the other room eating, I fling out onto my desk the New Delhi newspaper.

The overhead bulb turns the front page yellow: a train car derailed; doctors on strike; a ten-wicket sport victory. . . .

The dread I feel is like a ghostly presence outside of me, fighting the very lift of my arm as I turn the page, spread the paper wide. To look at the news, after so long . . .

Fast as my eyes can move, I scan: news of "Pak-trained ultras" and authorities who have been negligent in some other state, an ad for a ski resort offering "thrilling excitements." The Saraswati, too, could advertise its excitements. My eyes dart across the pages. Laughter bursts in the other room; my guests are all the same. I have sat with more two-night faces than there are paving stones in this city.

I can find no word in the front section.

So casually I asked the boy from Amsterdam for the loan of his newspaper, as if it were nothing.

A political cartoon shows goonish men with their parties written on their bellies. I don't care about these details. I want only that the danger cease. My finger slides down the column of editorials—a hanging stayed, and then: "Clash in Varanasi."

"Calm holds today in the face of violent incident."

"Holds today . . ." as if it might collapse at any moment.

"Charges of police excess . . ." my eyes swallow the paragraphs whole; "houses entered to search out arms." Searches in the Muslim sections would only sharpen and focus the fury.

I have gripped the paper until there are crumpled handholds on either side. I was wrong to pick it up.

Ramesh knows of these events and has not wished to tell me.

What do I do? I have no recourse. Only Ganga herself holds sway over him.

Better that there were no river, that we faced dead, stinking mud. . . . Let him worship that.

It is more than fifteen years since I have descended those steps. Yet where else is there to turn?

CHAPTER TWELVE

MARIE GRIPPED her cane, felt her way forward another step. Sunrise was supposed to be soon, yet the *gali* was so dark that if it weren't for Natraja's pale hair faintly visible up in front of her, she'd think she'd gone blind. The air had the damp-dust smell of a basement.

Natraja was moving too fast. Twice, Marie had asked her to slow down. She was acting like a child, not thinking somebody near eighty with bad knees might need to go one slow step at a time. Up ahead in the dark, her sandals slapped onward.

Marie felt for the wall to get her bearings. Her hand touched stone coated with a sticky dampness. She drew it away. It had been a mistake to insist on doing this. She could simply stand here on this spot until the light came up, then find her way back to the guest house by herself.

A bell clanged from a rooftop just above, so loud and close she could feel waves of vibration all the way into her teeth. The sound died away; then came more ringing from a merciful distance.

With her cane, she located the next little ridge and dip in the stones, carried herself forward another step.

"How much longer?" she called up to Natraja, now lost but for the sound of her feet. How could the path to the river be so long when the water was right in front of the house?

"A few meters." Natraja's voice sounded muffled. "We're almost there."

One near stumble at a patch of jumbled paving, and suddenly the two of them were out, standing on a wide silent street in ordinary darkness that was rapidly thinning. Marie felt a rush of gratitude to be out of that tunnel. People were slipping past them, ones, twos, groups walking together, heading toward the steps that led down to the river. She had the feeling she should whisper, but Natraja spoke out loud: "This is the vegetable market just above the main *ghat,*" and pointed out a man nearby who was bent to unpack great bundles. Other vendors, Marie now noticed, were arriving.

The sky was growing lighter, darkness fading from the direction of the river. Dawn would be here in minutes.

They stood at the top of the *ghat*. Beyond the milling people, the wide river threw off a matte glow; the light was up, if not the sun. Getting herself down these steps to the water looked impossible; she'd foolishly imagined the worst was over when they'd emerged at the market. A two-foot drop from one step to next. It wasn't as if the Indians had such long legs. People weren't built for this.

She looked to see how others were managing. A girl carrying two big babies took the steps quickly, absentmindedly, following a passing boat full of tourists with her eyes. A boat tour—that was obviously the way she should have done this.

"Madame, madame!" Two eager young men were racing up the *ghat* toward her.

They came to a halt on the step below, made a latticework of their crossed arms, and held it up to show her. A chair—they had in mind to carry her.

"Please, madame," the taller one said. The other one smiled up at her and pantomimed sitting, poking his butt out coyly, daring her to do the same. If this was a service they performed often for tourists, they would know the English words for it. She was about to become a spectacle.

With a quick look over at Natraja, she left her cane standing on its three legs. Facing away from the water, she felt as if she were about to launch into a great arc of a backdive into the river. Then, rising around her: four arms, two chests, the smells of curry and hair. Her feet left the ground; she was riding backward, pressed between the two men, their muscles tight as wires.

People turned on every side to watch her pass, and the splashings of water grew gradually louder behind her. Then she was tilting forward—ejected, her feet touching down on wet stone not six inches from the lip of the concrete, level with the water. Bits of flowers and dry grass, odds and ends of cloth and paper and trash floated, collected against the bank. She held on to the hard thin arms of the young men until she was sure she had her footing. Michael had been a big man, not what people expected of a pianist; he was broad in the shoulders. These two seemed so small.

She handed them each some rupees, a generous stack of small bills, and looked around quickly for Natraja. Maybe she'd decided to wait at the top. When she turned back, the men were gone, vanished into the crowds of dark faces and bright clothing as if they'd been erased. Slipping away—that was the way to die, not the way Michael had gone, straining for oxygen.

Her eyes wandered along the *ghat*. There was Natraja—three quarters of the way up the towering stairway to the city, easing herself down to a lower step, balancing with Marie's cane. How could she have missed her—that bloated shape wrapped in yards and yards of sari the same mud color as the river? She watched her reach again with a foot, tentative, concentrating, for a second exposing a wide white triangle of calf. The woman was huge. How could she even walk? And yet here she was, out where she hadn't set foot since she was a girl in her twenties. It was surprising how easily she'd acquiesced.

Nearby on the lowest steps, some men were laughing, Marie realized, at Natraja. "That's enough of that," she called out before she'd thought twice.

First one and then the rest abandoned Natraja to gape at her; Marie felt their curious eyes travel over her, pausing at the hanging folds beneath her chin, at her still-admirable bosom, her loose pleated trousers. You'd think they'd never seen an old woman.

From behind her and then from another direction came a sudden burst of singing, women's voices. More choirs began, then, all up and down the bank. The sweetness of the voices! Groups of women singing together—seated, squatted, kneeling, each gathering a circle facing a cloth piled with flowers, fruit. When had they come? They swayed as they sang, heads covered in saris, facing one another then down the river. Each group was like a bouquet: the brilliant saris, orange, pink, turquoise, shimmering green, some of the silks edged with heavy gold brocade, one a deep ruby red.

She was standing at the edge of the holy Ganges. Across the river, a rim of light pushed onto the horizon.

She heard Natraja step down beside her, winded; the handle of her cane returned to her hand.

The sun was going up so fast, a half circle visible. She couldn't help but think it: like a baby's head. The bottom half of the curve was easing into view.

Ahead of her, down in the water, thigh deep, a man with a wet string running the length of his torso was praying. He chanted out loud and offered handfuls of water toward the sun. She could see the shine on the water in his hand, and beyond him, little gleams of light hitting all across the river.

She braced one hand on Natraja's wide arm, lowered her cane, her foot, then slowly her other foot down into the water. She stood calf-deep on the submerged step, soaking her pant legs and, in seconds, the water filling her shoes.

The sun was up.

"Morning," she said to herself, the way her daughters had called out when they were children playing house and the moments-long pretend night was over.

Beside her, Natraja stood, looking into the sun the way you're not supposed to, the faintest rim of water shining in her eyes.

But the moment was already over. The man who had been offering handfuls of water to the sunrise was soaping an armpit now. A woman her age was washing herself up under a bright yellow sari that was virtually transparent with the weight of the water. She could see the woman's fat middle, her big slumped buttocks. This was like a city with no internal walls, people washing and brushing their teeth, elbow to elbow. She was glad she'd lived to stand in the midst of it.

Natraja stared out across the river, the pink bright in her cheeks, the hem of her sari soaked and swaying with the motion of the current.

It had been minutes, and Natraja didn't stir. She stood steady as the concrete edge of the bank. The intentness of her eyes was like a yearning animal's, at once expressive and unreadable.

Marie felt a sharp twist of envy. All she'd been doing herself in the last year was staying alive, dutifully chalking up new experiences. She wanted to be seized by something—something other than grief.

CHAPTER THIRTEEN

THE RICKSHAW pounding across another break in the pavement, the fat of my abdomen quivers on its surface like liquid.

The driver struggles at the pedals, rocking his weight from side to side. I feel feverish, glands in my neck swollen and tender from the shock of all I have eaten.

A small boy in the cab of a passing auto-bike fixes his gaze on my bare rolls of stomach exposed by the sari; he nudges his sister to look.

I could rise to my feet howling, pointing my finger at them and their parents and the aunts and uncles crammed in around them. The sound is coiled in my throat: it would bring these crowds to silence.

Chowk is crowded tonight, always crowded, always rush hour; nothing has changed. I shift to fit myself better onto the narrow red bench, its neat plastic cushion. It is years since I have been out to ride, eight or ten at least. I want to keep traveling, that is all; the driver has instruction to go where he likes. My house is now stained at its very cornerstone with the Muslim's blood.

More shouts and jeers at my driver from other rickshaw *wallahs.*

There, near the wall, a knot of people surround a man crushing sugar cane in a press in the bed of his cart; selling the sweet juice. The smell comes at me over the heads of pedestrians, a boggy, intoxicating waft laced with the dust that hangs over this twilight uproar.

Sunrise at the river has stirred me; the new guest has upset me: she tells me to come to the river, and I do it. Since then, smells are too strong, and the memories, all day, such odd bits: a school stairwell with its stale-gym-clothes smell; milky blue floor wax widening into a puddle on linoleum. I suspect these thoughts. I suspect my revulsion at the thought of the foaming sugar cane juice and the rush of giddiness it brings. I fear anything that disorients me, the bits of memory that might rise.

Better for death to slip over me quickly, when I am not expecting it. I give permission for this to happen.

Tonight, my guests lingered at the dinner table as I left, still reaching for another *chapatti,* and another. Ramesh eyed me with reproach; he sees what I have taken from the kitchen, all of the rosewater syrup, the steamer of leftover rice. He does not know I went to the river this morning and this is where it has led. He knows nothing of Neavis.

Marie behind me in the dark this morning, I thought of a time sitting in the car with Mama, the old black Nash broken down late at night by the side of the road. Part of Mama's face shone in the yellow glare from a security light up on a pole nearby, strands of her blond hair lit almost white. We could have walked to a phone to get help, but she said somebody would come along. She fiddled with the radio to find the announcer she liked, the velvety voice of the man on "Our Best to You"; he read poetry: *"Ah, Cynara, I have been true to you in my fashion. . . ."* When there was music, she leaned her head against the seat, staring straight ahead, and told me stories about her family.

The circle of the lighter on the dash and the ash of her cigarette glowed orange in the dark, brighter, dimming, bright again, with a bitter smell. I must have been eight or nine, Mama still talking about how she and Vic were going to find us a place at the beach to live in one of these days.

The windows closed against the cold; the air mixed cigarette smoke, Mama's perfume, and the faint undertone of gasoline. I could hear the rustle of burning when she took a deep drag. The next day at school, I could smell smoke and flowers in my hair.

Was it gardenia perfume? I am not sure.

That was the bush that bloomed at the corner of the house; the sweet aroma came through my window at night, bringing me unconsciousness.

"Driver," I call out. "Driver."

He peers over his shoulder at me. "Here?" he says, slowing, angry bells going off all around us.

"Take me to a scent vendor. The closest."

"Scent?" A flicker of amusement crosses his face.

He guides us again into the flow. We ride.

Night is falling; soon I will be hidden from all eyes, even from the passengers of rickshaws skirting close by us in the darkness, running without lights as they do, racing past with only a rush of voices and the whirring bicycle bell. The road dust feels thick in my throat. Tonight I ate nothing as I sat at the table. I had changed my clothes after bathing from the bucket. But still I feel smeared in sticky filth from the afternoon—three boxes of candies, enough rice and syrup-dripping bread to feed a family.

The crowd widening up ahead—I recognize this market from years ago. Over at the near corner, a scent man sits cross-legged among the bottles in his open window, visible in glimpses through partings of the traffic.

"Here!"

Lowering myself to the street, the rickshaw barely drawn to a halt, I step around the wheel of a bicycle, over the little open stream of water running at the side of the road, and arrive to stand before this man who sits in a window at the level of my waist.

"Madame." He leans in a sinuous motion to greet me. He is young, with a light, smooth, almond color to his skin, an angular face.

"Good evening." My lungs pant from this exertion.

"You would like to try, madame?" He is waving a hand over his best sample bottles in their wooden case; so many scents in one oily invisible smoke; it is heady, this blend. Behind him are shelves and shelves of glass-stoppered bottles along the two walls of his stall, disappearing behind him to glitters in the deep dusk of the little hall-like room.

"Jasmine," my scent *wallah* says. "Sandalwood. Marigold. Very good." He is holding one of his cool glass stoppers to the inside of my wrist. I want to press my face against that coolness in his tapering hand.

"Give me gardenia."

"I have it." He wipes it on, next to where he has placed the jasmine.

"This does not smell like gardenia."

"I am not deceiving you, madame."

Taking the stopper from his hand, I try it on the inside of my elbow, far from the other shiny streak of oil. It smells like a fresh-cut tree, pine. "This is wrong. It's nothing like gardenia."

"Marigold," he says, offering a different stopper with the barest flutter of frustration across the darks of his sleepy-lidded eyes. "Very good marigold."

Where is my driver? We'll find another vendor. It may have been Vic who planted the gardenia bush; I'm not sure.

The low light in the house seemed to make the smell heavier; it drifted along baseboards, around corners. The big squat shrubs around the place kept the rooms constantly dim—unless you cut on a light—and damp, which ate away at the boards on the porch.

"Fill one of those little bottles with the jasmine," I tell the man.

The scent man picks up the medium-sized. "No, there, the

smallest." I point to the tiny ones the size of a Christmas-tree lightbulb. "I want the smallest, the very least."

Disappointment clouds his face. "Only this, madame?" He glances over what he can see of my body.

I was not always like this, I want to tell him. I can feel how thin my legs were, one against the other, as I lay on my side. . . . I had on short shorts, a sleeveless summer blouse with pearl buttons, Reggie close beside me, the dirt underneath us giving off its cornfield smell. For one second, he pulled back from kissing me: "Are you my girl?"

I murmured again that I was, I always would be. "In just a couple of years," I said, "we'll be old enough to leave. We'll ride separate on the Greyhound bus to Miami, acting like we don't know each other. Then we'll take a boat to the islands, the Caribbean, where nobody will care that one of us is Negro.

"Reggie"—I said his name out loud, forgetting to whisper.

Quick, he clamped his hand down over my mouth, listened, one ear on the ground, one to the air.

The fronds of the corn rattled in the breeze. A bug buzzed.

He waited. I didn't stir, though his fingers were wrapped so tight across my face I could feel my teeth cut into the inside of my cheek.

Glass clinks against glass. The waiting scent man is giving me a sideways look, his bottle lifted, the hot clamor of the street all around us. I want to lean over close to him until my lips brush the folds of his ear, whisper to him what I want.

"Jasmine," I say. "Nothing more."

He shakes his head mournfully, pouring a stream of amber oil that runs like a thin shining string from the mouth of one bottle into the other.

It is just verging toward nightfall when the rickshaw steers in the direction of my *gali*. The time has passed so slowly. I crave the darkness. We have ridden in circles, I think; until my mind has begun to settle. Sitting high on this seat, erect, I am a queen, smelling of oils heated by the night and my own flesh. It is no different, really, from my perch on my roof.

Up ahead, there is a disturbance—the clashing of metal, and shouts.

The rickshaw has stopped, all are stopped around us.

I raise myself to see, but I know what it is: this is not serious; violence would be quick and nearly silent. It is only some parade, not even a demonstration.

There, just ahead, it passes on the cross street above the crowd, the rigid head and shoulders of a deity image carried high; I have not seen a Kali procession in so many years. Handing my driver a week's wage, I let myself down to the pavement.

Boys step aside for me.

The noise grows louder.

The *murti* procession is breaking a space through the crowd: another Kali figure, nearly as big as a human, is propped on the seat of a rickshaw. She comes closer: the dark goddess, her red pointed tongue protruding, her sunken eyes rimmed red, a string of severed heads around her neck.

This is Kali, the fierce and bloody consort of Shiva.

The shouting around me grows more feverish; bodies press close against my arms. Young men are approaching with the goddess rickshaw: gyrating, banging their cymbals, pans, drums. Their eyes are bright, their lips and teeth shine. Kali rides high above them, the motion riffling her long hair.

A cracker blasts only meters away.

Closer: the face, the eyes, the tongue, her breasts bare—she wears only a girdle, the linked hands of dead men, her red lips made to gleam as if with blood, like the live, wet lips of those dancing at her feet. My tongue licks at the night air. The man nearest, his black hair shining, his dark mouth—I want to pull him into the *gali* with me, force his face between my legs. A circle inside the top of my head whirls. The crowd sways.

When I open my eyes again, a small boy, standing close, gazes at me. The crowd has thinned; people follow the goddess to the river. The boy stands in the pool of blue-white from an early streetlight, solemn face and dirty shorts, feet bare. I have the mad impulse to tell him what it was he saw on my face. The little snake of pleasure can still twist forth from where it is buried, even after so many years.

I like his somber gaze; he is not a bad boy. I make the face of Kali at him, eyes wide, tongue hanging, teeth bared, holding out my arms as she does to hold a sword and severed head.

He laughs.

He snaps at the elastic band of his little shorts, and giggles.

He holds out his stick arms, rolls his eyes, lets his tongue hang out the corner of his mouth, and falls to the ground, pretending to be dead.

"Get up."

He closes his eyes tighter.

"You must get up from there." I push at his bare waist with my foot. He lies limp, trying not to laugh. His ribs like twigs—

A cold, bad taste rises in my throat—I must go. The boy's body laid out before me, and all around the street is emptying for the night. A Kali parade—everyone knows how passions are stoked. . . .

Stumbling in my haste, rebalancing—this is surely the direction, down this alley. The boy—but I can't look back. He will be safe when I am home within my walls.

CHAPTER FOURTEEN

YOU WOULD like some postcards?" The man's narrow shoulder kept edging in front of her.

For the tenth time: "No, thank you." Jill kept walking.

She'd thought she'd be able to wander unhindered out here on the river in the middle of the day. Her plan had been to hike the length of the city along a lower level of the *ghats,* parallel with the water that slopped onto the bottom step a few feet below.

The hawker had locked into pace with her, his face so close she could feel his heat. He flipped open a book of out-of-register scenes of Varanasi. "No." She turned her head, looked out at the water; it didn't matter that she needed postcards, that Ben would be expecting one.

"Boat? Madame, boat?" A boy was at her other side now, walking a step below. They were closing in. She looked at the bright open space up ahead: it would grow more distant as she approached, like a mirage. Hawkers had been at her elbow since she stepped out of the house.

Even the big guy from Florida had complained last night at dinner about being hounded, and if anybody could make them stop, he could.

"Very good boat, very cheap."

"No boat. No postcards."

The card hawker riffled through his stack, a blur of India pictures held so close to her face that the fanning of the air made her blink. Before she went home, she'd get some shots of these wildly exotic buildings to sketch from, maybe the smaller mosque behind the Golden Temple. "Look," he said, "only a moment."

Then the other guy: "Boat. One hour. Forty rupees."

"No." And more vehemently: "No." It sounded feeble even to her own ears.

"Thirty rupees only." He pointed to one of the long, open rowboats stationed below at the bank.

"No boat."

"Thirty rupees," he said sternly, as if she were a child defying him.

"Good-bye." She dodged left, up the steps, away from the water.

The hawkers followed, holding their places. Now the one with the postcards was holding up a jar of red powder, and another of bright pink. Was it makeup? She wanted to grab the jars and hurl them as far as she could. There was no peace in this holy city.

Heading for the top of the *ghat,* she leapt up the steep steps.

The two of them stayed with her.

She stopped, looked one, then the other, in the eye. "Go away." She felt a surge of wicked delight at saying such a thing.

But neither man was giving up.

"No boat ride?" The boatman was pleading with his eyes.

She shook her head. His woeful look made it more difficult.

He hopped up the step to stand beside her.

"You are very nice lady," he said. The postcard man, catching sight of another tourist, suddenly darted away.

"This is the fact," the boatman said, his face earnest. "Many of the tourists, they are not nice. They treat us like dogs. It is true."

"I'm sorry to hear that." She did know what it was like to try to sell a product, and you had to admire these guys for their persistence.

She began walking again, slowly. He came with her.

"But you are not this way," he continued. The shape of his eyes—they seemed almost to curve upward at the outer corners, like in the profiles of people in early Egyptian art. He had a mustache, a day's worth of stubble.

She thought she should remind him she wasn't buying so he wouldn't get his hopes up.

"Truly"—he stepped around a row of drying cow-dung patties—"I can see you are very different from the others. Once I have seen an American man. He pretends every day he is deaf and dumb. Every day he is pretending this. He is having no boat ride, no silk, no burning bodies, no postcard." He shook his head sadly.

"Do many people buy something?"

His face clouded. "Oh, yes, very many. At home," he said, brightening, "you have babies?"

"No." She'd been warned people would ask.

He put a hand on his flat belly. "There is some problem?" He smiled with a friendly, patient interest and the clear assumption that if there were, she would tell him.

"Not that I know of."

"No babies," he said, shaking his head. "I have three. All boys. Only three. Many babies make many more problems."

"Well, that's wise."

"You like massage?" he said.

"I like what?"

He was opening a little book he'd taken from the folds of his *dhoti*—thin-leafed, like a Bible, nicely bound. "You read here." he held it in front of her. She read:

> Shiv is an expert at loosening the muscles.
> Different from the guy at the Y at home, but just fine.
> Well worth the rupees. Joe Seabrook, Tucson, AZ.

The entry was six years old. He took the book from her hands; holding it so she could see, he flipped past dozens of testimonials in faded inks and different languages. Another in English. He handed it to her.

> My shoulder was a little stiff and troubling me until I came upon Shiv out here on the river. This is a talented young man. He did very well with my touch of arthritis. Marie Jasper. Cincinnati, Ohio, USA.

A recent one. This very week. Could that be Marie from the guest house, with the cane?

Jill flipped to another page. Here was one in French, which she could read a little.

> Cet homme a les doigts et aussi l'esprit qui sont le plus. . . .

Shiv was massaging her free hand, pressing into the center of her palm with both his thumbs. She felt a tingle behind her knees.

She could stop him.

In the distance, the flopping of wet wash, swung against the concrete riverbank in an even rhythm, slow—she waited for it to fall again. He was pushing down into the web between her thumb and forefinger.

"Come to my place," she heard, close by her ear; they stood closer than she'd realized. "It is only just near."

His place?

"There." He pointed to the top of the *ghat.* She saw nothing but wall. "Outside location. Near Ganga," he said. "Come."

Holding her hand, he started up the steps. She followed. He hurried, faster, skipping up the last few risers to the top of the *ghat.* She picked up speed, keeping pace behind him.

Single file, they walked along the top step, following the edge of a building at the lip of the bluff where the city began. The wall was stained dark up to a level several feet above her head, marked from the floods of monsoons. She put her hand up to touch how high overhead the water had been. The block radiated a baking heat.

Shiv stepped out around the low pedestal of a Shiva *linga;* on the other side, they stopped at a spot where the step widened, heading toward a *gali*. Another young man was sitting cross-legged against the wall. Spread in front of him on the pavement was a six-foot length of burlap.

"Here." Shiv motioned toward the burlap.

His place was a patch of scorching concrete in sight of anybody who passed. Shiv straightened a wrinkle in the burlap as the other man got up and wandered off. "Lie this way," Shiv said, showing her the end where she was to put her head. He patted his chest and pointed to the ground, indicating she was to lie facedown.

She wanted to take a shower first; it was so hot, she probably smelled.

He waited; his indulgent smile seemed professional, like the psychologist her parents had taken her to in ninth grade.

If old Marie could sprawl out here, she could, too.

She glanced around to see if anyone was paying attention, then quickly dropped to the ground, lying with her face against the sacking, a few feet from a stack of rusting water pipes. The hot pavement made the rough cloth smell like hay. She felt as if she were hidden: flat against the pavement, the hawkers would never find her. Shiv was no longer one of them.

On the street, she'd seen men getting shoulder rubs, but none of them lying down. And no women.

Shiv's hands pressed into her tight lumbar muscle.

Her eyes closed.

It was like lying on a beach, a boy putting lotion on you, house-party week in college. The sun was making her drowsy.

Her face toward the river, she could see the noon sun glinting on the water. Strange that darting light could be so soothing.

The ends of his fingers lifted gently, as if she were a piano keyboard, and descended onto her again. He was spending a long time on one spot, there at the small of her back. Her legs felt limp, as if they were drifting out longer and longer behind her; she was dissolving.

As a kid, ten or eleven, she'd taken a plastic raft to the lake in the summer, day after day, lying out there, floating. Her legs would sink down through the sun-warmed water to a cooler layer beneath.

He was working his way up her spine, now, his fingers prying up under her shoulder blades. The flat, buried bones seemed to come loose in his hands, floating. . . .

She lifted to get air beneath her, pulling the wet shirt away from her skin. The sun on the river was bright, even with her eyes closed. Facing her head to the other side, she looked into the open end of one of the water pipes only a few feet away.

Was something moving in there? She squinted.

She saw the glint of eyes. A rat? She could feel her pulse in her stomach where it pressed against the concrete.

The animal was coming out, low and flat, at her eye level. If she made a sound, it would jump at her.

Shiv's hands held still.

Half out . . .

It was long, like a ferret, holding still in the mouth of the pipe, tense and twitching.

"Madame? There is a problem?"

"There," she whispered, nodding toward the pipe.

"Yes, yes, a mongoose," he said, a delighted lilt in his voice. He clapped his hands.

The creature sprang into motion. Jill jerked over onto her side as it hurried away from her down the outer side of the pipe.

"It is very good." Shiv smiled, his eyes shining. "A mongoose is a good omen. It has always been so."

"Omen of what?"

"Not what," he said. "Only good." He pressed her gently back down onto the burlap.

"One small surprise," he said, "and you jump. Every day you should have the massage and then you will not be jumping."

She sat back up. Every muscle in her body tight again, her mouth was dry and sticking.

"I need to go," she said. Where was her other shoe? She didn't remember taking them off. What had possessed her to lie here in a stupor? The sun must have baked her brains; all the hawkers in the city would be after her, they'd never leave her alone.

Shiv sat back on his heels, perplexed. "You are having some problem?"

"No problem. Time for me to go."

"Go?" He looked wounded.

"It was a very good massage." There was no point in making him feel bad. "I just have to leave."

"Mongoose is nice," he said, his eyes searching her face, the low open neck of her Indian shirt.

"How many rupees?"

"One hundred." He hesitated, assessing. "And fifty." He repeated: "One hundred fifty rupees."

She paid him, getting to her feet. She felt light-headed, steadied herself with one hand against the side of the building.

"You like to write in my book?" He dangled it before her.

Automatically, she took the book and the pen he was holding. "Excellent massage," she wrote. That ought to satisfy him. Now that he had his money, his hurt feelings were gone. He looked her over with affectionate amusement. Her mistake had been in lying down at all, she thought, not in getting up. "Relaxing," she jotted. and handed back the book.

Reading it, his face was neutral.

She repeated to herself what she'd written. It was too short, she realized. It paled beside the leisurely praise of others.

He was tucking the book into the wrappings at his waist; she should ask for it again to give him a quote he could use, so she wouldn't feel bad later. It was crazy, she knew, to have to do that.

CHAPTER FIFTEEN

A WAITER approached with a tray of steaming teacups. T. J. put his empty down, took another full one. The party was humming around him, out under the night sky. The women looked spectacular in the light of the torches, draped in their silk and brocade. He'd wandered by pure accident into some fantasy realm of lustrous dark beauties, the men in their pale pajamas fading into the background.

Mrs. Rai kept coming and going from view. She wore a scarlet sari so vivid he could look at it and taste raspberries. But she was talking with Jill, who had volunteered at the dinner table how she'd love to go to an Indian party. Jill appeared to be getting the same attentive charm treatment from Mrs. Rai that he'd had; or so it seemed from the animated way Jill was talking. He felt a twinge of jealousy.

So he stood with several of the water-chemistry faculty, who carried on their conversation around him; he took another sip of the Indian tea. The Baldev family—friends of the Rais—had closed off an entire end of a street to have this party in honor of their son Dr. Baldev and his wife, who had moved back home to India. The young man was a cardiologist. "England-returned" was what it was called in the ads for marriage partners in the newspapers.

This felt like a wedding, it was such a lavish spread: musicians playing sitars and tablas under one tent, and another tent, big as a house, for the buffets.

Beside him, Rai, suave as ever, was holding court on a matter of departmental politics. Three or four of the professors were laughing but nervous. One kept looking around to see if anyone was overhearing.

At his other elbow, a voice rose in agitation. A man in Western shirt and tie was nodding indignantly toward the other side of the tent: ". . . two guards following him around. Let us speak the truth, why does he need two guards to show himself at a social affair?"

T. J. looked across the tent; he could see an eddy in the crowd, someone working his way through. It was a beefy-looking man with slicked-down hair and a smirk. A couple of men in police-type khakis were trailing him, their eyes scanning the crowd in a trained motion. They carried rifles slung over their shoulders, the tips of the barrels riding above people's heads.

"Who am I looking at here?" T. J. asked Rai.

"One of our local political leaders."

"I see." The men around him had given up pretending to go on with their conversation.

"It is a very sad day," said Amitabh, the paunchy metals expert, "when I see this on such a happy occasion."

The others nodded their agreement.

"What can we expect?" Rai said. "He is created by conditions we have allowed to build. A creature such as himself, exploiting hardship and animosities, is inevitable. If it were not him, it would be another."

"Dr. Rai, I must tell you, this does not satisfy me." Amitabh eyed the man who was passing like a shark only a few feet away.

"Nor should it satisfy anyone," Rai said.

"Please understand me." Amitabh raised a finger. "Men such as this aren't born of the conditions, but instead are manufacturing them, keeping anger alive and directing it to their own purposes."

"You take a noble view of the common man," Rai said in his easy, lofty manner. "I suspect myself that he is happy to be offered a scapegoat." He turned to T. J. "The individual we speak of lives here in the neighborhood," he said, as if to explain the man's presence.

"So, are you having a good time?" It was Jill at his side, freeing him from Rai. Over her shoulder, he caught a glimpse of Mrs. Rai.

"Impressive get-together," he said.

"Whole families have come from a thousand miles away," Jill said. "They're staying with people all over this neighborhood."

"You've been doing some research."

"Someone I was talking with said the man with the guards caused a violent incident last year in another city not far from here. He didn't do it, but he was behind it."

"He certainly had a nasty air about him."

She laughed, looking flushed from the firelight and excitement.

"So, you read his aura," she said, smiling, "like Natraja."

The glow of her attention was flattering, but he checked himself. His heart was given to Mrs. Rai. "Does she claim that?" he said.

"I think Natraja claims to do anything that will keep people at a distance but paying close attention," Jill said. "I noticed last night . . ." She was starting to detail Natraja's cryptic comments to Dov.

Jane had some of that about her, though she could get away with it better—because of how she looked, for one thing. When they were first together, he'd thought she had an air of mystery, found it enticing.

The last couple of years, though—maybe since she was pregnant with Elizabeth—she'd pulled deeper into her own fog. No doubt his griping had made it worse, and truly he could deal with introspection up to a point. He even admired her for it. But he'd tell her, say, what he had in mind for the weekend and she'd only give him a weary, distracted look. If he leaned on her for a response, she'd get her feelings hurt. He was left slamming kitchen cabinet doors in frustration.

Once, about a year ago, she had told him to stop "issuing pronouncements on everything." With two children, she didn't have time to listen. That had hurt him. She wasn't the only one taking care of the girls. He had stopped trying with her for a while.

But he'd recovered. And those few weeks of strain hadn't seemed to please her, either.

Since then he'd come home from work—so many times—resolved this would be the day he got through to her; about what didn't matter, he just wanted to see the old Jane in her eyes, mysterious but *there* with him. He wanted some reaction to what he was saying. Because if he did what she seemed to want, if he just let her fall into that dreamy way of going through her day, it would be the same as losing her.

The tabla player started drumming over in the other tent, a light-fingered kind of pounding.

"Or maybe," Jill was saying, "it's something about me Natraja doesn't like; I don't know."

"It's not you. This afternoon," he recovered himself, "I was walking past her in the doorway of the inn. She was eyeing everybody who came in or out, with that sneering, critical look on her face."

"Good evening, sir." It was one of the grad students; he remembered the guy's glasses that sat slightly askew. T. J. introduced him to Jill. "You are also a biochemist?" he said to her, eager-faced.

From three feet away, Natraja had smelled like a dirty undershirt, with perfume on top of the sweat. She had asked—so imperiously—where he was going.

"Oh, down to the river," he'd said. "Thought I'd rent a boat, get out there and row a little."

One step out the door and he was wondering why he'd told her. He didn't have to account to her. When he came in again an hour later, the foyer was empty. He sat down in her chair.

He waited. It still felt warm, the caning stretched and sagged. He feared for a second he was getting a hard-on from his little power play: he felt triumphant, wallowing his ass in her heat.

When she walked into the room, he saw her expression the moment she caught sight of him, her eyes coming forward at him out of all that fat.

"Get up."

"Yes, ma'am." He smiled, still seated. "Just wanted to see what it felt like to be lord of the manor. I don't get that chance too often." He'd said it in a friendly way, uncrossing his legs slowly.

"Get away from there or I will kill you."

He'd laughed, stepping away from her chair and the table she used for the hotel desk. It was just like her to threaten murder instead of simply telling him to pack his bags and go.

"This part of town," Jill was saying, "is so different from the old section of the city around the guest house. The wider streets and buildings that are obviously apartments . . ."

"More like Delhi, don't you think?" the grad student said.

She didn't answer. T. J. looked where she was looking. There was a big commotion about fifty feet away at the edge of the crowd. What now?

All around him, people were turning to look, a young servant craning his neck to see.

Then the crowd parted, opening a wide path. Walking in the center was a man in a long-coated white Nehru suit and an immense orange cone hat, with a scarf flowing off it like he was Guinevere, and unbelievably, people were bowing to him from either side.

"It is the maharajah," the waiter said then, dancing from one foot to the other. "Of Benares. The king. He lives in the palace across the river. You have seen." T. J. hadn't seen any palace.

He took quick note of how people were greeting him, two hands together almost up at their faces, a little dip of the head. It was an abject posture, putting yourself at the other's mercy, like wolves signaling surrender.

T. J. made up his mind that he wasn't going to do it. But then, he didn't want to make a scene by not doing it.

The maharajah was glancing this way and that, nodding to people. He had a pleasant, warm look to his face, and carried himself in a manner that was almost humble, shoulders forward in a constant slight bow—so grand he could afford to be gracious.

Then the man was right up in front of him.

His eyes hit on T. J.—a momentary gleam.

T. J. nodded, the way you do from the cab of one truck to another.

The king's genial gaze lingered on him. He returned T. J.'s nod, looking for a second like he might speak, but then moved on. The crowd closed behind him, excited conversation rising up in his wake.

T. J. stared until all he could see was the orange point of the hat. There was, in fact, something majestic about him. He hated to admit it.

He scanned the crowd, looking for Mrs. Rai to see how she felt about kings. He knew how Jane would feel: she'd fall in love with him and marry him, then tell him to tone it down a little.

CHAPTER SIXTEEN

JILL TUGGED at the bedsheet, trying to unwrap the tangle without pulling down the mosquito net. Four twenty-three.

This would make three nights of almost no sleep. If she'd known about these rope cots, she thought, she'd have trained at home, lying on bare wicker or a bed of nails. She'd given up all hope for this trip. This wasn't any place to try to relax. If it weren't for looking like a quitter, she'd pack up and go home.

Four twenty-four. From the corner of her eye, she could see when the lighted green number jumped. She reached carefully beneath the edge of the net and pushed the clock facedown.

She willed herself to relax. With each inhale, she imagined herself drawing in an opiate that caused deep, heavy drowsiness. She pulled the sheet over her nose and mouth: an anesthesia cone; in minutes she would be unconscious. Already her thoughts were slowing. At the party, she'd felt as if she'd had one too many glasses of wine, though alcohol hadn't been served. It was the anonymity and excitement of a big crowd, the torchlights and the shining silks that were near intoxicating. At least here there was no phone: no decision about whether to call somebody you might have offended during the day—or Ben. People hadn't seemed at all upset about the cow walking into the middle of the party. Wasn't there a song about a cow, late at night? *There'll be a hot time in the old town . . .*

She'd masturbated hours ago—twice—and that just woke her up more.

The window was open, but the air didn't stir. Looking through the net made the darkness hazy, as if the room were full of swamp mist. It was probably more than a hundred degrees. She'd gone to bed naked and wet from the bucket bath, her hair dripping. The evaporation had kept her cool for a while. Now her whole body felt sticky again.

She twisted onto her side, but her breasts felt like clutter in the way of her arms. She didn't want any part of her to be touching any other part of her. It kept her awake.

T. J. hadn't seemed interested in her. Married, but even so, she'd have thought he was the type who came on to women. She had focused too hard on him; it was a reflex, whether she was interested or not. On the phone before she left, her mother had asked when she was going to stop being a skipping stone.

She called up an image of Ben—shirtless, coming in from a run; then showered and tan in his white hotel bathrobe, reading the paper and drinking decaf on her apartment balcony. He looked like an ad. She thought of having to impress someone every day for the rest of her life. It was easier to have the prospect of love somewhere up ahead, the possibilities open. She'd had fantasies about relaxing here, more easily hooking up with somebody, maybe a European.

She lifted the clock to face her again. In half an hour or less, the noise would begin: bathers coming out onto the riverbank, temple bells ringing, people walking down below her window. The city kept up a constant, unbelievably high-decibel roar from sunrise until mid-evening. Yet at night it was nearly silent.

Her legs prickled as if she had a day's growth of stubble. But she'd shaved, standing next to the drain in the bathroom floor, pouring dipperfuls of water over her legs. While she was washing, a monkey had scrambled across the outside ledge of the window. That would be a story to tell when she got home. . . .

When she opened her eyes, she had to squint against the light, groping for the travel clock. It was after seven. That was three hours of sleep. The mosquito net was bright white, now, in the morning light. Jill thought she heard muffled voices from somewhere inside the house, but the walls were so thick. She shut her eyes and pulled the sheet back up around her face. Then she suddenly realized how quiet it was. How odd. She didn't hear any noise outside. Usually the singing and chanting from the riverbank woke her up. Maybe it was some sort of holiday. A good day to sleep in, she thought, and sank into the pillow.

By the time Jill was headed downstairs to the dining room, it was mid-morning, after ten o'clock.

Everyone would be gone except Natraja and Ramesh, and she hesitated at the thought of dealing with Natraja alone. She was groggy even though she'd gotten five hours.

It was actually easier to come down the stairway backwards. She held on to the thick rope rail along the curving wall, stepped down and around and around, pretending she was rappelling, a fast drop without a twinge of fear. Rock climbing, she'd always preferred the trip up, digging with the tips of her fingers at any edge of rock she could use.

People were in the dining room, though, their voices muffled by the thick wall and the corkscrew stairway. And when she stepped into the downstairs room, the place was full of people: Dov and Gersh, Marie, T. J., around the front table. Natraja, sitting with her eyes closed, was pretending to be asleep. Eric and Laura sat at a second table, sipping tea and reading, with another couple she hadn't seen.

She looked at her watch again. Ten-fifteen. Then at T. J.

"Problems," he said with no particular friendliness.

Natraja spoke from her chair at the end of the table, eyes still shut: "The city is under curfew. There has been an incident in the night."

"What kind of incident?" Jill dropped into the chair next to Marie.

"A retaliation." Natraja roused slowly to look around the table. "To avenge an assault against a Muslim man. Three Hindus were killed." She stopped as if she had said all there was to say.

"Was it the same men? How did they—"

"With knives," Natraja said.

All had paused, waiting to see if she would say more.

In the quiet, Jill could hear the rub of Ramesh's bare feet on the floor as he came toward the table, putting down a plate of toast and a cup for tea in front of her—two discrete knocks against the table. Her gaze followed the stiff set of his shoulders as he returned to the kitchen.

Three was not so many; surely that many were killed in Atlanta on lots of days.

"Is it people you know?" she asked Natraja.

Natraja shook her head. "No."

Jill grabbed a piece of toast, bit off a corner.

"No need to rush," T. J. said. "We're here for the duration. That's the part Natraja didn't mention."

"What do you mean?"

"The whole city is shut down, a day-and-night curfew. All businesses closed. Everybody stays indoors—every one of our nearly a million people."

"What time does it end?"

The rest of them laughed, exchanging glances.

"The curfew is indefinite," Natraja said.

"It could be all day?"

"It could be days, or weeks. We do not know."

Jill put down her toast. "I have a train day after tomorrow. A flight out of Delhi."

"Everyone has something," Natraja said, pointedly dismissive.

"So we're stuck here? That's it?"

"That is it." She seemed pleased to deliver bad news.

T. J. was rocking the bottom of his teacup in a circle in his saucer.

"There is one redeeming factor"—Natraja looked at Jill—"which I have already mentioned to the others. Curfew does not so much apply to you. If you choose to go into the streets, the police who enforce this decree on the Indian citizens will not see you. It will be as if you do not exist. Because you are not Indian, neither Hindu nor Muslim, no one will care if you go about. You may go out for a walk when you are ready. But you will find that the city is empty, no rickshaw driver to take you to your train. All are hidden in their homes.

"There is this, too," Natraja went on, overriding Dov, who'd opened his mouth to speak. "For today at least, I do not advise your wandering. When there are fresh wounds, not so much is predictable. Perhaps you have brought to India some book you would like to read." She let her eyebrows lift theatrically and slowly fall.

Jill stared at her, sunk down in her fat like a huge frog. What was she telling them? To go out, or not?

"I will tell you this, too," Natraja said, her eyes leveled on Jill. "You need not blame me. I am not the one who has imposed curfew and spoiled all your plans, whatever they are."

Jill felt her face flush.

Natraja laughed.

"I don't understand," Jill said.

T. J. crossed his arms and looked up at the ceiling.

"Come, now," Marie said, "we're all a little on edge. Madame Natraja has the worries of the household on her shoulders at a very troubled time. That may account for her tone and her behavior."

Natraja sat placidly indifferent, hands clasped across her stomach.

Dov and Gersh looked sideways at each other, like a couple of nine-year-olds. Dov, Jill suddenly realized, was a foreigner who could be mistaken for Indian and get himself killed. And Natraja was sitting here, telling him it was safe to go out. There was silence from the other table. The fan made a ticking sound with each revolution.

T. J. was studiously taking no part.

"Well, since you are the peacemaker," Jill said to Marie, "maybe you can do something about the people out there knifing each other."

Marie smiled a tight little smile. Seeing it, Jill felt awash with shame; it was Natraja she was mad at.

Natraja's eyes glittered again toward Jill. "With curfew, no one is out killing this morning," Natraja said. "Go and look for yourself. I invite you. I urge you. The streets and the *galis* are empty. Marie would find no one out there to make peace with. Only here can she find knives."

CHAPTER SEVENTEEN

MY GUESTS are scattered through the house, on the roof or hidden away in their rooms. I sit alone at my dining room table, my tea grown cold in front of me.

Three bodies were found on the street with their throats slit open like chickens draining; police stacked them in the footrest of a rickshaw to carry away.

Varanasi is closed.

Not one has left the house. If they wanted, they could easily stay clear of the places where trouble is expected. At the edges of the Muslim neighborhoods, police and soldiers are posted with their guns and riot shields, with orders to shoot if anyone so much as steps onto a balcony. At least this is the word Ramesh has heard passed down the *gali*.

On any other day it might be difficult for a tourist to know whether a lane is Hindu or Muslim. In Sambhupura or the other Muslim *mohalla,* there would be a few women in the crowd, veiled and shrouded in their dark *burquahs,* and the smells of Persian spices drifting from a market, a *biryani* rich with animal fat.

At the edge of the colored section, the oily vapor of cooking grease hung in the air, coming from out a sagged-screen window, the smell of snap beans simmering with a bit of meat. A clay rut road ran between the paint-peeling shacks. I was trying to catch sight of Reggie and see in his eyes that everything was still fine. If anybody asked, I would say something about finding yard help. Nobody came near. But the word spread in an instant down dirt streets and alleys: he appeared out of nowhere, loping out from around the corner of a house, his eyes big, rasping at me from six feet away, "Girl, what are you thinking, coming here—"

My hands are suddenly wet on the arms of my chair, my breath shallow.

Where is Ramesh?

I call for him, but I make no sound.

The room grows dark. I can't breathe—

Please—

Air . . .

Gagging, I wrench my head away. I am on the floor, the rung of a chair near my shoulder.

"You're okay." A man's voice: "Can you tell me your name?"

"Stelle Wilson," I say, gulping air. My face is wet. I know his voice.

"You blacked out. Do you know where you are?" He looms over me, dabbing with a cloth—the smell of lighter fluid—at my face where it's coated and sticky. My stomach sinks again, then convulses. "I had to get you breathing." It's T. J. He's had his mouth on my face.

As I push up to sitting, the windings of my sari fall half loose. Layers of flesh spill out. Grabbing for cover, I gather my breasts in a crumple of cloth. He has ripped my blouse.

"Sit still." He scrambles to his feet, keeping his face averted. "Something might be broken. I'll get Jill to help you. Tell me how to find a doctor."

"No need for a doctor. I am recovered."

He waits for me to yield to his wishes. "Thank you," I say. I cannot begrudge him that. "Truly, I am well."

"You may have had a heart attack. You have to let one of us go for help."

"My name is Natraja. Yours is Clayton. It is your luck to see me so humiliated. Obviously, I lost consciousness for a moment: the shock of recent events." My hip, where I hit the floor, throbs. "I thank you again—I know what you have done, and how it must have disgusted you. Please, now, leave the room."

Silence. And then he says, "Yes, ma'am," in that tone of sweetness and seething threat that makes me know how well I know him. He resettles the weight of his shoulders and walks out of the room. His face, hard-set, shows in profile as he turns to go down the first-floor hall.

CHAPTER EIGHTEEN

So you venture out from your room," Natraja said coolly when he walked into the dining room for breakfast. T. J. ignored her; he'd decided this was how he would handle her. "People asked after you at dinner last evening," she said. "I trust you had snacks stashed away to tide you over."

He nodded good morning at Jill and Marie. "*Chai,* please," he said to Ramesh, who was coming toward the table. He pointed to Jill's teacup.

"I figured I'd have plenty of time for sitting here." His eyes roamed across Natraja's face: a bruise ran along her jawline; she couldn't pretend it hadn't happened. He fluffed out his napkin and spread it in his lap.

"How long are we up to, now?" he said to no one in particular. "Twenty-some hours of 'cor-foo,' as Ramesh calls it." Ramesh, heading for the kitchen, cocked an ear toward the table. T. J. could feel the man taking stock of him.

"Twenty-eight hours and forty minutes," Jill said—she would be the one to keep count—"and no end in sight."

"People do come to India to stop rushing around,"

he said. And to Natraja: "How are you feeling today? Better, I hope."

"Were you not feeling well?" Marie leaned forward, concerned.

"I am well." She said it with such finality it was surely obvious to all there was more. Marie waited.

"T. J. is referring," Natraja said, "to his coming to my rescue yesterday when I was momentarily unable to catch my breath."

"She was passed out on the floor," T. J. couldn't keep quiet. "Right there." He pointed just behind Natraja's shoulder. "She'd had the wind knocked out of her."

He could see a purple spot on her throat next to her windpipe where he'd dug in with two fingers to find a pulse. If she'd died, he thought, they'd have been trapped in this heat with her rotting corpse.

"What in the world?" Marie was saying to Natraja. "Is it your heart?"

Natraja's hot stare focused on a spot in the center of the table.

"I'll tell you what," Marie said, "we'll talk about it later on. I'm glad you're feeling better." Marie, he could see, had begun thinking about her own health. "This is not a good time to have an emergency," she said.

Jill was looking a little white around the mouth. Maybe everybody should come clean about medications and ailments, since calling in a doctor looked to be out of the question. It was also time, after breakfast, for someone to get into the kitchen and take stock of how they were set up for food.

Early afternoon, the temperature at its peak, and the sounds of their footsteps, his and Jill's, echoed down the long empty market street, up against the fronts of the buildings on each side.

Jill had wanted to get out of the house, talk about something; surely she could see this was no place to talk, when people you might not see could hear you. The streets were empty, but the buildings were surely full.

With the people gone you could see how the pavement was cracked and jutting in places. A trickle of sewage ran along one edge.

Ghost town, neutron bomb, plague, Pompeii—all the clichés of devastation ran through T. J.'s mind. They walked on a layer of settled dust, milled by traffic to a grain as fine as talcum powder. He kicked at the dirt; it rose up in a cloud, following him. "It's like walking on the moon," he said.

"Do you have the feeling you're being watched?" she said, not looking at him, her eyes scanning the street.

"The commercial buildings are likely empty," he said, "since curfew was called at four in the morning. But it's hard to tell which ones they are."

"So, what happened with Natraja?" Her voice was so low and even, he wasn't sure he'd heard right.

"Is that what you wanted to talk about?"

"Yeah." She cleared her throat. "I wondered."

"I walked in and found her on the floor next to her chair. She wasn't breathing. I thought she was dead, but her pulse was strong. Likely she blacked out and her weight knocked the wind out of her. I don't know, though. She doesn't confide in me."

"I heard her shouting at you after breakfast."

He laughed. "That was a whole different thing. She didn't like me taking inventory in the kitchen."

"There has to be some way to get food, with this many people—"

"There is. I talked with the fellow over on the next rooftop. A few vegetable vendors, medics, people like that, have curfew passes, pink tags they wear on a string. He said last night, cops broke the arm of a doctor they'd caught out on the street. They were on him before they saw he was wearing a curfew pass."

Jill was quiet for a moment.

"She didn't say why she passed out?"

"No." Why was she still going on about this?

"She was mad at me," Jill said, "just before it happened."

He glanced at her to see if she was serious. "You think she fell out over something you said?"

Jill looked alarmed. "Do you think that's possible?"

"No, I don't."

"You don't?" He could hear the beginning of relief in her voice. "But what are you basing that on?" she said.

"Jill, it's got nothing to do with you."

Her face had turned bitter; he'd let her down. But it was clearly Natraja's weight. Her heart had to be a time bomb, and he couldn't understand how she'd persuaded Marie to back off.

They trudged on, silent. He wasn't sure how close they were to the Muslim sections. They'd need to keep some distance.

"Over there," Jill said, keeping her voice down.

Two policemen, a hundred feet ahead, stood half hidden in the mouth of a *gali*—but Jill's step didn't falter. Their feet hitting the pavement fell into a rhythm.

T. J. kept his eyes fixed on the men, close now.

The nearer one had sharp features, slick black hair that shone around the edge of his beret. He was the rifleman. They each held a heavy bamboo club as well, which scared T. J. more. One of those things could be deadly as an automatic weapon but quicker put to use.

He and Jill were pulling even with the men. He readied himself to speak—*Namaste*—as if everything were normal. But the police, only a few feet away, weren't looking. It was true: he and Jill might as well be invisible.

They'd moved past, now, leaving the two men behind. He listened for footsteps following, strained to hear, but there was nothing.

Jill smiled her usual bright, social smile. He was surprised; he'd have pegged her for the panicky type.

He looked down the length of street, and out of the corner of his eye saw a flash of movement.

A face showed in a second-story window. Another appeared beside it. It was two kids, a turbanned Sikh man in the shadows behind them. T. J scanned along the second floor of the buildings: more faces filling the open windows.

Dozens, maybe hundreds of people were up there, staring down at them.

He laughed. Jill gave him a pointed look.

How many people had stood at their windows and watched when the doctor was beaten? he wondered. On this street, the snap of a twig would echo.

A man in a red Western shirt stood on a rooftop farther down, leaning over the low wall and monitoring their every step.

T. J. waved at him to see what would happen. The man continued to look but made no answering sign.

Just ahead, the road opened into an intersection. Without the usual throng of people, it looked as if it were a mile across, a dried-up lake. On the other side was another pair of cops.

"I don't know that it's so wise to be out here," he said to Jill. "Any time you want to head to the house is fine with me."

"Sure," she said, "whatever you feel like."

They did an about-face, and in ten minutes or so of brisk walking, they were almost back at the guest house.

They were just across from the *gali* that led home when T. J. heard the sound of running steps behind them, then feet scuffling against concrete.

Grabbing Jill by the elbow, he twisted around and in the same instant heard a thud and a muffled yell. Across the street, a policeman, his bamboo *lathi* raised, was descending on a boy who cowered along the wall, forearms raised in front of his face.

The boy yelled in Hindi, motioning toward the *gali*. The policeman had cut him off, trapped him against a wall. He whipped the stick through the air. It made a whistling sound: a warning swing.

Jill gasped. Everything hung motionless in the bright light.

"Hey," T. J. shouted at the cop, setting out across the open street. "Hey, buddy." The man glanced behind him, annoyed.

The instant his attacker was diverted, the boy dashed for the *gali.*

The policeman whirled around, his face furious. Then in two long steps, he was standing at the mouth of the *gali,* the cane drawn back hard at waist level, held like a bat in both hands.

The *lathi* sailed out of his hands, close to the ground and spinning on its center, thrown with a skill that stopped T. J. where he stood. In the next second, he heard a scream, the sound of it echoing farther into the lane.

His eyes blinked shut—it would have caught the boy at the shins or the knees.

The policeman stood, staring down the *gali.* T. J. lunged after him.

"T. J. No!" From behind, Jill was grabbing hard at his shoulder.

He threw her off. She was on him again. "Don't," she said, her voice sharp in his ear. "You're making it worse."

CHAPTER NINETEEN

MARIE STUDIED the list of questions in her red Hindi primer. She and Ramesh sat in a couple of the old lawn chairs up on the roof. Ramesh kept shifting his big bare feet against the concrete. She wished he would relax.

All she needed was help with pronunciation and a few basic rules; surely the two of them could have some rudimentary conversation. He seemed like a sensible man who could say—with the help of sign language, perhaps—whether Natraja had a heart condition and if the city was going to be shut down for a month.

Here was a good one: "Why are you silent? Why don't you answer"? She could read that off to him in Hindi, but then she'd never understand his answer. She needed yes/no questions, or questions with one-word replies. She flipped to another page.

"'When does the train arrive?'" The Hindi was spelled out in English letters: *"Gari kab ati hai?"*

He scowled, pressed his lips together. He was trying not to laugh. "You say it, then," she told him. He didn't understand.

"You say," she said, pointing to him in the middle of his chest. He was wearing a Western shirt over the *dhoti* he wrapped around his waist and tucked up between his legs. "You. *Aap.*"

This time he got it, repeating the words in a slow, teacherly way: *"Gari . . . kab . . . ati . . . hai."* No wonder he'd been confused. There must be ten different pronunciations of the letter *a,* half of them in that one sentence.

She looked again at the book; she had opened to the section on "Traveling by Rail" and some of these phrases seemed to put too fine a point on things. She read down the list:

There is not even elbow room.
Food is not good.
See the swarm of flies.
See the lavatory is dirty.

She tried it out loud: "*Pakhana ganda hai.* The lavatory is dirty." She said it once again, looking up at Ramesh to see if she had it close to right.

Ramesh's eyes had widened. He looked alarmed.

"No, no, Ramesh." He thought she was complaining about his bathrooms.

"Not this lavatory. The *train* lavatory." She put the book in front of him, showed him with her finger where it was written. *"Gari,"* she said. "Train."

She saw his eyes take in the Hindi words, the understanding pass over his face.

Then he started to laugh, perusing the rest of the page. He had a deep, rich laugh that was startling.

She wanted to find out more about him: how long he had worked here, and where his family was, when he had the chance to see them. He slept every night on a rope cot that he pulled out in the dining room. She'd discovered this one night when she couldn't sleep and was up and walking. She flipped through her book, trying to find something she could use.

This was close: She said it slowly in Hindi, then in English, "*Apke ghar men: sab log thik hain?* How is everybody in your family?"

He was eyeing her warily.

She gave him time to think it over.

He repeated the phrase in Hindi.

She closed her eyes in frustration. "No," she said, pointing to him. "*Aap,* you." She repeated the question again in Hindi: how is your family?

He said a few tentative words. He seemed surprised to be asked. He spoke slowly, as if that would make her understand him, and when she didn't stop him, he picked up speed.

After that, he didn't let up, talking on steadily as if she would understand. His hands moved with the sound of his voice in a way that entranced her. She had the strong sense he was talking about a son, but couldn't have said why. The sound of his talk was pouring past her, all the gesticulating and the sweet rise and fall of the language itself. It was tempting to think she could seize on some meaning, but all she was doing was catching a word or two when he slowed.

She broke in: "*Kitna* . . ." How many, how much, she knew that from shopping. "Ramesh, *kitna* babies?" She said it with an Indian accent: "beh-bees."

"Beh-bees." His eyes lit up. *"Tin."* Three. He was holding up three fingers in case she didn't understand, pointing to himself and saying, *"Ek."* One like himself. Pointing to her, *"Do."* Two like her.

She leaned back in her chair. So, two girls and a boy, and they would probably be in their thirties. Her own children were old now; Richard, though he still had his wiry track-team shape, was only two months from being a grandfather.

Ramesh was turning pages now, twisting the book one way and another to read the charts of phrases. She waited.

"Me beh-bees," he said. "One . . . professor."

"Professor, Ramesh?"

He was nodding. How could he possibly have put a child through college?

She reached for the phrasebook, but he held on to it, flipping pages. She had heard the tuitions were really low, if you were one of the one in a million to get in.

"America," he said, nodding to himself.

Marie felt taken aback. That professor son should be sending money home. Ramesh should not have to work day and night at his age. "Ramesh," she said, *"kyon aap Saraswati?"* Why you Saraswati?

He looked away. She shouldn't have asked. It was so hard to be diplomatic with only a few words. He kept his eyes on a cow picking its way along the *ghat* at the edge of the water.

"Sar-vess," he said finally.

She repeated his words. Did he mean service?

"Ji, han," he said, smiling. Yes, she had it right. But that still didn't explain.

He was searching the book again. She wanted to know why a man like himself should have to be in service to anybody as difficult and peculiar as Natraja, not to mention tourists coming and going.

Then, "You are happy journey?" he asked with difficulty. "Why?"

She leaned over and took the book. With a little hunting, she found the words to say, "Husband. Die." She pointed behind her in the direction of the river, he would understand that. She'd now told him a lot more than he had told her.

Ramesh nodded, *"Ganga-ji."* She reminded herself: when you add the *ji,* it becomes an endearment. Dear Ganges. The river—it seemed to be the simple answer to everything. Perhaps it was the river he was serving; working here certainly was a way to live just next to the water.

Ramesh-ji, she thought, trying it out. He was such a gentleman. She didn't dare say such a thing; he would wind up misunderstanding her.

When she looked again at his face, he was staring past her at the river. Like Natraja out at the sunrise, he had tears standing in his eyes.

For dinner, Marie was wearing her *salwar kameez* that she'd bought in New Delhi, blue and red print with a gold brocade decoration on the front. It was a little dressy; at the same time, the drawstring pants were so comfortable. Her friends at home would cackle, but then they'd be looking for a catalog to order the same thing.

The room had its usual after-dinner feel—or at least what had become usual these last few days, with everybody cooped up together. Evenings were now a social affair of sorts.

Laura, the nice young Australian woman, was talking about the Indians living in London and how you saw Muslim women out in public there in their hoods with holes for the eyes. "I got used to seeing it: we spent about a year in England. It doesn't seem to me so odd now."

"It might if you were wearing it," Jill said.

Laura thought it over. "Actually, the reverse might be true . . ."

A tinny rattle came from out in the *gali.* In the sudden silence, Marie heard the heavy rustle of the canvas that hung over the open doorway in the other room, and the murmur of hushed voices. Natraja tilted her head to listen.

"It is only the man with the newspaper," she said after a moment.

"I'll get it," Marie said, rising from her chair. She was feeling kindly disposed to this group.

She searched the little pocket of her *salwar kameez* for the few notes she carried with her room key, just in case. Pushing aside the canvas, she stepped out into the *gali.*

She looked around as her eyes readjusted to the dimmer light.

There, twenty feet away, was the newspaper boy with his little cart, curfew tag pinned to his shirt. From other doors down the lane, people were taking a step out to get a paper, then rushing inside again: a soft scurrying in the dim light.

She held out ten rupees to the boy.

He shook his head. *"Hindi."* He dismissed her.

"Mainh Hindi pasand hai," she told him. I am liking Hindi.

He gave her a second look and muttered in a cross voice. There were a million things he could resent: her money, the fact that she could get on a plane and leave this trouble. Swatting a paper into her hand, he took the rupees and pushed on past. Maybe he was mad at his mother; she'd heard that Indian matriarchs wielded a furious power, avenging whatever constriction they'd suffered as girls.

She carefully retraced the few steps to her own canvas curtain, realizing she had not brought her cane. At the step up to the door, she stopped. The newsboy was already gone. The others had disappeared too, so quickly.

She looked up at the ribbon of sky, a pale twilight above the *gali.* It felt strange to be out here, away from the others, as if she had passed over into different, silent territory.

At her age, she couldn't be *so* far from death, however charmed a life the newsboy thought she led. Her arm was braced against the doorjamb for balance, her loose flesh hanging, the skin crumpled. But for the moment, she was here, alive in all her particulars, arthritic knuckles, spotted stick of a wrist. Inconceivable that anything so fully articulated—down to the dark red nail polish the girl had insisted on—could simply cease to exist. She wanted to remain herself—Marie—not dissolve into some great mishmash of souls like raindrops falling into water.

The door flap was drawn aside. "Any problem?" It was Eric, come to see if she'd been taken hostage.

"No, I'm coming." She'd be glad when this curfew was over and she could get out and walk a bit in the open air.

Back in the dining room, she handed the newspaper to Natraja, who flopped it out on the table and began skimming the headlines. Marie settled into her chair. Jill was spinning one of the little pieces of the *carom* board game that she and T. J. had played most of the afternoon; it made a gliding sound crossing the board, and a click when it hit another piece or bounced off the sides.

Natraja studied the paper. Finally she looked up. "There is a reprieve," she said. "Tomorrow the city is open for four hours, all neighborhoods. From ten until two."

No one cheered.

Jill's hand held still on the game piece. "So, we can go out, leave town if we want to?"

"That is correct," Natraja said.

Jill stared blank-faced into space, taking this in.

T. J. sat with his chair tipped against the wall; he looked skeptical, as if he wouldn't believe Natraja wasn't withholding some part of the news.

"If we could get to the train station," Dov said to Gersh, "we could stay there until the next train out. The rest of the country is not under martial law."

Gersh nodded, thinking it over. Everybody had fallen into befuddlement; this was not at all the excitement she would have expected.

For herself, she wasn't sure what she wanted. Her daughter would tell her to pack up tonight.

Should she sprint for the train station? She could go with the two boys, if they decided to go.

No one was talking. T. J. had let his eyes fall shut; he looked tired.

She'd read that sometimes a prisoner didn't want to leave his cell when he had the chance. Certainly she wasn't ready to leave this city.

"I hate to just walk away," she said, "for all we know, the trouble is over."

"And for all we know, it's going to go on for years," Jill said.

"All of you," Natraja said, getting to her feet, "should pack your belongings and go. Do it while you have the chance."

The conversation broke off. Marie looked to see if Natraja was starting one of her fits of pique.

But the dull look in her eyes, as she stood slumped and staring at nothing, was more like fear. It was hard to understand what would frighten her now, with the trouble apparently coming to an end.

"I want every one of you out of my house," she said.

T. J. gave her a weary glance. Even Jill looked patiently condescending.

"Did you hear what I said?" Her voice was petulant, like a child's.

"Natraja, sit down here with us," T. J. said in the forgiving tone of a parent.

Natraja obediently eased down into her seat, her gaze fixed on T. J. Her fat face as she looked at him, the way she ducked her head and hunched her shoulders, gave off an air of submissiveness, of ingrained defeat, so abject that Marie was certain she could smell it, a faint sultry odor. It faded as Natraja simply let her eyes close, lacing her fingers together across her stomach, for all the world as if she'd drifted into sleep.

Marie glanced at T. J.; he shook his head, apparently equally baffled.

CHAPTER TWENTY

TEN MINUTES before curfew was to lift, Jill slipped through the canvas curtain, out of the house. She wanted a head start getting to the airline office, which would no doubt be mobbed with tourists trying to get out, though she still wasn't sure whether to confirm her flight tomorrow or delay it a few days.

Several men in skirtlike *lungis* were already walking up ahead of her. Farther in front of them, the lane was full of walking traffic, men pushing bikes, people carrying buckets and baskets for shopping, and the last fifty feet of the *gali* was packed solid with people come to a halt, more stopping behind her. The front wheel of someone's bicycle rested against the side of her leg.

Over the heads, she could see at a distance the bright sun out on the open street. Then, without any signal that she'd heard, the whole jammed mass of people surged forward in one unit. She moved with them, careful not to stumble. Carried by the noisy pushing flow, past the two cops with their rifles, she was out and standing in open air.

From every direction, more crowds poured onto the wide street. Metal overhead doors slid up, revealing the hole-in-the-wall shops. Everywhere, the vegetable vendors, bangle and makeup *wallahs* were settling in, a *puri* boy already frying his puffed breads. A man selling wooden flutes meandered through the crowd, blowing a tune on one of his Krishna reeds.

It had taken less than a minute, and it was all here as if it had never been gone: the heavy smells of cooking, the haze of dust raised by the traffic. This confusing, overwhelming uproar—she hadn't realized how much she'd missed it, the shiny reds of the rickshaw seats, everything so soaked in color. Looking there at the orange, pink, and magenta silks so quickly strung up in front of a bare stall . . .

She felt herself smiling, an unaccountable delight welling in her.

It was nice, this feeling, light as vapor. And in the same instant, a wild exuberance rising . . .

Gone—nearly the moment she noticed.

Yet the echo—of whatever had just happened—was playing across her still, faint and delicious.

She looked around her at the stall and the passing traffic. All she'd done was admire the silk. But for one quarter second, she'd felt a relief. She strained to recapture it precisely: it was a trustful feeling, free of any burden, but so potent, full of the possibility of anything, everything.

She closed her eyes, opened them again to stare straight at the brilliant display. She focused on a brocade edging, gold thread on watery green silk, trying for it again: the mental pause.

She was making the silk seller uneasy; he watched her over the top of his teacup.

Maybe by trying, she was keeping it from happening.

She walked on to at least get out of range of the silk man.

She had less than two hours now to make up her mind: leave or stay.

She walked, trying not to step on any of the squatting vendors or their wares. The way they piled so close together, there was no real path. She was afraid of stepping down on a propped hand, onto somebody's only good piece of burlap.

During the night she'd gone over it, most often thinking *leave* first, which might be significant. But *stay* was what she inevitably ended with every time she ran the choice through her head.

It seemed clear in the light of day what she should do: fly out tomorrow as scheduled, or even go out to the airport now and get on the next flight; it was possible the city would be shut again tomorrow.

But if she were to miss out on her time here, she might regret it forever, not that she could say why. Obviously, this wasn't the sanctuary she'd imagined. But maybe it would be, once the curfew was lifted and life was normal. Still, to stay would be pure self-indulgence; this was a time she needed to be in the office—

"Madame, rickshaw." A man in a Nehru cap was leaning out from behind the wheel of an auto rickshaw, shouting to her from the edge of the market.

"The Cantonment," she said as she crouched to get into the little cab. "Airline offices."

He wheeled the *tempo* into traffic. "So, you are wanting to leave our holy city." He threw a quick look over his shoulder.

"I don't know yet whether I'm leaving. I had originally planned to fly out tomorrow, but now—"

"How is this?" he said in an exaggerated tone of surprise. "You do not know if you are going or coming? This is very good. To achieve such a state is the dream, I think, of Americans who come to India. You have reached *nirvana,* yes? And so it does not matter whether you are here or there."

T. J. was standing in one of the little telephone-call stores, the rooms around the city where you could pay a man to let you use the phone.

A young fellow was on his hands and knees on top of the desk where the phone sat, scrubbing the worn wooden surface. He didn't look up. A couple of other boys lolled in folding metal chairs along the wall.

"How does this work?" T. J. said finally. "I want to make a call."

"Sixty rupees a minute," he said, bending into his work.

Two dollars. Not exactly a bargain.

"So, what do I do?" T. J. tried to keep the edge out of his voice.

The phone man climbed down off the desk with a show of weariness. "Sit," he said. "Give me the number." He passed a sheet of paper and a pen over to T. J.

Country code, city code: T. J. wrote it all out. The other two boys still stared. He looked past them; above their heads were shelves with movies for rent. He read the English titles: *Sex Sirens of Chicago, Hot Biker Girl.*

The man was dialing, T. J.'s familiar number lighting up in red on a digital panel. He pictured the phone at home on the rickety side table by the open door out to the screened porch. Right next to it would be an old *Better Homes and Gardens* with a rumpled circle on the cover where a glass of iced tea had sat. The adjacent corner of the sofa was Jane's reading spot. The magazines on the end tables were there mainly to use for coasters, though. What she read more and more was romances, for "escape."

Fifth ring. No answer. It was eleven o'clock at night there. She and the girls had probably been asleep for an hour.

Then the man handed him the receiver.

"Hello, hello," he heard Jane saying. She sounded sleepy; he'd woken her up.

"Jane."

"It's you. Hey. Are you . . . Where are you?" She cleared her throat, as if she were about to speak in a business meeting.

"I'm in Varanasi," he said, "Finally had a chance to get to a phone. You got the message I'd arrived?"

"Yeah, my new assistant said the connection was terrible. Are you all right? Do you like it?"

All three men sat, staring at his face. When he shifted his feet, all eyes went to his feet.

"It's okay," he said. "Some complications, but I think everything's worked out now."

He pictured her in one of her long nightgowns, the three buttons unfastened in the front.

"How are the girls? Is everything going all right?"

"It's fine, they're fine. Sally got to play in the soccer game Saturday. I don't know if you remember, she'd been on the bench."

"Of course I remember." After the first game, the child looked like she'd actually gotten smaller; sitting silently in the backseat of the car. He'd wanted to turn around, go back to the school, and back the coach up against that chain-link fence for a talk. "Was she real pleased about it?"

"It's all she's talked about."

"Not complaining about missing her old dad, is she? Have my postcards been getting there?"

"No. No postcards."

"It takes a while, I guess." The nearest man leaned closer until his face was not even three feet away, watching with his chin in his hands.

The monitor said he was up 220 rupees. It flicked to 221.

"Jane, is it . . . Should I let you go back to sleep?"

"No, you're not disturbing me."

"You seem quiet."

Outside the open doorway, a tired-looking bullock was pulling a long flat cart piled high with lumber past two men in rag turbans riding on top of the load.

"Things are fine here, T. J. The girls are doing great." But her voice sounded strained.

"Well, okay, then, that's good. How's work? Did the rest of the audit go all right?"

"Yeah, we're on to new problems, now. I'm trying to get authorization to replace a defective monitor; in the meantime, work is piling up. I'm fed up. I'm thinking seriously about finding something else."

He scanned along the line of video titles. "Like a new husband?" It came out of his mouth before he knew it. Two of the Indian boys exchanged glances.

"Let's don't start something on long distance," Jane said. "You'll be home soon."

"That should give me something to think about here for the next few weeks. How about we talk now?"

He could hear the faint clear mouth sounds in the quiet on the line. She was agitated.

One of the Indians giggled, his friend nudging his arm and egging him on.

T. J. stood up. "You"— he pointed with the receiver at the laughing one—"out of here. All three of you, get out."

The two hangers-on shot a wide-eyed look at the proprietor who reached over and disconnected the phone. "Sir," his face impassive, "that is four hundred sixty-two rupees, please." The boys' mouths gaped in delight.

"You cut off my phone call? You little shit—"

"It is four hundred sixty-two rupees. Pay now."

He grabbed the man by his arm. "Not one minute of privacy to make a phone call—"

He felt a tugging at his hip and whipped around. One of them had snatched his wallet out of his pocket and was pulling out cash.

T. J. grabbed the wallet, but the boy had the money. Flipping through bills, he said something in Hindi to the boss.

The boss said in English, "This is only three hundred fifty-six rupees. Please pay now the rest."

He should demand to be reconnected! But it was impossible to talk here. He hauled his neck sack up through the collar of his T-shirt. It was filthy, he could smell it: a week's worth of sweat. He peeled off some bills and threw them on the desk. "You cut off my call," he said. "I ought to report you to the police."

Stepping down into the dirt edge of the street, he could hear the three of them behind him, laughing over their triumph.

She had to know he wouldn't hang up on her.

But a hot feel of alarm was traveling up his gut. A rickshaw rattled past, overloaded with young men yelling and laughing: pack of hyenas.

"This feels like Coney Island," Marie said to Dilip as she walked ahead of him down a *gali,* festive with jewelers' stalls along both walls. She was delighted to be out, with the city alive again. "I keep thinking of the boardwalk arcades when I traveled east with my dad. That's a long time ago."

"No, madame, it is not far. Very soon."

Dilip had virtually disappeared over the last few days, keeping company with Ramesh in the kitchen or in some other part of the house. Exactly on time, though, he'd reappeared for the break in the curfew to see where she needed to be taken.

She needed to go first to the Golden Temple and see the most revered Shiva *linga* in all India. The black shaft, her book had said, was set in silver and situated just beneath the gold-covered temple spire.

Reading during curfew, she'd been struck by the descriptions of the *linga* as so much more than just a statue of genitals: it stood for the very forces of the universe, the woman's parts as the expanding circles of energy that create the physical world; the man's as the still center of all of life, one balancing the other.

Gawking at the statues, though, the Western tourists didn't tend to be so interested in symbolism.

There, now, across the lane, was a little *linga* set in a cubbyhole in the wall, a few fresh flowers at its base. They were everywhere. And in the neighboring jeweler's stall, a mother and daughter were poring over trays of gold earrings. It was a strange choice of errands for the first time out of the house in days.

In one way, she could make sense of the ebb and flow the *linga* represented. With Michael, over all those years, she'd had a sense of a natural motion. She would reach toward him for a time, then again she'd draw into herself, wanting to be alone or with the babies.

After the more than three years since his death, she was beginning to see that underneath all she remembered—as vividly as if it had happened this morning—there had been a constant rhythm, now halted. She felt motionless and dry.

Up ahead, voices rising. Was there more trouble? No, only a cow coming past, she saw it now, curved horns riding at chest level through the space that opened for its passage. Her hand relaxed on the grip of her cane; she backed close against the wall to let it pass.

"Some very nice necklace today, madame." A young man had stepped in front of her, daintily smoking a cigarette. She gave him a reprimanding look, and he stepped to the side. Still, he had a Clark Gable amused gleam to his dark eyes, the same glossy sweep of hair.

"You would like to see some sights? Burning bodies, Golden Temple?"

"I don't need any help today." She tried to pick her way on past him, but he stuck with her. "Golden Temple is very handsome," he said. "I will take you."

"I have my guide." She waved a hand in the direction of Dilip somewhere behind her.

The man looked back at Dilip, straggling along. "But this man is not Banarasi," he said with a semblance of alarm. "He cannot know Golden Temple."

He was helping himself to a thorough study of her, assessing the quality of her clothing, noting the sag of her neck. Did he think she wouldn't notice?

"What is your country, madame?"

"The United States."

"Aah." He flashed a smile. "California."

"Not for a moment. I'm from the Midwest."

"America!" He was not discouraged. "So you are knowing my friend Ram Dass. This man"—he looked away modestly—"Sri Ram Dass, he is too good to me, giving me his special address." He pulled from the folds of his *dhoti* a business card worn gray and fuzzy at the edges.

"Very nice. Indeed."

The steady stream of faces that came toward her, single file, was shadowed in the low light. She could smell something oily cooking, the heavy odor filling the tunnel. Dilip walked just behind her now, keeping a sharp eye on this new man.

"After Golden Temple, you are liking some stars? I know very good astrology guru. He will tell your future."

"At seventy-six years old, I think I have some idea what's in my future."

"You are so old? Oh, no, it is not possible." He laughed, tossing his head of black hair.

She kept walking, conscious again of the familiar aluminum clack of the joints of her cane.

"But there are many things in your future," he said. "I am knowing this much. I am astrology student. My name is Jagdish. Baba Gomati is my teacher."

"So, it's the job of the student to bring in the business?"

"One day I will sit and let my student bring to me. It is very nice."

"I'm sure it must be."

"Here is Golden Temple," he said, as if announcing a train stop.

She looked down the lane. She looked up along the roof edge several stories above. She didn't see any temple. Although on the left there was a pretty tiled doorway, a multicolored floral design on white tile. She leaned closer to see if it was paint or mosaic.

"No, no," Jagdish said. "That is temple to Annapurna. Not Golden Temple." He pointed upward to a spot above the lane on the other side. "There is Golden Temple."

She looked up through the narrow space between two buildings, no more than a crack for slowing the spread of a fire. She could see a slice of it, a glimpse of the sun on the spire; it was like looking into a different, brilliant world up there above the alley, paved with gold. From where she stood, the tower seemed to float. She looked back down at the *gali* floor to get her balance.

"Three quarter ton of gold," he said.

She scanned the wall of the lane for the temple entrance.

"It is there," he said. Maybe he would make a good psychic, he did seem to anticipate her every thought.

"But of course, madame cannot go in." Pressed by the crowd, he was standing close.

"What?" She leaned away to get a better look at his face. "Why?"

"Madame is not Hindu, I am afraid. Hindu only can go in."

Her book hadn't said a word about that; or maybe it had and she'd forgotten.

A large family, steadying their matriarch by her elbows, was coming out the doorway where others were now gathered to go in. From behind the wall came the sound of chanting and a sudden harsh clanging of bells. She wanted to be inside in the midst of it all, to walk in the courtyard of *lingas* that was somewhere in there. She felt the disappointment spread across her face.

"Oh, please, you must look here." Jagdish was pointing down low in the fire space, at ground level. "See inside," he said. "Excellent temple peephole."

"I beg your pardon?"

"Peephole." He made a ring with his fingers and put it to his eye.

Fifty feet or more into the crevice between the buildings—and it was barely as wide as one person—a big pale Western man was crouched at a grate in the wall of the building, peering in. Several more tourists had lined up single file behind him. Not one of them had more than two inches room on either side.

"I'm not going down any alley to peek at people." She'd feel buried alive standing in that line, someone blocking you in front, someone behind.

"No?" he said with genuine dismay. "Then some astrology, madame. Yes, you must get your future prediction. Only very close from here."

It wasn't the sort of thing she'd consider for a second at home. Dilip was resting against a wall, haughtily ignoring the insult of Jagdish's presence but clearly pleased also not to have to work.

"What is your name, madame?" Jagdish said.

"Marie Jasper," she said, yielding to him further.

"Come, Mrs. Marie. We go to Baba Gomati."

Before she'd had time to think, he had taken hold of her arm. They were hurrying along the lane, faster than she was accustomed to traveling.

Michael used to say she had a weakness for the young men. It proved she was alive, she told him, though at that stage she hadn't needed to prove it.

Jagdish led her through the labyrinth of lanes for what must have been three quarters of a mile. The grandchildren, especially Alex, would love playing in this maze full of hiding places and all kinds of livestock walking around unfettered.

"Mrs. Marie, it is here." They had come to a stop at a brightly lit open-sided room set into the wall, like a stage two feet above the *gali* floor.

"Sit." He motioned to the edge. "Just one second." He vanished into the crowd.

Dilip stationed himself a few feet away, fraying the ends of a bit of twine.

At the sound of footsteps behind her, she turned to see a plump-cheeked, big-bellied man with an overflowing beard, the look on his face at once sweet and smug. "This is Baba Gomati." Jagdish reappeared, climbing down beside her. "Very good astrology. Your life, your health, everything."

The astrologer had sunk down into a Buddha pose on a cushion, waiting for her to get herself over there and join him. Putting aside the indignity of it, she scooted backward into the room. Dilip, at the last moment stirring himself to be useful, tossed her cane in after her and settled at the room's edge.

The guru smiled serenely.

"How much do you charge?" she said.

"Five hundred and one rupees." He let his eyes close. That would be twenty dollars; by Indian standards, a staggering amount.

"Extra rupee is for good fortune," he said.

"The five hundred isn't too bad a fortune in itself." She could already feel the ache in her lower vertebrae from sitting without support.

The astrologer eyed her, his head canted. Dilip and Jagdish sat in attendance.

"Let's get going," she said, "before my joints give out."

He nodded in his magisterial manner. He took up a thick notebook and flipped through to a clean page. "It is excellent for you that you have come to me."

She stifled a comment.

He settled to his task, writing down her date and hour and place of birth. She was born in the dark of early morning, she told him, in the bedroom closest to the kitchen on the farm in east Iowa. It was in the winter of a year when blight had done terrible damage to the corn. But he wasn't listening; instead, he was hunched over, examining her right hand. He rocked his body and rolled his head around on his shoulders. This performance lasted five minutes or more.

Finally he began to talk in a high singsong, continuing to rock. "I am seeing that you have had a very long life."

The audacity . . .

"Most excellent family," he said, "very good husband, many grandchildren." It was entirely predictable.

"I see in the present," he said with a theatrical lift of his chin, "that the planets have changed." He hesitated, for effect. "You visit India today; last year you have traveled in some other place. Not good, not bad. But now I see coming change."

He began describing the alignment of planets in tedious detail, referring to ascendants and whatnot.

She interrupted him with a wave of her hand. "What change? And how long do I have? To live."

"Extremely long. Many, many years."

"You're toying with me." She glanced at Jagdish and Dilip. They were solemn as acolytes.

"No, madame, it is true. You will live more than one hundred years."

She heard Jagdish murmur: "Madame is most venerable."

What would she find to do with twenty-five more years? She couldn't imagine. She wasn't doing herself or anybody else much good now.

"What about my family?" she said. "They are in good health for a very long time?" She winced, realizing she'd imitated him.

"I cannot say. Too many people, and I do not know their hands or stars. It is not so easy."

Her list was not intended for a life that went on so long. Sitting in the living room at three in the morning, about six months after Michael's death, she had written out a list of assignments for herself: learning Italian, searching out every childhood friend or third cousin of hers or Michael's who was still alive, getting a computer and figuring out e-mail. It had taken her hours to select the items, because each one, however trifling or difficult, was a vow. The sun had come up before she was finished. Sleep by the Ganges was number thirty-eight, though she certainly hadn't been doing them in order.

Gomati was speaking. "This time is important moment for your life. These very curfew days. You have come to Varanasi when there is much trouble." He waved a hand. "For the silk merchants and the vegetable *wallahs* who cannot sell their goods. For the guru astrologer who cannot see so many people to read their charts. When the tourists go away, all is lost."

She opened her mouth, but he overrode her: "You come in this difficult period. There is danger. And who can say where it will end? Yet your chart is telling me you will think of this time until you are more than one hundred." He spoke slowly and carefully. "Because you are not, what do you call it, a spectator? You are not this. Though I cannot discern what your part is. Only that you are coming to Varanasi to find your way through these narrow *galis* with your three-point cane like the trident of Shiva, and it is not only for the touristic pleasures. Or even to learn the moment of your dying. You are a very important person here."

Then he blinked his eyes one time ceremoniously and cleared his throat. "So, that is five hundred and one rupees. I thank you."

Jagdish and Dilip were staring with new respect.

It was exciting—the prospect of having some calling, some importance. It was heady.

She thought again of Natraja's face that first morning out on the river; emotion, like violent weather, had transformed her in just moments as she'd stared at the river. Marie had envied that passion, whatever it was about.

But she knew better than to take any of this fortune-telling folderol too seriously. She reached for her cane, her pocketbook. It was nothing more than a boardwalk amusement, like the game where how hard you swing the sledgehammer tells you whether you're a good lover.

Gomati sat with his chin lifted, smug as a camel, ready to receive payment and praise. The two guides looked at Marie as if she might be a deity just descended to the earth.

There was no reason they should be so surprised—that was what she wanted to tell them as she got to her feet easily, like somebody forty years old with things to do. She had always been a ball of fire.

She reached over and patted the guru's beard: springy. . . . He managed to hide his astonishment.

It was a little embarrassing to be this awash with gratitude at merely knowing someone still saw the life in her.

CHAPTER TWENTY-ONE

RAMESH SHOPS in this market—he must be here.

From the bench of this idled rickshaw, I will spot him.

The plaza so jammed with people swarming in every direction, yet the heat is stagnant, trapped between the buildings on either side. It is a decade since I came out at midday.

He had no reason to leave the house ten minutes before break began. It shocks me he would do this. Did he think the vegetables would sell out? He knows his vendors and surely realizes they would put aside for him.

This sneakiness makes me suspicious. I could have him followed. He would never involve himself in the violence, though he might well be part of some effort to stop it.

A woman shouts—the bean-and-cauliflower seller whacking her stick across a goat's sharp spine; his hooves clatter against the stone as he ducks away. I have heard Ramesh speak of this woman.

"Bahar jao!" she screams after the fleeing creature. *"Jao."* Get away.

The goat has come to a stop near where I sit. His jaw works, trailing the ends of string beans.

He collapses to his knees, felled by a whistling blow—by God, she has followed him. The goat springs away again, this time disappearing beyond the milling crowd.

The vendor's retreating back, as she hurries again to her vegetables, looks spare and mean in its dirty cloth.

"You—" I am startled to hear myself. *"Gali na dijiye!"* Do not abuse. Vendors and shoppers stare at me up on my perch; a policeman standing near looks toward me, lifting his chin.

I cannot stop myself: *"Ainda aisa na karna,"* I call out, up off my bench. Then louder, in English: "Never do it again."

She raises her stick and gives me her evil eye.

The policeman—or a soldier, is it?—comes toward me, carrying his bamboo club. But there is no law against shouting.

"What is the problem?" he says in Hindi. His heavy-lidded eyes are haughty, as if he is bored with his work.

"The problem," I say, taking my seat again, "is the killing you gun-and-club men have not managed to prevent."

He is silent, looking me over. "I have seen you threaten that woman."

"I threaten no one."

His left hand fingers a ridge of his club. He looks not more than twenty, with the stance of reckless authority.

"It is you," he steps closer, "who has sent an Indian man into the street, forced him to break curfew for your errands."

"No," I say, shaking my head. "I didn't send him."

He hides a smile—I stop.

What have I done? He will blame Ramesh. Ramesh will be arrested.

"No, he does not break curfew. I swear it." The man is withdrawing, smiling; he does not listen. "Sir!" I call after him. "I am certain you are thinking of some other."

It must be an hour I have sat, searching the passing crowds. If I stir, the truth of what I have done will break open inside me.

I have brought danger on Ramesh.

He could be in jail already, though the man with the club remains in the range of my vision.

More likely he has quickly gathered the supplies and gone to pray in a temple. But that is where they would look for him—the police—at a shrine or on the riverbank: his devotion is well-known.

No one should go to the shrines today; there could be no more logical place for an avenger to strike.

The shoppers circle past. I had only to keep myself indoors.

He will have to pass this guard to get home, unless he prowls through hallway and courtyard on some secret route.

I have endangered him—

Focus—what do I see: fissures in the dry ground; a dog near the wall gnaws at the wound on his leg, flies crawling in his hair. I have had sores like that, red-rimmed yellow craters beneath the folds of fat.

I'll get down and walk—out of the guard's sight. He watches as I grip the side of the seat and lower one foot toward the ground. Strings of my hair stick to my shoulders where I am bare. The squash-and-potato man in front of me packs up his sacking, letting his eyes run over me.

People stared in Neavis, too. I could not step out our front door without the passengers in passing cars twisting to look. In front of me now: glass bangles. They clink on the arm of a girl who admires her wrist. Under my sari, my thighs slide against each other as I walk. The flesh slaps, loud as my heartbeat. The man coming toward me in a *dhoti*—his bare legs are no more than sticks. I weigh as much as three of him. The fat of my abdomen hangs below my sex. In recent days, I have eaten even beyond my usual habit, and in the presence of people.

This boy up ahead will sell me fried bread. I must have brought money. Yes, here it is. A warm morsel will soothe me. The wafer is still hot, oozing grease as it crunches in my mouth. It is the rhythm of it, bringing food to my mouth, that helps me calm. The boy, serving another customer, eyes me sternly. "I will pay," I say, covering my mouth full of food with my wrist. "When you are ready."

He can pack me up a full parcel; there is time yet to have it delivered to the house. What I need will be more than I can carry.

"Memsahib!"

"Ramesh!" I cry out, forcing the mouthful down. He is here! I want to prostrate myself and sob. I want to strike him for leaving.

"Curfew has descended." His voice is urgent. "Please, we should go—"

A metal door slams down then in the wall of the building a hundred meters away; a second bangs shut, closer by. Something has happened; word is spreading. The bread boy wants his cash. I hand him a bill without looking.

"Where are Mrs. Marie and the others?" He is heading us toward the mouth of the *gali* where the sentry stands, face angled slightly away.

"They scattered, the guests. Wait. We must take some other route."

"No time."

As the policeman brings himself around toward us, Ramesh's face goes rigid. He lets out a hiss of scorn.

"Have you gone mad?" I rasp at him.

"It is that lout," he says sidelong, all the while moving us toward the *gali.*

"Whoever he is, do not utter his name or he will see."

The two of us go forward in an uneven rhythm.

We enter the lane, the cop on my left, Ramesh at my right. This indolent boy in uniform casts his gaze across me at Ramesh. "This is the old rag picker who broke curfew," he murmurs, close to my ear.

I lay my hand on Ramesh's shoulder, feel his surprise at the touch. In the next moment, I sense beneath my palm his very fiber receiving the message, the reminder that—usually—even the roughest will not take the law into his own hands while a white foreigner is near. Ramesh holds himself stiff as we walk, both of us fixing our eyes straight ahead.

CHAPTER TWENTY-TWO

FROM HER bench at the edge of the trees, Marie could see swarms of monkeys playing and screeching. This temple, a little distance from the *galis,* and surrounded by gardens, was so much nicer. In front of her on the brick path, people in their church finery were coming and going.

She fanned herself with her folded city map, watching an odd creature that looked like a small llama grazing at the edge of the crowd. She'd left Jagdish shaking his head at her coming to another neighborhood with only an hour until curfew. But she wasn't going to waste this time, no matter how many more years she had.

It was so pleasant to sit out under the trees. She hadn't seen so much as a bush since the taxi ride from the Varanasi airport. These banyans looked 500 years old, with their shaggy hanging vines, which, she'd been interested to read, were actually an above-ground root system.

Across the way Dilip stood, talking to the man at the booth selling sweets and garlands for offerings. A young couple—the woman carrying a sleeping two-year-old—came past on the brick walk. Sitting outdoors again in the midst of so much life and activity, with the chanting drifting out the open doorway, she felt as content as that baby. The August they'd spent at the Maine shore, she'd gone to sleep every night to the sound of waves breaking, the deep uneven beat, and a light rushing that washed over: men's voices, and women's.

A break in the chant—oddly abrupt, but she knew so little about Indian music. She waited for it to resume.

Perhaps the ceremony was over.

A tight cluster of family and a straggle of others hurried from the temple doorway. She looked for Dilip. The man in the sweet shop was reaching to shut down his awning.

Something seemed amiss. She reached for her bag and cane, spotting Dilip across the way. But there were people still arriving: here was a man coming up the path by himself. He looked oddly familiar. He stopped short of her bench, watching from under the canopy of trees as more people emerged.

The temple was certainly emptying. She should go.

The man near her held a white package tucked under his arm—a box of sweets, no doubt, that he'd brought for an offering. She could see the red print on the lid; it looked exactly like the sweet boxes Natraja left piled in the trash.

Yet she could not stop the sudden thought: bomb. He has come here to leave that bomb. Rajiv Gandhi only months ago had been killed by a woman stepping forward to greet him with a bomb hidden under her clothes. At home, through a long night, she'd watched the funeral on CNN, the lighting of the pyre. But that had been a different part of the country, with different factions, and he was the head of state, the son of Indira Gandhi.

Getting to her feet, she noticed how her heart was beating.

Perhaps she was more nervous about the violence than she'd thought.

She squinted for a better look at the man's face; to see if he really looked like Dana, as she had imagined for a moment. He was gone. Of course, he hadn't looked like Dana; last time she'd seen their foster child, he'd been only eight years old.

A group of women glided past her in their elegant saris, talking and laughing. They didn't seem worried. She looked back to where the man had stood.

There on a bench, twenty feet away, was the white box with the red print.

A young girl had perched on the other end—barefoot, braids dark against the red of her little *salwar* shirt.

"Get away," Marie shouted, motioning with her free arm. "Run!"

The child stared wide-eyed, started to laugh. Marie was backing, now twenty-five, now thirty feet, away. "Go." She pointed the girl to run. Still seated, the little girl laughed again and called to someone.

The monkeys had noticed the box now and were scampering, the first spidery hand pulling at it.

The child, making a face at the monkey, slid off the bench.

Marie ran, fast as she could, stabbing the ground with her cane, heading for the gate. She twisted to catch a glimpse over her shoulder. The girl was ambling.

The silent flash spread wide, blue-white. In the next instant, the sound smashed against her shoulder and face; she strained for air—she was falling, seeing it all happen in one instant above her: the monkeys swallowed up in smoke, the mango tree bent at the middle.

Then it was silent. Marie lifted a hand to touch her ear, but her arm was pinned beneath her. She clung to the ground, leaves and sticks dropping on her.

From some distant neighborhood, far beyond the silence, came the faint singsong of a vegetable man.

Then sounds of screaming and running rose up all around her.

Was that the little girl crying?

She raised her head. "Over here," she called out. She tried to get to her feet; one arm wouldn't push. "Dilip!" Someone crouched beside her, a rag tied across his nose and mouth.

"Help me up, help me, there was a girl . . ."

She heard him calling to someone.

Two men lifted her and ran with her. Jostled, half dragged out of the courtyard, she saw dark shapes appear and vanish in the dust; a sharp wail rose from the ground close by. But it wasn't a child's voice. She closed her eyes against the smoke and grit.

Lying on the car seat, she heard the voices of men in front.

She fumbled at her side. "My cane . . ." then she realized where she was. She'd lost track.

The car bumped along, pain shooting the length of her arm.

"You are needing to rest." He was a policeman. She tried to sit up. One eye was burning and watering so she couldn't see out of it.

"We return to your hotel," he said. "They will be having a doctor."

"Was there a girl—"

"You must rest and have no worry."

He was facing forward again.

She slowly straightened her arm, felt along the bone. Nothing was broken. Dilip was likely safe; he'd been standing at a distance.

"But did you find a child?"

The man didn't answer.

The car rounded a curve, then another. Had she told them where she was staying? She couldn't remember.

"Sir . . ."

He looked at her again—the yellow whites of his eyes were bloodshot.

"Sir, did I—" She was starting to cry. "I should have yelled, 'Bomb.'"

He leaned closer. "The bomb you have seen?"

"I thought I was crazy, I would look foolish—"

"What is this bomb?"

"I should have warned people." She tried to collect herself.

"Please, madame, what did you see?"

"A white box, sweet box."

"You have seen someone place this box?"

"He wore a long scarf." Her nose was dripping. The officer handed her his bandanna. The sulfur smell of it burned in her nose.

The silence after the bomb: she'd felt that emptiness in the hospital room when Michael's next breath hadn't come and she felt the life go out of his skin.

Outside the car window, the street was empty. She saw a monkey running along the edge of a roof. She shouldn't have come to India by herself.

"Madame, what did he look like?"

She imagined the scene in her mind, the brick path, the shade. He was short, had black hair; he was dark-skinned. She was crying again. "I'm sorry—"

"You are needing to take some tea," he told her, "have your rest."

Rest was not going to help. She searched his face. He looked exhausted, as if he hadn't slept in days. "At your hotel," he said, "you will have peace."

CHAPTER TWENTY-THREE

ON MY roof in the hot night air, I eat my cakes as if nothing has changed. The child has died—and another more distant bystander struck by falling cinder block. The evening's paper has given the names.

The police had to lift Marie up the step into the house. Her clothes pulled all awry, eyes dull and frightened. They'd found her a few feet from the lethal edge of the explosion.

Tonight I look down the riverbank; I have never seen the city so still. Under the security lights, the concrete steps are empty. Not one breaks curfew.

Marie went to bed not knowing. Tomorrow she will blame herself for not saving the girl.

A bomb in a box of sweets. The Shiva worshippers have it right: sweet and deadly all in one. It is more cruel that way, adding the element of betrayal. My mind lingers on betrayal. It would have been easier for me if I'd never had feeling for Vic. It's bitter in my mouth even to think it, that I had loved him. But I was a child. Silent, brooding as he was, I knew—or thought I did—that in time of trouble, he would do anything for me.

Down below, a Shiva shrine sits at the point of the next *ghat*. I see the shadow in the moonlight. Am I supposed to offer prayerful thanks to the gods that Marie is alive tonight? The man who set this bomb—I could rip his throat open with any ragged edge at hand, the lid cut from a tin can.

It is all I do, daydream and eat. I disgust myself. Year after year I sit, comforted by rhythm and sweetness, all sensation blunted. Rocking, filling my mouth—the shredded coconut fresh and oily. These sweets tonight are like little birthday cakes. I remember the photo on my birthday at ten—one of the last pictures from before—showed me scraggle-haired, my elfin face bright and open.

Mama, when she couldn't get things out of her mind, would sew lace and ribbon onto the edges of pillowcases, all the time singing her mother's old hymns.

Rock of ages, cleft for me,
Let me hide myself in thee.

Familiar phrases running together, fitting into one tune.

Blessed assurance,
Ancient of days,
This is my story
All the day long.

Heaving upward to my feet, I take an unsteady step—drunk on sugar—holding the guardrail, keeping my balance.

God of our fathers, whose almighty hand,
Born of His Spirit, washed in His blood.

"Ganga!" The name has a different rhythm from the hymns. The heat so heavy and smothering seems almost to coat the sound. In Neavis, I had no warning, no chance to pray or beg. Spitting acid to the pavement below, "River," I shout as I lift my head.

There is not even an echo.

Louder, each sound distinct: "River goddess—you protect Ramesh!" The hot night swallows up my words.

River and city are silent. My cupped hand, wet and full of food, rises to my face.

"Memsahib." Ramesh's voice behind me. He is holding my arms. "Madame, come to your bed."

"No, you must leave. I am doing my *pujas.*" If he comes too near, the gods will punish us.

"You must sleep," he says. He holds the backs of my arms; it is not accidental. I can't resist. He steers me.

It's almost noon," T. J. is sprawled in a chair at my table. "Do you think we should check on Marie?"

"Let her sleep," I tell him; it is not as if he would be the one to go into that room and rouse her to face the day.

"We should have left when we had the chance." Jill sits at the edge of her seat, jiggling one leg. The sight makes my head pound.

"Stop that."

She knows what I am referring to: she stops. T. J. stirs his tea. It's down to the three of us and Ramesh, and Marie in her bed. All the others have left the city, Marie's Dilip included.

Jill casts a searching look toward T. J.; it is possible some intimacy occurred between them last night in the scramble of emotions.

"Here she is." T. J. is getting to his feet, the perfect gentleman. "We had begun to worry about you."

"No need for that." Marie pushes her cane, with its clacking sound, out in front of her with each step.

Ramesh sets down a fresh pot of tea, pouring out a cup.

Marie looks past it. "What did the news say?"

"Two were killed." I keep my tone void of expression. T. J. is glad to leave this for me to do. "Several more injured."

"The little girl?"

"A young girl is one of the two who died."

Marie's eyes are hidden by the light that hits her glasses. Her pallid face does not change. She seems not to hear. The other two have grown dutifully somber. There's a rustling out in the *gali.* . . .

"You warned her," I say, "and got yourself to safety. It was the right course."

Jill busies herself with looking toward the kitchen after Ramesh.

"I am sorry you were so unlucky," I say to Marie.

"I was lucky," she says.

T. J. shifts as if he would speak, but he does not. I have an impulse to ask about his time in the army, about how many he killed.

Out in the *gali*—it is surely some animal. I listen for Ramesh. Silence, then from the kitchen the knocking of a spoon.

Marie sits, holding the edge of the table, tightly composed. "I think I hear something outside," I say, getting up to go to the door.

Pushing aside the canvas flap—we must have this door locked—there, down the corridor, I see a lean foraging goat. He noses his way along the stones. His ribs show. Snuffling, he comes closer; he is dirty gray with dark blotches. "Stay here," I say to him. "For one moment."

In the dining room, my guests are staring this way and that, T. J. idly tapping the end of his dinner knife on the surface of my table. No one wants to look at Marie and see how her face has fallen slack. I should have put her on the train at the first break in curfew.

"It is only an animal," I say, but they are not paying attention. While Ramesh isn't looking, I slip my plate from the table.

Lemon rind, bread crusts—I slide them onto the ground. The goat does not give me one glance of thanks, no more than does Marie for my efforts with her.

The corners and bits of toast scatter and disappear as if a vacuum were taking them up. Lowering myself with difficulty to sit on the concrete stoop, I put out a hand and touch the stiff prickles of hair along the ridge of his back. Yesterday, Marie folded herself against me like a child, clung to my arm; and Ramesh last night guided me to my bed. I had forgotten, in these years, the damp impress, the gradual heat of another's skin.

In the shed where we hid, we couldn't see each other, Reggie and I, not whole, just an eye or a piece of shoulder caught for a second in light from between the logs. When we heard the voices—right at that instant, my hand was roaming up inside his T-shirt. We had our shorts on, but that wouldn't have mattered.

The two of us held perfectly still. I felt the sweat come out on his chest.

From outside: "We may as well take it all with us. To the house."

They stood a few feet from where we were lying. "I sure don't see the reason for that, when we can lay it up right here in the shack."

"Do what I said."

Reggie's heart was hitting like a fist, so loud I thought they'd hear.

The dragging of something heavy outside vibrated the ground. Whatever piece of farm equipment they were pulling, they took it to the house with them. Nobody ever so much as walked up to our door.

CHAPTER TWENTY-FOUR

JILL YANKED at the corner of her mosquito net, trying to hike the sagging center out of her face. All day and night, the air had felt muggier than usual, the airmail stationery sticking to the side of her hand.

> Dear Ben . . .

It didn't matter what she wrote: she'd heard the mail had stopped going out and letters in the street boxes would be dumped.

> I started thinking about how long
> we've been seeing each other . . .

That sounded like she was going to put pressure on him. She began again on a fresh page.

> Dear Ben,
> I think we've wasted the last five months.

Startled, she looked at what she'd written. She crossed out the "I think," and went on.

> There's trouble here; the whole city is under curfew because of religious riots. I don't know how many people have been killed.
>
> Stuck here like this, I can't pretend to myself about us. I guess I was excited at first but then kept on just to have somebody to go out with, and I've thought all along you were seeing me until you met somebody. We could still go to a movie, have sex, maybe, I don't know. It's what we're doing, anyway; it would be more companionable somehow to admit it . . .

T. J. must have gone mad from the heat if he really thought she'd made a pass at him. Stopped for a second in the hall after dinner—they'd been talking about Marie—the next thing she knew he was looking embarrassed and saying he had to go. All she'd done was put her hand on his arm. She'd meant it to be friendly.

> although I may feel differently about that when I'm home, if I ever get there. I nearly got Marie killed, the old woman staying here. I had told her about a temple with a garden that I'd read about. But then I didn't go with her because I needed to reschedule my plane flight. When they carried her into the guest house and I heard where it had happened, where the bomb had gone off, I threw up on the kitchen floor. Ramesh, the cook, held a wet towel on my face before he rushed over to Marie. He must have a wife somewhere, I can't imagine he wouldn't.

She stopped to wipe the sweat; her nightgown was soaked through.

> I'm going to push this letter down in the toilet. It's nothing but a shit hole with a foot ledge on each side where you stand, or squat. The sewage probably runs straight into the Ganges with all the ashes and garbage. If you die in Banaras you don't have to be reincarnated: it's over.

Closing her eyes, she imagined her body tied to a bamboo stretcher, wrapped tightly round and round with the silk bindings. Long and thin, she was the shape of a knife. Lying on the pallet faceup, she was carried. And she could see, even though her eyes were covered: drifts of smoke were rising from the pyre down near the water.

Her eyes opened.

She stared at the inky tip of her ballpoint, then crushed the letter into a ball.

Pushing the net out of the way, she flung her legs over the side of the bed.

The hallway along this first floor was dark except for the one small night-light up high on the wall. She could hear the windup alarm clock ticking inside Marie's room. At the end of the hall, the bathroom door was standing ajar.

She reached in, groping for the pull string of the light. She hadn't dabbed any perfume under her nose, so she sucked in air through her mouth. Where was the fucking string? The open window up high let in a block of moonlight that made everything else darker. She waved her free hand overhead—nothing, it must be caught up on something. The chemical cleaner was almost worse than the stench.

She tried to imagine riffling though the pages of a magazine, a fat *Vanity Fair,* sniffing the breeze of mingled perfume ads.

From outside the high window came the whisper of river water against the *ghat*. It sounded so close. Maybe there was a stronger current than usual, more runoff coming down from the mountains.

She felt with her feet for the places to stand over the hole.

The murmuring was louder—no, it was her imagination. She balanced herself with a hand against the wall, dropped the balled-up letter in.

The whispering outside was somebody talking.

She should have torn the letter to shreds. She wasn't even sure if it had gone in. If somebody found it, they would know who had written it.

The voice rose again; someone was singing.

Was that . . . ? She listened hard. It was Ramesh. He was outside at the corner of the building, just on the other side of this wall. She'd seen him there once before, sitting cross-legged with his brass kettle of river water. But at night?

She stepped across the toilet hole to stand below the high window ledge. She could tell from the sound that he sat a little to the right of where she stood.

On tiptoe, ear almost at the level of the window—it was definitely him, seated at the level of her feet and the lip of the toilet hole, out there in the moonlight, singing his river prayers. He sounded like the cantor she'd heard at a funeral, his voice mournful and soothing. She leaned the side of her face against the wall, gripping the concrete edge of the sill with both hands.

Outside, his voice meandered higher, rose quickly higher still. She held her breath and waited for a storm of grief to break from him, some relief. He kept on, a keening whisper; she couldn't stand it. Each note pushing against the next as if his sorrow were an actual weight coming up.

Tears rose in her eyes; her cheek pressed against the bumpy concrete.

Holding her balance, she reached out sideways, guessing at the place on the wall that would be just behind where he sat. Satisfied for no good reason that she had found it, she pressed her hand there as if to comfort him.

CHAPTER TWENTY-FIVE

TWELVE PUSH-UPS and the sweat was plopping off him in big drops. It was dark, not quite five in the morning. He'd been too antsy to sleep, had finally gotten out of bed and come up onto the roof.

It would be a reasonable time to call and catch Jane.

He pushed his weight up slowly. Last night when he got back to the room, there was the telegram that he'd since memorized: *T. J., call if emergency, otherwise please write or fax office. We're okay. Love, Jane.*

"We're okay." Did that mean the two of them, or her and the girls? For the hundredth time in the last few months, he'd taken a step toward her and she'd taken two away.

A bunch of chittering monkeys scrambled along a rooftop several buildings away.

He lowered himself again toward the floor.

The concrete had a fresh-washed smell, rough against the side of his face.

He could go to see the Rais. He needed to get away from here; he was hovering on the verge of losing his temper most of the time. Before curfew, Mrs. Rai had insisted he come for tea any day.

He rolled over faceup. The sky was navy blue with a

few pale unfamiliar stars. He should have packed a star map. Rai would have one, though, in his library.

Maybe Jane had decided that she liked his not being around, not butting into everything. Now with him gone, she'd have solitude to think and brood. She'd read in bed. She'd sprawl on the ground, playing some make-believe game with Elizabeth. Hurrying the girls into the car in the mornings, she'd go off to the office in her suits and heels, leaving clean laundry cooling in the basket and the kitchen full of the chalky smell of detergent. Tears came to his eyes, so rooted in his brain was that smell of home with her there.

He couldn't imagine her telling him to leave. But she hadn't said no. . . . The concrete he was lying on seemed to spin and wobble like a Frisbee.

This was crazy, to get himself agitated. They were good, the two of them; they loved each other. He needed to put things in perspective, get away from this house.

At dusk, T. J. hiked down the steps of the *ghat* to the river. He'd been advised to walk until he came upon someone with a boat who would paddle him up to the other end of the city. The river was the closest thing to a safe zone, Natraja had said; there still were a few men in rowboats willing to take a customer. At the same time, she had assured him she would not risk herself or anyone else if he got into trouble.

He walked along a step, following it downriver; didn't see any boatmen, though. The city was so quiet, like the marshes at home. The way the light hit the riverbank and the skyline at this time of day turned everything gold. With each step, he could hear the grinding of grit against the paving. The whole city, all the exteriors, could use a good hosing-down.

"Sir, you are liking boat?"

A young boy had pattered up silently behind him. The child

pointed down the steps to a long rowboat. Squatted in the stern was an older boy, who motioned him to come.

They headed down the steps. "Where you are going?" He had a cowlick right in the front; couldn't be more than eight.

"Up to Naya Ghat."

The boy didn't hesitate. "One hundred rupee."

"That's a whole lot more than usual, isn't it?"

The boy shrugged. "One hundred rupee. Come."

"I guess you're charging extra since these are sort of difficult times."

The boy smiled. "Come."

T. J. followed.

They stepped across three empty rowboats to reach the one he'd hired. The boy scampering ahead of him seemed almost weightless. T. J.'s own bulk dipped the bow of each successive boat; as he stepped to the next, the one before would bob up again in the water.

He settled onto a bench at the stern. The older boy put the oars into motion, sliding out, pointing them toward the far northern end of the city.

The water was glassy.

At home, the river'd get choppy with the slightest breeze, good-sized waves so that a little motorboat was always bucking and throwing up spray. Where they were situated on the Nagacochee wasn't that far from the coast.

He let his gaze run along the high steps that paved the whole river edge of the city. The way the *ghats* were built, it was as if the city itself had been finished with a beveled edge. One little girl was out scavenging for cow dung in a raggedy dress, a big straw basket balanced on her head. At a hundred yards, you could see that the dress was falling off her.

He reached down in his pants pocket, where he had half a candy bar. "You boys like chocolate?" He handed it to the nearest one.

"Yes. Chocolate." The little guy broke it in half and passed the other half on to his brother.

They smiled at him. The little boy seemed to be on sentry duty, scanning every minute.

"You worried about being out here?"

The older one answered. "The river is more safe."

"But not really safe?"

The boy laughed and took another long pull on the oars. The light was getting lower. It would take a half hour or more to reach the far end. This was the time Natraja had said he should do this, if he was going to. They were pretty far out toward the center of the river, maybe half a mile. The tourist boats usually ran along the horseshoe shoreline so people could see the bathers and the burning bodies. This boy was taking a shortcut, a straight line between the two points. There was only one boat between them and the shore.

The little boy was twisted around, nodding his head over to the other boat 150 or so feet away.

His brother started pulling harder at the oars. "Do not look, I am telling you," he said.

T. J. looked. At the side of the other boat, two men leaned toward a white shape in the water, half as long as the boat.

It was a body, wrapped in white.

What were they doing out here? You were supposed to burn dead bodies; dumping wasn't allowed.

The men were bent over what they were doing, the one at the stern, the oarsman, faced T. J.

"Sir, mister, do not look there."

T. J. couldn't look away. The body was tied to a board and weighted by two huge stones at the ends.

The voices of the men floated across the water. They let go, and he saw it roll, dark-stained on one side and on the head.

"Sir, you must stop."

He wanted to stop.

A splash of water went up a foot high or more at the spot where the body went under.

He looked at the boys and only then thought of what he had

done. The older one was pulling, fast as he could go, swearing in Hindi.

He had made them witnesses.

He started to look again toward the other boat, to see if they were following. He caught himself.

"Are they coming after us?" he said to the bigger boy. "Can you see?

The boy kept rowing. He didn't answer.

T. J. listened for the splashing of a boat coming up behind them. He couldn't hear anything but the roiling of the water beside them. Onshore, the skyline was zipping past. They seemed to be flying, the angry-eyed boy on the oars rowing like a demon. The sun had gone down on the other side of the city, the light out here down to almost nothing. He'd screwed up. If this had happened at home, he'd have gone straight to the sheriff with his story and descriptions of the men; he'd have gone to the boys' parents and let them know what was up. But he wasn't at home, and his normal, automatic responses were of no use now at all.

The street was wide open to the night sky. The walls along each side of the road guarded houses that, from what he could see of them, looked like gardened cloisters. He hadn't appreciated the wealth of Rai's neighborhood when he was here before. He sauntered along, making a point of not hurrying. He was glad to see a streetlight though.

When he'd gotten out of the boat, he'd paid the older boy, apologizing again. He asked for his name, but the kid wouldn't give it, just took the money and shoved off into the water, not looking back.

T. J. consulted a scrap of paper with his key-ring flashlight. It had to be close. In the wall across the street was a gate that looked right, rising to a point in the center. That was it—he recognized the shape of the roof and the mass of vines on the balcony.

He rang the bell. Behind the gate, the front door opened. It was Dr. Rai, silhouetted against the light of the interior.

He stepped out, barefoot, holding open the door. "Dr. Clayton, good evening. Please, hurry and come inside."

The two of them stood in the half-lit foyer, Rai looking him over. "I am surprised," he said, "that you have ventured here in these circumstances." Switching on lights, Rai ushered him into the living room, where he'd eaten breakfast only last week.

From the dim archway into the dining room, he saw Mrs. Rai.

"Mr. T. J., I am glad you have come to take some tea."

She did remember that he'd been invited. He fell into the first easy chair.

Rai sat across from him, pretending to be relaxed. Mrs. Rai had gone, he presumed, into the kitchen.

"So, did you have any problem in finding us?"

The fan was turning slow enough that you could see the shadows the blades cast on the ceiling.

"Out on the river," T. J. said, "I saw a body, a corpse."

"Yes?"

"It was dumped by men who'd towed it out there, keeping it hidden just at water level. It was wrapped in a bloody sheet."

"Aah." Rai was nodding. "Aah," he said again.

The house was so still. Both their children, he'd said, now lived in London.

"So, what should we do?" T. J. said.

"Do?"

"Yes."

"I am afraid there is little that we can do. I am glad that you have come to no harm."

"But there are the two boys."

Rai looked puzzled.

"The fellows who rowed me here."

"These boys will be careful to take care of themselves. I think that you do not need to worry."

He heard the teacup set down beside him.

Mrs. Rai was bent near him, her face two feet from his, arranging a plate for him. Her hair was pulled back from her face in a shiny coiled braid. The diamond stud in her earlobe glinted blue, then yellow against her skin. She smelled good.

Rai was watching.

"Mr. T .J. has had an eventful journey to find us tonight," he said to his wife, who was settling herself into a chair, her filmy sari in little folds around her. "He has witnessed on the river a suspicious event, perhaps the result of some foul play."

"What is happening in the city is a tragedy." She looked up from her teacup and met T. J.'s eyes.

"I fear what the lingering effect of the Ayodhya dispute will be," Rai said.

"Which dispute is this?

"In the city of Ayodhya nearby"—Rai slid into his lecturing mode—"militant Hindus favor pulling down a Muslim mosque to replace it with a temple of their own."

T. J. opened his mouth to speak, then remembered that the Rais were Hindu.

"There was originally a Hindu temple there on a sacred Hindu site. Muslims tore it down some centuries ago," Rai said, as if anticipating his rush to judgment. "People are upset on every side. I do not like to think where it may lead." Rai rearranged the face of his watch on his thin wrist. "People in Varanasi take such religious matters very seriously."

"I am sorry"—Mrs. Rai turned to T. J.—"that these difficult times occur while you are here. I want our special guest to think well of India."

"Oh, I do respect the culture, very much."

"My husband serves diligently on the city's peace committee. So I can only believe that we will soon return to harmony here."

"That's admirable, indeed." His fantasies, though, had depended on her being drawn to him as the man of action, robust, in contrast to her self-contained, elegant husband.

Rai gazed modestly into his teacup.

"When you come to visit us again," Mrs. Rai said, "you must bring Mrs. Clayton and your two daughters. We can go out to Sarnath together, the children can run in the park and play. Have you been there?"

"Not yet." He kept seeing the way the body had pitched forward into the river, as if it were bending a little at the hips. He would never let Jane and the girls come to India.

"How is your research?" Rai said. "But then, it may be impossible to work just now, isn't it so?"

Mrs. Rai glanced toward the plate of food beside him that he had forgotten. "Haven't been able to do much." He picked up the dish, took a spoonful of the pile of peas and rice mixture.

The peas were cold, sweet. Dessert peas—he'd expected scones or little shortbread cookies. He washed down a swallow. Rai waited for him to finish.

"It is surely understandable," Rai said, "under the circumstances, that you would not be able to proceed."

Rai was sitting in the same chair when T. J. came back into the room at mid-evening for dinner. He'd cleaned up, then rested a bit on the narrow bed in the room he'd been assigned. The Rais had insisted he stay for the night; he'd humbly accepted their kind invitation, secretly thrilled at the thought of clean sheets on a proper bed, of quiet and a break from Natraja.

This bedroom obviously had been the son's with its closet full of soccer balls and athletic shoes, a rolled *Rambo* poster he'd had a peek at, Sylvester Stallone strapped with grenades.

Mrs. Rai came to the doorway. "Perhaps you can help me in carrying things."

"I'll be glad to."

He followed her into the brightly lit kitchen. The servants he'd heard rattling earlier had disappeared.

"I hope you enjoy eggplant," she said.

"I'm very fond of eggplant."

"Usually my guests are not allowed to come into the kitchen. But you are a person of such warmth and home-loving. Both my husband and I feel this."

He took the bowls of sauce she handed him, careful not to spill. "That's kind of you both," he said, eyes on the full-to-the-brim bowls of runny tomatoey liquid.

He walked slowly—feeling for the edge of the straw carpet—into the living room.

"Here you are, sir." He put the bowls down on the table beside Rai.

"This is a very rare occasion when my guest brings me my dinner."

"I think your wife is trying to keep me busy and out of trouble."

Rai smiled, demure as a cat.

When they all had settled to their meal, T. J. could feel every small break in the silence. His fork, clumsy and foreign to his hosts, clanked against his plate. He heard the small rustling of Mrs. Rai's sandal on the floor, his own gulp of tea.

"Dr. Rai, let me ask you a couple of questions," he said finally, "along the lines of my research here."

Rai nodded, a bit of *roti* held neatly at the tips of his fingers.

"Say that you have a large number of residents in the habit," T. J. said, "of routinely relying on the local river for a particular use. For example, your laundry people—"

"The *dhobis.*"

"Yes. Hundreds of people doing wash for a whole city out there on the water, pouring soap into the river. How does the cleanup campaign try to reach those people? There doesn't seem to be any enforcement of regulations that I can see."

Rai focused his gaze on an imaginary audience in midair over T. J.'s head. "It is a difficult problem. The *dhobis* have been given no other place to do their work. Where can they go, if not to the river? And if you want a clean river, they are thinking to themselves, what could be cleaner than soap?" Balancing his plate on his knees, he held out his hands, palms up, lowering his gaze to look T. J. in the eye.

"You cannot simply regulate away the livelihood of a whole class of people," Rai said. "Not with impunity. The river is our lifeblood, in many different meanings of the phrase."

T. J.'s mind went again to the dark stain on the wrapping, the body rolling overboard. The bite of bread and eggplant stopped in his mouth. He forced it down. He wanted to talk to Jane.

Instead he was sitting here, talking to strangers in this shadowy living room. He had no business here; he'd come to the wrong side of the world.

Mrs. Rai stepped in to fill the quiet. "Do you have some similar situation," she said, "in your own town? People who rely on the river there in this way?"

"Farm runoff is a serious problem," he said. "It's difficult, as you know, to control non-point sources of pollution."

"There are many complicated problems in the world," Rai said.

"Fortunately, we do not have to solve them all here tonight," Mrs. Rai said.

T. J. took up a forkful of something he couldn't identify. "This is just excellent," he said to her. "I'm going to have to find out where I can get some Indian cooking when I get home."

"You will not find cooking there like Mrs. Rai's," Rai said. When he looked at his wife, for that brief flicker, there was no sarcasm in his manner. For a few seconds, he was a softened man.

T. J. caught the plate that was tilting in his hand.

In the bedroom, he fell into sheets that were starched and cool.

He sank gratefully into a real Western mattress.

Out in the living room, he'd been struggling to stay awake for the last half hour, Rai telling a long story about the different scientific institutes.

The fan overhead made a light whir. A quiet little boat motor. He saw the water rise up over the body as it went under. Going to sleep was like that, dropping weighted into a river.

The light was, all at once, too bright. He looked around him. He was standing in the middle of the living room. Rai at his side—Rai, hair rumpled, in a baggy shirt dress. A servant stood near, a young boy, looking frightened.

"You must come, Mr. T. J.," Rai was saying, holding him by the elbow. "It seems you were walking in your sleep."

He looked around the room. One lamp was on, a little ottoman knocked over on its side. Mrs. Rai was not there. "Good God, I hope I didn't . . ." He felt a panicky need to assemble himself, to make sure he was properly covered.

"There is no harm. Nothing to worry about."

"I must have been dreaming," T. J. said; his mouth felt sticky. "I was swimming, trying to get there in time—"

CHAPTER TWENTY-SIX

MARIE TRUDGED along the edge of the empty plaza, holding the arm of Sankar, the newspaperman, his curfew pass fluttering from his top shirt button; Ramesh had helped her make this arrangement, since Dilip had decamped.

The sight of the vacated market was familiar now, the green parrots, the blank-faced buildings. She hadn't hesitated to come out. She felt a bit weary in spirit, but as she'd told them at the table; people do die, and sometimes violently. She had no patience with anybody who had to hide their eyes.

Sankar nodded. "Here." He pointed. "Baba Gomati." They stepped into a *gali.* This was the one that usually was full of peddlers selling the little carvings of the gods.

She let him haul her along. She didn't have extra energy for figuring out the route.

After a dozen or more oddly angled intersections, he came to a stop, rapped on a metal shutter in the wall.

"Baba." His voice reverberated down the *gali.* "Baba . . ." and a string of Hindi.

She heard a footstep from inside; the wide shutter rose like a garage door. There Baba Gomati stood on the mattress of his little astrology room, tying up the pullcord, hair wild and eyes puffy, as if he'd been sleeping. He nodded them to come in. Sankar—not as charming as Dilip could be, but much more useful—helped hoist her up, got her to her seat on a pillow.

"Sorry to rouse you from your nap," she said, though it was nearly time to get up for dinner. As she'd left the house, T. J. had been heading out to tea.

"So," Gomati said, when he had settled himself, "you have returned so soon. It must have been a good fortune that I have given to you, yes? I am not yet remembering all the details." He shuffled through the pages of star charts in his ledger and seized upon a sheet, thin as onionskin.

"Aah, yes. Of course. Mrs. Marie Jasper from America who comes to stir up our city and leave us all in confusion. You seek the counsel of Gomati again." Victory was plain on his face.

She had always admired a sturdy acceptance of things, but he seemed altogether too lighthearted after the recent events. "I came again," she said, "because I want some further explanation—"

"You come during curfew. You surprise me, madame." He shook his head. "The difficulties drag on and on."

"How is it, Mr. Gomati, that you tell me I am centrally involved in the business of the city and it's not an hour later that I am standing next to a bomb?"

"Bomb?" His eyes widened. "That is very bad, a bomb."

"Two were killed." Her voice shook. "One of them a young girl."

Gomati nodded. "I have heard of the incident. It is very distressing."

"You shouldn't be surprised. You all but told me about it in advance."

"I have never said this word *bomb.* Never."

"But you knew; you said before that I would be right in the midst—"

"Madame, please." He rolled his head. "Anyone can look at you and know you are in the midst of whatever is happening. It is your nature. When has it ever been other? Have you once in your life stood at the sideline? No." He smoothed the folds of his *kurta.* "Do not trouble me with accusations of knowing too much. Gomati knows only what he should know."

She looked at his dark eyes that were so big he might have a touch of thyroid. He was right, of course. She'd never stood off to the side.

But that didn't really explain anything. "I'd like to know how you arrived at what you told me about my life. And I have a few other questions."

"Always other questions. Is there no satisfaction? Is there no 'enough'?"

She sat silent.

"So, I see we will have the beginner astrology class for the American lady; you may go home and tell the future to all your people. I charge one hundred rupees extra for the lesson."

"That will be fine."

"Ah, but there is nothing to explain. The planets tell all, and what is not there, I see in your face and the palm of your hand."

Sankar, who'd insisted on remaining down in the lane pretending not to listen, nodded sagely.

"If you don't mind, I'd like to look at that book."

Gomati pushed it toward her, his head tipped in a haughty manner. The page looked like a trigonometry problem.

"This is your map of the skies," he said, "as it was at the moment of your birth."

"What are these marks?"

"These are the glyphs that are showing the signs of the zodiac."

She looked at the sheet; it was pointless to try to understand.

"It is taking many years of study, Mrs. Marie." He reached for a blank sheet of paper, drew a circle, divided it into pie sections, making little notations as he went. "You see, you must mark off the Ascendant degree here in each part of the circle, anticlockwise, join each to its opposite, First House below Ascendant."

He caught sight of her expression, put his pencil aside. "I think we waste our time in this discussion. What concern brings you to me?"

She hesitated. She wanted proof that he knew what he was talking about or that he didn't. And she wanted to know so many things: if she would live to face the death of one of her children; if Michael, her parents, her sisters still existed as themselves, and if they would be reunited.

Things he had no way of knowing.

"Do you see any big changes coming?" she asked instead. "In my life."

He dared to laugh, rolling his head from side to side with delight. "It is more than one hundred rupees to know all the secrets of the universe."

She frowned; she'd asked him a simple question, a starting point.

He patted his lips as if to tamp down his amusement. "Some pilgrims who come even want me to say if the river has washed away their sins."

"What do you tell them?"

"I tell them it is the job of the river to know."

He glanced down the empty corridor of the *gali,* his smile fading. "I will tell you in earnest, when it comes to this question of yours about changes, you must ask Ganga, because already I have told you what I know."

The river: it was the easy answer to everything.

"Also I will say this. The city, Varanasi, for many it is a crucible."

"I've been tested already," she said, then felt embarrassed at such a claim. Her life had been easy. The loss of Michael was with her every moment; but they had had fifty-two good years together.

"Anyway, I didn't come here as a pilgrim. My trip is simply one item on a list of worthwhile projects—"

"We come by different routes."

His tone was unduly patronizing. She reached for her purse.

At the house she could sit up on the roof with Natraja, have a cup of tea. Last night she'd dreamed about their foster child, Dana, which hadn't happened in years; she'd woken up calling out his name.

Gomati sat impassively as she paid him.

Dana would be almost middle-aged now, in prison in Missouri, the last she'd heard. They'd had him for two years, long enough to fall in love with him, before his relatives got custody and took him away. She pictured him at the swimming pool, skinny and shivering in his wet bathing suit, wanting a dime for an orange Popsicle. She'd seen no sign he could shoot a man.

"Perhaps there is some item on your list," Gomati said, his voice now surprisingly gentle—sadness must have crossed her face—"something for you to do in this city while we wait for the trouble to end."

"Perhaps," she allowed, though she wasn't sure if he was serious and didn't at the moment care.

With Sankar's help, she began the project of maneuvering herself off the ledge and back down into the *gali.* She felt tired, the way she remembered feeling in the days after her stomach surgery: severely weakened, her mind and heart and all her bone marrow taken up with unseen things.

CHAPTER TWENTY-SEVEN

DINNER IS done, and still it is dusk, the open air damp on my skin as we step out of the stairwell onto my patio.

"Vijendra," my haughty neighbor Nirmal calls from the next rooftop. He speaks to Ramesh, just behind me, by his last name, ignoring me as usual.

"You have not heard?" Nirmal is saying to him. "Only in this last hour, barely one kilometer from here . . ."

He does not address me, and so there is no need to listen.

I face away, upstream. This is my rooftop, where I am to be left in peace.

Behind me, Ramesh, agitated, demands to know: "What? On which street?"

The sunset upriver is muddy yellow, the sky full of dust. Birds wheel in the bright light.

Nirmal, his voice so shrill. He must stop this raucous shouting, building to building, and Ramesh, too. He does not wait for an answer before firing his next question.

Nirmal again: "It was across from that yarn seller—a massacre, Vijendra, that is the truth of it. . . ."

I hardly recognize Ramesh by his last name. He

must come stand here beside me in this mild twilight. We have matters to discuss, the planning of meals.

"The bodies of four women," Nirmal will not stop. He has seen them carried from the street, knows there were more, the blood so deep it coated the bottom of motorbike tires.

My ears ring. Why does Ramesh linger over there?

The shocked cries of others listening float from other rooftops. They are like birdcalls, soft on the air. A sharper voice calls, "Yes. It is true," buildings away. "Those savages have butchered nine."

Out over the water—oh, it is magnificent. Ramesh must throw aside these terrible rumors and come to stand with me and look: a great gold dome of sunset sky. I know it has never been more beautiful. I cannot take my eyes away.

My bed is full of crumbs, the sheets foul.

With morning light, the room has the closeness of a damp basement, no space for a table or chair. All these years I have spent my waking hours downstairs, or planted on the rooftop in the sun. Here in my bedroom, I am a foreigner, a *videshi.*

If I were a sick child home from school, Mama would bring me Coke in a glass of shaved ice. I'd hear her in the kitchen swinging the dish towel full of ice cubes against the counter.

But the knocking I hear is surely a boatman banging an oar to shake off tangled debris.

I do have a view of the river from my bed, framed and narrowed by the window casing. A boy fishes from the prow of a moored boat; near him at the edge, a woman scrubs her shining metal plates and jugs with wet dirt. Hindu or Muslim, she should not be out today, no matter if there is a curfew break in her neighborhood.

The violence that came yesterday—the shock of it propelled me here. And yet Ramesh, no doubt, stepped forth this very morning into the dark *gali,* walking barefoot as he always does when he goes for his bath.

Reggie would have been coming out of the field at the end of the day, carrying the empty fertilizer bucket, the slat-side truck humming on the dirt road there, along the boundary.

I saw that very sight so many times, when I'd go out to help with loading, get to ride in the back of the pickup.

Walking his loose-jointed way, bucket swinging, he heads toward the truck, Murphy and another man standing at the tailgate.

Can't he see? Why doesn't he drop the bucket and run?

"Come on, boy." It's Murphy yelling to him, Murphy who treated him like backdoor family. "Hurry it up."

In my mind's eye I want to scream: *Get away from there . . .*

He steps along, hoisting his pail up onto the gate. Murphy doesn't turn, the side of his face blotched like he's been drinking.

"Where're the other kids?" Reggie says. There'd been a bunch starting out.

Around front, the door to the cab opens, screeching back on its hinge—

I did not want to know the details, yesterday, of the slaughter. Yet Ramesh repeated them as if I had not heard Nirmal's voice, that it was Muslims killed, some of them pulled from rickshaws, the women's long cloaks stripped off. I tried to interrupt, but while he spoke to me there on the roof, it was as though word of death came again to my house on its own; a faceless, colorless wraith appearing beside me on the patio, drifting out beyond the rail of the roof, then coming toward me again, only to dodge once more away.

I pray Ramesh has not left the house again this morning.

Living in this room, I still can rise up on my pillows and watch his morning bath. It is likely I will not go out again. I can converse with the river from here. Ganga surely must know my voice by now, even muffled by these thick walls.

I wonder if I will come to a state when I cannot eat. These sacks of peanuts beside me are warm from my body heat.

Marie and Jill can take their meals in the dining room without me. I expect T. J. will stay on at the Rais, assuming he did arrive there.

The walls around me radiate their presence; I understand how the blind can know they are approaching a large object. These walls are a companion; they make a sound that is almost within hearing. I learned when I came to India of the immured saints, those who literally wall themselves off from the world. A man will have a room the size of a coffin built close around him, leaving only a hole for vision, a larger slot for food and his bucket of waste to be passed through. He will stand locked in this box for the remainder of his life, devoting himself to worship.

I have immured myself too late.

CHAPTER TWENTY-EIGHT

JILL HAD been walking since early afternoon, following the step third up from the concrete lip of the bank. It was the hike she made every day, for exercise and to find what she could of the holy city's magic, in spite of the trouble.

She half expected the river today to be running red, to hear the cries still echoing. She wasn't scared, not for herself. Her head felt hollow, though, her body full of wind and electricity. In less than twenty-four hours, she'd heard so many different stories. Nine had been killed; then it was thirteen. It was at the corner near the policemen's stand; no, it was not in the street at all, it was in the market for the garland sellers. Natraja had said one of the killers was a woman.

She searched up ahead for some movement along the shore. It was still as a painting except for the glittering light on the water, the haze of the body-burning rising from Manikarnika Ghat far down the bank. Her eyes skittered over it all.

She shouldn't have tried to compliment Ramesh on his singing; he had frowned and walked away. She'd pantomimed and tried to sing something like the sound of it, so he'd know what she was talking about. He had probably thought she was making fun of him.

Walking at least made a little breeze, cooling the sweat on her face. She'd dreamed she was swimming laps in the bubble-top pool at the Hyatt. The water had looked clear, but she knew from the current underneath her that it had snakes. A lifeguard with red-stained teeth had lazily waved her to get out of the water; she'd kept trying to explain that she'd just gotten in and couldn't leave now, no matter what the water hid.

Maybe Natraja would translate her compliment to him—though, now that she thought about it, he'd been praying, so maybe a compliment was inappropriate.

There was the tilted spire, standing out in the water.

She stopped—once again—to look it over. This little temple had lost its footing more than a hundred years ago, sliding partway into the river. It had held there ever since, interrupted in the midst of its fall. Poised at eye level, she could see the finely carved stone: a steeple-sized piece of stonework, a bit like the top of the Woolworth building in New York.

Design was one of the things that might interest her if she ever could clear space in her mind. She still had her Erector set and her LEGOs. She'd build a subdivision like nothing Atlanta had ever seen, cottages with thick medieval walls and tile roofs, and central hearths that opened in two directions, maybe a garden wall of big river stones, all of it drawn on the deliciously orderly grids of graph paper; it would at least make a virtue of her exactness. She might also—weird thought—like to make lace by hand as a hobby. She imagined a single hooked tool in her hand, bringing each thread, *punkt,* as her grandfather liked to say, to the precise place it should be; that was the principle of delicacy, that precision.

Slowly, she put her feet into motion. The drunken spire, half in and half out of the water, was hard to walk away from. Incomplete, it seemed in need of attention. She imagined climbing up the *ghat,* stepping into a *gali,* and finding a tableau of a stabbing frozen in the same way.

But there, up ahead—what was that? A great block of something had appeared since yesterday. It looked like, of all things, an empty four-poster bed, with a pillow and a bright spread.

Closer, it looked like there might be—yes, sunk into the pillow: the head of an old man, his body so thin it made no rise in his bedspread of fresh flower garlands. She slowed to get a look from a respectful distance.

His eyes were open, staring out across the river, his face like candle tallow poured over thin bone. She saw no definite sign of life, yet was fairly certain he was alive.

She walked up a couple of steps, passing above the head of the bed, seeing the old man's view.

He must have been brought out here to die, his wish to have this last look at the river. A couple of boys idled at the top of the *ghat,* but they seemed too casual and unconcerned to be relatives. Hard to believe he'd be out here alone—did someone bring water?

She wanted to step down and stand at his bedside, know for sure if he was dead or alive. But she walked on, feeling his unsettling presence in the bed behind her.

From a window up in the city, Hindi TV soap opera music blared, gradually putting a barrier of sound between her and the dying man. She walked on until she no longer could hear it, arriving finally at the *ghat* topped by the mustard-colored building that had become her regular stopping place. She swung around and headed back toward the guest house.

High on a balcony up to her right, she spotted a stocky, shirtless man. Faced away from her, he swung over and around himself, from hand to hand, what looked like a long-handled sledgehammer, the head of it big as a forty-pound weight. It was a solitary dance, this primitive exercise.

She usually ran on a stair machine in the crowded roar of the health club at six o'clock on a weeknight. If she'd left as scheduled, she'd be there now.

The man's hard planes of muscle shone in the sun, from oil or sweat or both. It was a relief to see him, unmistakably alive and strong. The head of the hammer whirled around him. The shadow marking his spine held steady at the center of the flying weight.

"Madame."

Startled, Jill spun around.

"Madame." Standing before her, a man smiled patiently, as if he thought she knew him. "You are liking some more good massage today, madame?"

The massage man. Of course. She noticed again the almond shape of his eyes.

"You're still working during the curfew"—she searched for his name—"Shiv?"

"Oh, yes. Massage is always. But no one comes, this is the problem. Today I am happy, you have come." His eyes glowed; he reached for her hand.

His thumb pressed into her palm in a gradually widening circle. She hadn't noticed her shoulders were so tight.

"Curfew," he said. "We must go boat."

Boat?

He nodded toward the river. Dozens of empty boats were tied along the bank, more boats tied to those boats.

She walked with him, though undecided.

"Here," he said, next to a pointed prow touching the concrete.

"Here?"

"Yes. Please step." He steadied her as she stepped down onto the bow of the long, open rowboat. He boarded behind her, then hurried past to lead the way. He wore rubber flip-flops, frayed down to half length; his heels stood on the bare boards.

This was safe enough; he was certainly no terrorist.

She followed him from boat to boat, across four of the long, empty taxis, as if they were crossing a logjam.

Then they stepped onto one of the bigger vessels, a sun-blistered old houseboat of the sort that commonly anchored out beyond the rowboats.

It was what her father called a scow, the pale blue paint peeling in strips. The cabin, a shed on the center of the deck, had louvered windows. She thought of Humphrey Bogart and *The African Queen*.

"Careful your head," Shiv warned as they ducked low to go in.

It wasn't too late to dash back across the boats to shore.

The two of them hunched in the cabin, which was dim even in the penetrating afternoon light. "Sit here," he said. She sank down onto the board floor.

A bad idea, this whole thing . . .

He crouched and crawled along the wall; he was closing the shutters.

"No, don't," she said. "Please. I like the air."

He left the remaining two open, stripes of light at one end of the cabin, a sharp line of darkness where she sat. This couldn't be his boat, and he probably didn't have permission.

Water washed against the side; she put her hand on the wood and felt the pull of it rushing past. The whine of a mosquito was a faint steady ringing, amplified in the close space.

Shiv sat cross-legged in front of her, the light behind him; she couldn't see his face. She heard his long, slow sigh, and again he took her hand.

"I can't stay long," she said.

"Not long," he said. "Very small massage. Very good." He was curling, uncurling her fingers.

In the shaft of light, she could see the mosquitoes floating, rising, like dust motes.

"Mosquitoes," she said. She felt the pressure come and go at the base of her thumb.

"You are taking the malaria pills, yes? The tourist pills?"

"Yes."

"Then you have no reason, madame, for any troubling worry."

CHAPTER TWENTY-NINE

MY BED, parallel to the river, makes the upstream waters appear to be heading toward a spot somewhere close to me that I could almost reach if I leaned out to the side, letting the water rinse over my arm, climb cold across me as the weight and force of it draws me in.

I thought I was starting fresh, leaving Neavis after high school. I had imagined myself walking on an Outer Banks beach in winter, breathing in clean, salty air.

Lying on these sweaty sheets, it is my own salt odor I smell.

It would take a monsoon beyond any in memory to come and rinse me clean now, here on this upper floor. Though the brown water stood a foot deep and more in the downstairs rooms during the monsoons of my first year, the walls and floor and the *gali* outside smelling for weeks of putrid mud soaked in beyond the reach of cleaning chemicals.

Leaving Neavis, I had hope. At the Carolina Sands, I would go up to the third-floor porch on my breaks and gaze at the surf: a wave would rise, tower, blue-green, sparkling or glossy, depending on the wind.

Then so quickly the peak would reach forward, curl, the weight of the mass collapsing into foam.

I thought of those waves as social creatures, acquainted with each other, one rolling in behind the next, followed by the close company of another. I lived solitary, as I'd meant to, in a small, weather-tight room in the storage area underneath one of the summer houses. What I could see out my window was a paved garage, storage for a sailboat and bicycles. My room worked like a hollow column to support the house, the way the box for a furnace does. Around October, the living areas overhead would empty.

Sitting out on the beach on a day off, bundled in a coat and drinking beer, I looked around and saw a man I didn't know taking a seat a few feet away on the sand. His hands were cut-up; deep lines fanned out from his eyes; he was a commercial fisherman, and older. I was the age of the college girls who waited tables during the summer. I looked like one of them, long-legged and blond. But he knew from a glance I wasn't. I pushed my feet down into the sand.

"I've seen you in the Safeway grocery," he said. He had a true Outer Banker accent, mangled Elizabethan.

"I've bought a few frozen pizzas there."

"I make a pretty good fish stew," he offered. "Rock bass, some carrots and onions, let it simmer all afternoon. Then right before you're ready to eat, break an egg in the top; the egg poaches in the liquid, you know it's done."

His eyebrows were bleached from the sun until they were lighter than the rest of his face. Seeing me looking him over, he started a smile that came slowly across his face.

When we got married, all of three months later, it was in front of the justice of the peace. Friends of Donald's, the couple who ran the bait and ice store, witnessed.

The bedroom in our apartment faced northeast; wind rattled the corner of the storm window in early morning. When the alarm went off, there still would be an hour or more of dark left. I would lie warm in the bed with my head against his shoulder for a few minutes before he got to his feet and stepped into clothes.

Then I'd rush to make coffee, fry sausage, wearing for slippers a pair of his thick wool socks.

I've asked myself a time or two what he would think of the river. He was not a talkative man, not like T. J.; he had a look of being pared to the bone, as if he were long accustomed to deprivation.

It was only a matter of a few weeks, maybe two months, before a cold, drafty feeling began to come and go in me.

I would hear Donald moving in the kitchen and think for a second I was in Neavis and the sound of a chair sliding or a throat cleared in the next room was Vic.

Donald liked to stay concentrated on whatever it was he was doing; as soon as he finished eating, he would get up and go to scraping the dishes, as if his hands were the only set in the world. He was not somebody you could talk to about a colored boy.

Standing up on the hotel roof one morning, I looked out at the ocean and decided. Waves were breaking up on the slope of the beach, the water solid white. It was high tide and windy, my hair blowing across my face, strands getting in my mouth. Up on the corner of the roof, the hotel's flag kept making a hollow popping.

When I told him late that afternoon I was leaving, he stared out the sliding glass door in front of where he stood. "Go," he said, "get out," not once casting his eyes toward me. Outside, from three steps down the plank walk in front of the apartment, I could hear what he did to the glass door and the wallboard, and the sounds that came out of him. I grabbed my bags and started running.

CHAPTER THIRTY

SHIV WAS behind her on his knees, pressing down into her shoulders where the tension was.

As he shifted around to her side, light hit half his face. He was pulling, stretching the muscles of her upper arm and across her shoulder. A prickling sensation crept down her arms and sides.

If anything happened to her out here, she was going to look like an idiot.

Lying down, as he had magically rearranged her, her stomach and face pressed against boards that smelled like green moss and creek mud.

"Is this your boat?" Her voice sounded sleepy.

As if from a distance, she could hear herself worrying, but it was a thinner sound, one plucked note ringing and ringing.

Shiv laughed as if he were trying not to disturb anybody. His hands on her shoulders had the rhythm of water. Or was the boat moving? Was that the water that she was hearing, such a soft rushing she might be imagining it? She couldn't keep up with anything.

His hands were trailing down the length of her.

They were on her butt, coming up the two slopes of muscle there; it seemed as if hours had passed, that he had been a long time coming to this place, but she had lost track and missed it. His hands were moving, rolling the flesh so close to her crotch, as if he were opening her, tugging at her muscles until she parted.

He was on his knees, one leg outside her thigh, touching. One knee between her legs. She could feel the warmth of his leg there, as if his leg were breathing, its hot breath brushing across her.

Her whole body was sliding down toward his knee, gravity pulling her.

Her thighs locked around that leg, that tense knee; his hands on her waist pressed her whole body hard against the boards. She heard him make a sound as her crotch bore down on his leg, which came toward her. She felt a wave glide up through all the muscles he had touched. A widening ripple running through her, the ghost of the massage, and as the wave passed, those same muscles falling limp and loose.

She opened her eyes. The light was dusky.

Shiv hovered somewhere behind her.

She tried to get herself to stir, though all she wanted was to go on lying here.

The river was pouring past under the boat, sliding beneath her just below.

She was drifting with it, streaming out, as if she were giving off a vapor or steam that floated away with the flow.

Shiv's hand worked slowly up and down her spine. She imagined him drifting off, too, running one hand over her as if he were trailing it in water.

CHAPTER THIRTY-ONE

DINGY LIGHT falls across my bed. I have slept through this day. I will sleep more, I think.

Peanuts spill out into the covers, a few lodged underneath me, as buried as if they never left the ground. In my mouth, bits of shell shattering give off the flavor of burned dirt.

My body sounds—the smack and gurgle, the grunting when I shift to a new position—seem to my ear the workings of some other creature. The wheeze could come from an animal, a fierce dog lying out of sight below me on the floor.

They all should be in the house again by now.

I hope they are settled and I can sleep, uninterrupted.

I tried once before to slip away, long ago. I didn't get far.

The day after Bhushan lifted my doll figure before the moon and spoke his own vow, I left.

I knew of a monastery. In the two years I lived in the Joshi house, I had listened to the family tell wild stories they'd heard about the place.

The first time—it was Bhushan's nephew Gopal, I think, saying what he had heard at school—I sensed immediately it was a sanctuary for secret outcasts like me. I was so recently arrived, though, so new to the country and the family and Bhushan. India itself was still my place of refuge.

It was only my second day in the city when I met him. A boy who worked nights at the desk at my hostel had told me where to look for work. The place was not hard to find; a rickshaw driver took me to the door of the stair. The restaurant itself was a big dim room on a second floor near Dashashvamedh. I walked in half blind from the glare of sun outside. It was a moment before I noticed the young man at the cash register—stocky, full-lipped, with a shock of hair that hung toward one eye—going about his business at the counter but at the same time watching me. I told him I had come to ask for a waitress job. I spilled out the story of my work at the Carolina Sands. I was wearing, I remember, a pink Oxford cloth shirtwaist dress. It was 1971, and the sixties had only begun to arrive in North Carolina.

"Yes," he said, brow furrowed and earnest, "it is good you have your employment experience, since my family is also in the hotel business. I think there will be some position for you. I will speak on your behalf, and we will see." He told me his first name: Bhushan. He fumbled with the stack of receipts beside the register. It was past the time of the midday meal, and the room was quiet. He looked again at me—a slender twenty-year-old, pale as a dandelion—and broke into a startlingly sweet smile.

Not long after, I took a room in the Joshi house. It was as big nearly as the Carolina Sands, but massive and hidden, a great *haweli* deep in the *galis,* half business and half residence and all of it mixed together.

Within the family, to the older men, the children, and some of the aunts, I was an enchanting toy, unlike the sons, who carried family hopes and might well disappoint, or the worrisome daughters expected to go off with their dowry to join a husband's family. My position in their house seemed uncomplicated; of me, their American, nothing was expected. Every day, though, I watched the pulls and frictions of the Joshis. Bhushan, for one, had taken up the business more easily than his brother, but then was not complying in the matter of marriage. And Rupa, a daughter-in-law, would hide herself away, reading novels and sipping *lassis* when she should have been supervising children and servants.

Most of them had no idea, though, that Bhushan had in fact grown to have serious intention. If they'd learned, I would have lost my welcome. And had Bhushan followed me then, he would have lost both his family and his place in the world.

But how was I to resist? He was charming; he had the ease of a young prince. In Neavis, the only boys who sought me out after Reggie were furtive.

Better if Bhushan too had remained content with nothing more than his late-night visits to my room. Hours after the house was still, he would tiptoe in, crawl beneath the veil of mosquito net around my bed. So many nights on that narrow *charpoy,* we whispered and wound around each other in darkness. Usually he was quick, muffling his cry in the pillow. But often he brought fresh flower garlands, and the smell of wet roses and jasmine announced him. In the dark, he would pile them around my face, on my hair, or trace my breasts and the length of my body with the tips of damp petals I still can smell. In my bedroom the only window opened onto the *gali,* and if the moon was strong, my flesh had the color of dirty soap. Bhushan, so dark, was invisible. Even now, so many years later, I think I would know his young-man's body by smell and feel; yet even at the time I might not have recognized him naked by sight alone, other than his head and hands, his lordly stance and walk.

In the days and evenings, at work in the restaurant and at the table with the family, he and I were easily jovial, like playful brother and sister, talking about nothing, in English and soon in the Hindi that I was grateful to learn. The new language flooded in—I felt it remake my mind. I seemed to know only what I had learned to speak of in Hindi, the words I needed for that day. Nothing else existed. For more than a year, our playfulness together, his and mine, was an easy disguise because our hearts were so light. I rode to work in the mornings seated behind him on his motor scooter. At night we both would read *Indian Express,* swapping sections back and forth, while his mother and his father's ancient aunt did their stitching, talking in a dialect of Hindi I never learned, and the men read Hindi newspapers and financial reports. Then the two of us ventured to see Bhushan's cousin play cricket, and failed to return home immediately afterward. I watched his mother draw herself up in scowling disapproval. We didn't take such a risk again. What we had to hide was our nighttime meetings, and how Bhushan was changing.

In truth, I'm sure some of the family suspected there were trysts but would look away as long as there was no threat to their plans for Bhushan.

I had told him, again and again, that regardless of his family it would never be more than it was.

He didn't accept that. He said I did not know my mind and would come to see the rightness. At night in my bed, he would talk of making me pregnant with our first child, a wheat-brown boy with my long legs.

Once I locked my door. The next morning he threatened to announce our betrothal. I refused to meet his eyes the rest of that day and, feigning illness, missed dinner.

The following morning as we walked his motor scooter through the *galis* toward the road, he told me he would not come to my room again until he first had circled the city in a silver wedding carriage, with the sword of the bridegroom worn at his side. He would do this whether his family joined him or even if they stood against him, leaving him to make his groom's journey alone. In the meantime, he said, pushing the bike through the foot traffic, he would make arrangements for us away from this city. It surely would be possible to find some clerk position in the private sector without use of family connection. Or we could go to America, where we would not be forced into such secrecy.

He looked at me only once during this speech and otherwise kept his eyes on the *gali* winding ahead, the slant morning light full of dust.

"Are you crazy?" My tone was shrill and jeering, and I didn't care.

He only lifted his chin higher, pressing us on through the crowded corridor.

The rest of that day at work, he was impassive. And on the following day, he kept bitterly silent, even in the presence of his family. At dinner he didn't speak in my direction or look at me. To his father, he said that the restaurant was overstaffed and some should be let go.

"Is this how you would treat me?" I whispered at him later as we passed in a hallway. "It's clear I've made the right decision."

All the joy I'd felt had vanished. I was frightened by his intensity; I hadn't known him. He seemed a foreigner and not civilized; and the Joshis' medieval fortress of a house, its thick walls and carved doors and the shadowy dampness, now threatened me. Even the garrulous relatives at the dinner table at night made me suspicious and afraid. Thoughts began to flicker in my mind about their foreign ways that I hated myself for thinking.

My coming into their house was wrong; in the back of my mind, I'd known it from the start. I had no right to insinuate myself into their family. I thought with fresh horror of the snakes that slipped in during the high waters of monsoon. I knew what I was. A few days later, after a lunch service in the restaurant, I ate a full tray of leftover desserts on the sly, plates of soft crumbly *halwah;* it was the first time I felt my glands swell from eating. To the tips of my fingers, those small swellings in my neck bulged like poison sacs.

On the morning I left, the moment I'd decided, layer upon layer of panic began to lift off me.

I stepped out of the house carrying two folded saris as if I were taking them to the laundry, and underneath a sack of necessaries.

Everything else I left piled in my room upstairs. Along with a note for Bhushan.

On the first street beyond the *galis,* I hopped up onto a rickshaw. I hadn't felt as free as this even when I first boarded the plane for India. I told the driver the name of the street. That was as much as I knew. He cast a dubious glance but propelled us into the streaming traffic.

All around me, the colors looked new and fresh, everything clean, flying past. Up on the bench in the air, I hurtled toward a place where I could live as if there'd been no day before the present. My life would be a sequence of moments that were vivid merely by being unclouded. I was finished with Bhushan. And this was the end of my effort to live a normal life. I was giddy with relief.

I had seen the gateway to the *math* several times, opening off a little-traveled road. Whenever a rickshaw driver, avoiding the more traffic-packed routes, had happened to go that way, I would twist to look. The street in front, unusually broad, always had a deserted feel, pavement buckling in places as if there'd been an earthquake. And then the wall of the monastery, holding back trees—in such a dusty city, the jungle growth of the grounds seemed to me a green island, wide leaves spilling out over the top of the long whitewashed guard wall.

I had never believed the full extent of what the Joshis had repeated: that these people drank out of human skulls and cooked their food on cremation pyres. I did accept what Bhushan had told me, that people in this sect believed everything—even the grisliest parts of life—was sacred. They wouldn't turn me away.

On this day, when we came to the street that passed the monastery gate, the very air seemed of a different texture, lighter. My driver swung off his bicycle seat, suspiciously eyeing the entrance. He'd called over his shoulder twice while pedaling, saying that no one ever asked to be brought here. On either side of the portal rose totem poles of painted plaster skulls.

"Keep the extra," I said, handing him more than the usual fare.

He looked me over once again: another American hippie kid in a sari.

"I am waiting here for you," he said.

I shook my head no.

But he stood watching as I stepped inside the wall of the Aghoris' compound, my sack tucked under my arm.

Two steps inside the wall, into quickly deepening quiet, the greenery dense on either side, a boy stepped onto my path. "Please remove the shoes," he said. He was gone again before I could feel the start of surprise. I stepped out of my sandals and kept walking.

The cobblestones in the shade were cool against my feet. The leaves of a close-hanging limb were big as dinner plates. I held one against my cheek. It felt like skin, but cooler. It wasn't possible that in this place, so serene, anyone cooked food on the pyres of corpses.

I walked nearly half a mile. I had to be fast approaching whatever was hidden. Maybe all the ascetics were praying in their cells, or sitting one by one through the woods.

They couldn't make me leave. I'd clean latrines, do whatever they needed; I'd be their untouchable. Then one day I'd come back to this path and lie down on the fat stones, cover myself in giant leaves.

A bend ahead—the path opened out onto water, bright with glints of sun: a bathing pool, a *kund* larger than an acre. Out in the center, a small stone figure, mossy and green, sat at water level as if it were floating.

Scanning, I saw no sign of anyone. Paths led to breezeways and arcades, small shelters partly open to air, and shrines painted in bright colors; that *linga* was tall as I was. No sound but the birds, not the smallest splash.

Surely they knew I was here. Maybe they'd wait and watch me for a while. In Neavis a couple of times, babies were left on the steps of the church. Everybody knew Ricky Jarvis, at two weeks old, had been abandoned in the seat of the preacher's car. But I was not a baby; I had brought myself to the church door.

Namaste. Without warning, a voice from behind me. "How do you do, madame?"

I composed my face, to seem reasonable.

The man was paunchy, not the one from before. I made a formal *namaskar* bow, praying hands in front of my face. Tails of the cloth wrapped around his head dangled next to the rims of his glasses. He was harmless-looking, entirely ordinary; the sight of him made me want to laugh. Bhushan's mother had said they all had wild ropes of hair and burning eyes, like people from Jamaica.

"We have not expected you here today. How may I help?" His smile was pleasant, businesslike.

"I didn't send a message ahead."

He noticed the bag sagged at my feet, the saris now stuffed inside. He let his eyes rest there a moment before raising his gaze. I could see him trying to assess if I was crazy or dangerous.

"Come." He motioned me to a mat at the edge of steps that overlooked the water. I hadn't seen it: the perfect view of water and shrines. "It is teatime. We will take tea."

"This is a very beautiful place," I said as I dropped down onto the mat.

"Yes." He settled himself more slowly.

"Do many people come here?"

"No." He seemed alarmed by the question.

A boy arrived with a platter of cups and saucers, a delicate white teapot.

The tea was normal: milky and sweet. I swallowed carefully, to keep anything from going down the wrong way and making me choke. The muscles of my throat felt tight. He sipped, looking out at the afternoon light reflecting off the water.

"What is it that has brought you here?" he said finally, his impersonal gaze a little more sympathetic.

"I'm looking for a *math.*" I hadn't meant to say it yet.

His face was blank; I must have used the wrong word. "Monastery," I said.

"Yes?"

"I want to live inside. I want to live here."

He put his hand to his forehead.

I felt the despair come over my whole face, but he didn't see.

"You, madame? Here?"

I nodded, again short of breath.

"You are in trouble?"

I shook my head. "No."

His eyes took me in from top to bottom. "We have now and again taken in for short time an individual who has great trouble." He paused. "What do you know of us?"

"I heard you live apart from the world."

"And?"

I didn't know what else to say. "You drink from skulls."

He lifted his eyebrows, gave me a mock-quizzical smile. "And you are wishing to take part in this?"

I looked down at my tea, the cup, with its small pink rose on the side, a matching flower on the saucer.

"I didn't believe it when I heard that."

He pursed his lips, looked again toward the water.

He was going to sit and visit for a few more minutes and then break the news that I had to leave. The air in here was so soft, like the backyard in Neavis, where it was nearly dark under the water oak.

At the edge of the yard, though, the sun had hard-baked a strip of bare dirt under the clothesline. From the basket full of balled wet underwear, I would flop out a T-shirt, pin each shoulder to the line. There would be swipes of grease across the chest. Vic was in the shed, working; the clang of the hammer hitting metal vibrated out on the hot afternoon. He never said anything, nobody did.

"I'm sorry," I said to the *mahant* beside me. "I didn't hear you."

"There is some truth to the rumors," he said, enunciating carefully as if I were deaf. "We have no rules about what is proper to consume. No part of life is unclean. That is what we believe. What has been created is good; we are free to take of it."

So, did they eat the actual bodies, then? The skin on my forearms prickled with fear and thrill.

"But here," he was saying, "we do not go to extreme. If you search through the city, you may find those of our sect who perform the practices that are rumored. It is difficult to speak for all. Still, I can tell you we are Hindus, loving of Shiva. How long have you been in this country?"

"Almost two years."

He looked past me, nodding to a man who had come to stand at a distance behind us.

"It is the hour of *arati,*" he said, unfolding his legs; his bare feet were dainty. "I must go and prepare. I invite you to join us for this worship, there, where you see the flame behind the grate."

I looked where he was looking, up the small hill that rose from the water; maybe it was a cooking fire.

"I eat a lot," I said. He glanced at my bare middle. "You are thin as a village woman," he said over his shoulder as he moved away.

The surface of the pool lay smooth before me.

In the time we had sat, shadows had stretched from one side to the other. It would be night soon; surely he wouldn't put me out in the dark.

CHAPTER THIRTY-TWO

JILL OPENED her eyes into darkness, the sound of water near. Facedown, she tried to collect herself. Shiv was gone. The floorboards were covered with dew. She scrambled up, holding herself crouched so she wouldn't hit her head.

Her hand found the canvas of her backpack over near the cabin wall. Her neck pouch was in place under her shirt.

Her legs itched. Mosquito bites had swelled up hard, a rash of them she could feel through the cotton.

She sat still and listened—no sound but the water against the side of the boat, and the creaking of the wood. He probably had gone home—but surely not without getting paid, unless trouble had threatened. The cabin was stifling. The windows at the far end let in the only air.

If he or anyone else were close by, she told herself, they'd have heard her by now.

It could be two in the morning, or four. She had no idea. . . .

Head ducked, holding on to the ribs of the ceiling for balance, she felt her way to the door. The welcome open air hit her face, cooling under her baggy Indian clothes.

There was no one in sight. The steps of the *ghats* were long in the moonlight, edged by thicker lines of shadow. Not even a dog walked along the edge.

Then from behind, a loud thump against the deck.

Her hand flew to her chest.

Shiv had hopped down onto the deck from the roof of the cabin. A rumpled cloth rolled into a pillow still lay there.

"What time is it?" Her voice panicky, insistent.

"It is late." He seemed disgruntled.

"You've been here all this time?"

He rubbed his eyes, stretched. "Curfew," he said. "It is more dangerous at night. Also I am keeping an eye for you."

Awake now, he smiled, looked away toward the dark far side of the river, modestly playing down his efforts.

"Good massage?" he said. "You are happy?" He faced her again, the light from shore hitting half his face; she was glad it was dark.

"Yes." She coughed, cleared her throat. "Yes, happy."

"More massage," he said, "now you are awake. Very good. Very better this time."

"No. No more." The trip to the guest house loomed, an hour at least of dodging shadows.

Shiv had lit up a little *bidi* cigarette. He smiled when he saw her looking. She pulled up on the strings of her neck pouch, hauling it out through the neck of her shirt. "I owe you money," she said. "Let's get all this settled."

She could see half his frown in the shore light. "Later, please, and then settle."

"Last time it was a hundred and fifty; this time was longer, so two hundred?" She passed him the money; he folded it into the waist of his *dhoti.* His eyes did not give away that he had received it. But maybe he would buy himself some new flip-flops.

She looked down the long stretch of riverbank. At least it would be quicker at night. The rowboats still formed a bridge between this boat and the wall of the shore. She could go out the same way she'd come in; she'd be in her room at the Saraswati in no time.

"No, madame." He was shaking his head. "Danger."

"Danger for you," she said. "Not for me. I'm a foreigner."

"At night it is danger for anyone. Stay." He waved toward the cabin door. "Sleep until morning."

She stared back down the bank. She could run and get there in half the time.

"Foreigners, maybe they are not so safe. Already there is one American man missing. You have heard of this? It is not good to take this chance."

"What American man?"

"I am not knowing his name. I have seen him many times. Big man, buffalo, his face sunburn."

"He must have found a way to the airport."

He looked puzzled.

"That man is from my guest house."

"Madame." He sounded alarmed. "You must not walk to this place in the night."

CHAPTER THIRTY-THREE

It was night under the trees. An open-air portico at the side of one small building had filled with people. We stood close against a metal grillwork wall, looking through to the interior, where the *mahant* alone faced a raised hearth. Firelight wavered across his face. His ordinariness, the glasses that caught the light and blocked any view of his eyes, his smooth placid face, now made him seem sinister.

The others, pressed tight around me, looked like any twenty people you might see on the street, gathered here for vespers. We watched through the fretted metal wall as the priest made his preparations, catching only broken glimpses of his face—I had not learned his name. His hands tended a many-pointed gothic candelabra.

A crash just at the side of my head—the vibration humming in my teeth before I could even register my surprise.

The man beside me held up a heavy skillet, a ragged star-shaped hole punched out of the center. Stunned, I stared at his face a foot from mine. He saw my confusion and laughed. Triumphant, he struck the pan again.

Then from the rear of the gathering, someone hit a

drum, a beat without pattern; and a pair of cymbals, one dented, rose over the heads of the others, slammed together. A whang lashed out, sharp-edged, whipping in every direction. I shut my eyes, but a fresh shock of noise made them open.

A girl my age was striking a chime, over and over the same piercing note; then the man at my side was at it again. It was no more than a frying pan with a hole, I told myself, and a man banging it with a ladle.

The tight-packed mass pressed forward against the grate in the wall, starting to sing—no, it was shouting more than singing, weirdly dissonant. Fervent faces across from me in the half-moon of crowd, mouths moving—light from the fire darkened their eye sockets, reddened their cheekbones.

A conch shell howled, and I pressed my hands over my ears, tried to drop to my knees to escape. I wanted to crawl out, feel the bare dirt under my hands and knees, get away from this chaos that was rising. Yet wedged tight between bodies, I was trapped, unable even to sink. The dizzying smell of anise hung in the air, and oily hair tonic. The man behind me was held full against me, his penis distinct along the cleft of my buttocks.

Yet up in front of me, glimpsed between the bobbing heads and raised arms, I could see empty space, there inside the room where the *mahant* had left his spot in front of the fire. He carried the rack of tapers, trailing sooty smoke, to stand before one of the wall shrines, circling the candelabra before the god's staring face.

The noise rose louder; the bars that walled off the interior rattled and shook with the force of people leaning. I leaned with them, had no choice. I tried to cry out for it to stop but couldn't hear myself. The light shone hard red even through my closed eyelids. I slipped into a silent space somewhere out in the darkness.

CHAPTER THIRTY-FOUR

SHIV WAS asleep a few feet away. Jill could hear his steady breathing, her own nearly as slow and even. She was comfortable, surprisingly, as if the two of them lay here companionably every night.

In the open air of the cabin roof, the stillness felt like a light sheet over her, the water whispering. Now and then she'd hear something stir on the bank, a goat's hooves clicking on the concrete. She wondered about the old man in his bed—he might be dead by now. Having the covers of the bed heaped with marigolds while you die would be nice.

She rolled over to face upstream. Far down at the other end of the city, the palace of the maharajah hid in the darkness. Closer, maybe a mile away, burned the orange light of the funeral pyres, probably bodies from the rioting. From where she lay, she could see spots of fire, and in the faint breeze, she imagined she could smell the smoke.

These fires were burning human bodies—she turned that fact over in her mind—the flesh cooking like a roast before it began to burn to ash. As she lay out in the night air, it didn't seem so terrible. The flare-up and dying away of the fires—at this distance, she could see it had a sort of rhythm, of waking and sleeping, one continuing flow, with nothing she could do to stop it or alter it in any way.

She eased over onto her back. The sky was black, untouched by the sprinkle of riverbank lights. Even the stars looked small, dimmer and more distant than the bright pinholes they usually were. The night sky had engulfed them; it hung over her, protecting her, like the mosquito netting at the house.

Under this sky and all around her, the dark river was flowing. Shiv breathed, slow, in and out. Her legs, her arms lay still. She never had been so still.

She felt the night on her skin, and the joining of two boards where they buckled slightly against the muscle of her calf. She could feel everything, and there was nothing in this moment that needed fixing or improving, herself included.

CHAPTER THIRTY-FIVE

MY BAG under my arm, I groped my way in the dark to the path that led out of the monastery.

I cried as I walked and ran, following the trail by the feel of the paving stones under my bare soles. Hurrying, staggering in my rush, I felt the leaves and vines bat at my face and neck, pull at my sari.

In front of the open gate, the road spread wide and empty in the dim glow from a distant streetlight. I trudged off, wet-faced, with my zippered sack. The edge of my sari, pulled loose in the run, dragged in the dirt.

My ears rang from the clanging music—I'd heard of people doing that to wake up their souls.

A sharp jab at the ball of my foot: I bent close so I could see, kicking loose a rock hidden in the dark and dust. I'd forgotten my sandals.

At the side of my big toe, a flap of skin leaked blood.

I kept walking for a mile or more, the wound caking with dirt, then came to an intersection where there still was traffic. I spoke the Joshis' address to the first rickshaw man who stopped. That instruction—the thought of walking back into the house—sealed my defeat. There was no point, though, in trying to go elsewhere tonight. I wanted only to lie down.

As I rode, the street-side cooking fires threw shadows on the walls of buildings; I saw flashes of men's yellow-lit faces, clay drinking cups in their hands. The family wouldn't be surprised at my return—what could you expect of a pet? Sometimes they ran off. With Bhushan, though, the break was made; we would not remain long under the same roof, no matter what welcome his family might offer me, and I could not imagine my future.

I came up a side stairway, managing to avoid everyone but a couple of the children chasing each other, and they paid me no mind. Shutting my bedroom door, I took out a huge sack of peanuts I had tucked away in my bag. I fell onto the bed. The note I'd left was gone, though nothing else of mine had been touched.

In my hands, I held the 200 grams of roasted peanuts, a large bag shaped like a brick, rolled shut at one narrow end. As I opened it, the smell was like wet brown dirt.

I cracked the first shell, emptied two shriveled nuts into my mouth. They tasted bitter and meaty, the papery wisp of skin falling away. The next two were better. And as I ate them, I was splitting open the next, several at once, mashing the shells together in one hand.

I broke them by the fistful, letting the hulls drop and scatter. The motion of it fell into a rhythm. Growing up, I had dug for peanuts and potatoes, seen hogs butchered in the cold, and the greenish mold creeping over hams curing in the dark. I knew as well as anybody that food comes from dirt and manure and the slaughter of screaming animals. Huddled there on my rumpled bed, I hummed as I ate; sucking on the peanuts, chewing them to a gravelly butter or sometimes swallowing them whole like capsules. With the sack of nuts held close, I was snug, and could feel in the silence and concentration—chewing, swallowing—how I was putting myself in order again.

CHAPTER THIRTY-SIX

SUNBAKED AND empty, the bridge stretched out in front of T. J. The metal planks rang as he set out across. Almost twenty-four hours since he'd left the guest house—surely they assumed he was staying on with the Rais.

High on the bluff on the far side, the maharajah's palace hung above the river like a mirage. He should have asked Mrs. Rai for a bottle of drinking water.

This bridge was like the ones they'd built in Viet Nam—platforms on big floating cans, strung together. The quonset huts in Da Nang, too, had that same tin-can feel. He'd sat in one for a full year, dripping sweat onto supply forms, only a hundred yards from the morgue. Day in, day out, the choppers brought men in on stretchers. The hospital was in the same building, but everyone just called it the morgue. You could smell it the whole way from Perimeter Road. The rotted-flesh odor mixed with formaldehyde and the jet fuel from the runway on the other side—it seeped into the papers in his hands.

He'd been out on this bridge—it must be five minutes—surely half a mile; but the far end seemed no closer.

Last night he'd dreamed he was swimming toward

Jane, fighting a riptide. In a few weeks, he'd fly home, find out he'd worried for nothing. She'd be so glad to see him, they'd fall into each other's arms. She'd be near tears. Maybe not, though. Maybe she'd calmly tell him, sitting in her car in the airport parking lot, that the marriage was over. He was too demanding, too intrusive.

What Jane needed was somebody who could get along just fine without her. At least that was what she imagined she needed. It wasn't at all true; she liked being worshiped. Without him, she might not have the confidence to be so goddamned self-possessed.

He had the feeling she was watching him right now from somewhere behind him, up high: a tiny toy man crossing a model railroad bridge. Out on this span, he felt pitifully exposed.

At breakfast, his mind had fogged when Rai had reported, in his flat tone, yesterday's massacre; he'd seen the color leave Mrs. Rai's face. The thought of it went around and around in his head: the singling out of so many women, it was a calculated butchery. He'd sat still, feeling the knowledge leak into him.

He'd left the Rais as if he were urgently needed somewhere; along the way he'd decided where it was he was going.

Fifty yards to where he would step off this bridge. Thirty-five—he counted each stride as one yard. Finally, he put a foot down in the cut-up clay of the shore. Up on his right, the palace loomed, massive and turreted, its lower stories blocked by smaller buildings.

Climbing through narrow empty streets, one eye on those tall spires, he came to a long high wall. He followed it to the palace gates and found himself in the semblance of a military camp.

On either side, in the walls of the shadowy arched walkway, was a high open-sided room lined with cots, rows of soldiers' polished boots, sheets and shirts hung on lines to give a little privacy. He could see just the stocking feet of one man lying on a cot. Near the rear wall, three or four were playing cards.

It looked like fifteen or twenty men lived in here, camped out in the front door, seeing about as much action as he had. The soldier standing watch was giving him the eye.

"Sir." The man came toward him, rifle slung loose at his side. "There are no tours scheduled today." He was little. T. J. could see the top of the guy's beret.

"I wasn't planning to take a tour. Could you point me to the person I should see about an appointment with the maharajah?"

"I am sorry. This is not possible."

"The truth is," T. J. said, "I met His Excellency recently at a social function."

"Interview is not possible."

"Well, that's all right, then. I appreciate your considering it."

T. J. looked past the guard to the courtyard, a wide-open dusty parade ground enclosed by buildings painted peach, yellow, and aqua, with carved balconies. It was ornate but shabby, like the place where he and Jane had stayed in Venice.

He nodded in that direction. "Is that where the tours go usually?"

"Come here in a week or two, then maybe open."

"You think everything will back to normal by then?"

"I cannot say."

Swarthy little guys with guns were too much like Nam, made him feel like he needed to piss.

The man had stepped away, returned to his post.

T. J. stood, staring through the archway.

The guard looked back, pointed with his head toward a building inside the grounds. "The museum," he said, "it is just there. You may go and look once, if it is not locked. Then come out."

T. J. nodded deferentially, stifled a grin. He walked out into the bright sunlit grounds of the palace. He found the door to the museum unlocked.

Inside, the light was dim, the air hot and dead still.

He pulled out his little key-chain flashlight; what he could see looked more like a storeroom than a museum. He pointed the light to the other wall, stepped closer: it wasn't a wall. In front of him was a carriage, big as a stagecoach made entirely of ivory. Was that possible? He shone the beam of light over it: Cinderella's coach, made of ivory lace. His girls would love it.

Sweat rolled down his chest. It was fucking hot. He headed for the strip of light from the door he'd left ajar.

Outside, he leaned against the museum door shut behind him, put his hand up to shield his eyes from the light. Cooler, but still 110 degrees at least.

Across the court at the arch, a different soldier stood guard, young-looking, a teenager. T. J.'s eyes followed the uneven perimeter of the enclosure; another soldier blocked another doorway. He hadn't been in there but a few minutes. Through a smaller arch, he could see one more.

No one seemed to notice him, but they knew he was here, the way the policemen had on the street.

Just then a loud bang came from the other side of the front wall, and a second smaller popping. A soldier ran along the courtyard wall toward the gate; the men in the archway grabbed rifles. It was only firecrackers. Didn't they know that?

Across the way, a door had been left unguarded, its deep blue paint seemed almost to radiate its invitation. He'd come all this way . . .

T. J. sauntered across the fifty yards, forcing himself to keep an easy pace, as if he made this walk every day.

He opened the door and stepped in.

The hall was empty. He waited for his suddenly racing heart to settle down. He'd gotten in.

He was standing in a long corridor, wide and high-ceilinged, the only light coming from windows up high near the roof. At one end, a set of stone steps curved up and away.

He walked slowly toward the stairs, then up them, as if he belonged here.

At the top, he opened another door and stepped out on a balcony edged with a low carved balustrade. A woman in a blue sari rushed past below, carrying a platter of dirty dishes. He could hear the soft sound of her sandals on the path, the clink of one plate against another.

Down that path, wherever she'd come from, that was where he needed to go.

The door at the far end of the balcony led him down and out. He followed the path to another building, passing a man carrying a stack of neatly tied files. "Good afternoon," T. J. said. The man nodded, kept walking.

He was deep inside the complex, passing more people, all of them Indian, none of them looking twice at him. This was easy.

He kept moving, following the general direction of the traffic.

At the head of a set of stairs, he walked into a big room; one man sat working at a massive table in the center. The table had legs big as columns.

"Sir," T. J. said, clearing his throat.

"Yes?" The man's manner was stiff. "May I help you?"

He was an officious clerk, maybe thirty, maybe forty; it was hard to tell.

"Sir, I'm from the United States."

The clerk was staring at the dirt caked around the edges of T. J.'s shoes.

"Here on some government research. The maharajah, the king, and I had the opportunity to meet recently at a social affair—the name's T. J. Clayton—I'd just like a few minutes of his time."

The clerk adjusted his starched shirt cuffs.

"To talk with him," T. J. said, "about some issues concerning water quality."

The room was quiet, the floor covered with many carpets, overlapping so thick that T. J. felt as if he were standing on a bed.

"I am not understanding this fully," the clerk finally said. "You are telling me that you have an appointment?"

"No appointment—I just came on over."

The man's face displayed weary disdain. "Please remain here; I will ask."

T. J. nodded, almost a bow, which gave him a quick look at his dirt-streaked khakis. The clerk was probably on the phone now, calling the guards to come throw him out.

CHAPTER THIRTY-SEVEN

A LAYER of debris—bits of peanut shells, wrappings of hard candy—has pasted itself to my skin.

A day must have passed. The light has the look of morning.

I remember now how I groped along the shelf for the basin to use as a toilet: that is the source of the fetid smell.

The stink, if nothing else, will bring someone to discover if I am alive or dead. Though news of the massacre may have sent them all into their own refuges. Not Ramesh, surely—but I missed his morning bath, slept past it. All these years I have watched, every day, without fail, and thought it habit as much as anything, a focus for my mind.

My head has an odd ache, hurting in segments.

If I'd locked the house, as I've again and again imagined, when the trouble was over, I'd find his drawer emptied, the three folded white *dhotis* gone.

Ramesh could never abandon me unless I kept him from his river prayers.

At the first flare of this trouble, I could have assured his safety, but only by the very act that would drive him from me.

If he has gone out, that young policeman Jawahar will kill him.

But then, he expects to die on these banks and be freed from the cycle of rebirth. That is the gift of this holy city.

I count upon it for myself; I am Hindu: I have spent enough time with Shiva, the many-faced, the deliverer.

If Ramesh and I could die together, sinking into the river where he washes every day—the water cool, a dark soothing tea—I would barely see the shape of him beside me, though his hand might brush the side of my hip.

She would be gentle—Ganga—her sweeping current. I'd stand behind him so as not to see his face. He would be lost in his prayers, easily overpowered by the force of my weight as I drew us both under.

His bare back—it is my one intimate glimpse of him; and if I heard a cry from his mouth, I could not do it. I would come to my senses.

But then I know—as I have not dared to think in these twenty years—that I might well savor the feel of his body one second too long. I wouldn't be able to stop. He would die with me holding him.

CHAPTER THIRTY-EIGHT

THE CLERK breezed past T. J. and back to his desk. "It will be permitted for a few minutes that the king will see you." He shook his head extravagantly to make his own feelings clear, then returned to his paperwork.

"Thanks," T. J. said to the top of his head, "for arranging that." Another dark young man in Western dress appeared at the doorway and motioned him to come.

Now he wondered, did the king agree to see anybody who just wandered in? Maybe he had intelligence that kept him apprised of who came to town. The man ahead of him kept moving.

They walked into a room where walls and floor were covered with thick burgundy carpets, the air dusty and close. A man seated on a pillow was talking on an old black rotary phone. With muffled footsteps, they passed the cross-legged man and went out a doorway on the other side.

His escort pivoted and vanished behind a screen. T. J. followed, and they emerged into a high-ceilinged room. Tall windows ran the length of the far wall; it looked a lot like the sanctuary at First Methodist. T. J. could tell from the shifting brightness of the light that the river was just below.

A man turned, short, stocky. He'd been standing, looking out; T. J. hadn't seen him.

"Good afternoon." The man made a *namaskar* bow. T. J. recognized his big dark eyes and mustache. The maharajah was about his own age.

"Good afternoon. I'm T. J. Clayton from the United States." All at once, he felt shaky, the dehydration catching up with him.

A guard stood at each end of the room, looking but not looking.

"Come and sit down," the king said; he had an air of quiet dignity about him.

T. J. sat in the carved wood chair he was pointed to, and prepared his mouth to try to explain himself.

"You have come to make an official visit," the king said.

"I'm here from Florida. You have heard of Florida?"

"Yes, of course I know Florida."

The man was barefoot in flowing *kurta* pajamas of rust-colored silk. The buttons glinted yellow like tiger's-eye marbles. Of course he knew Florida.

"Though I am sorry," the king continued, "to say I have not been to your state. Perhaps one day I will have the opportunity. I might feel at home there, since I believe your weather is perhaps a milder form of ours?"

The maharajah was chatting T. J. up about the weather, placidly ignoring how he looked and how he'd gotten in here.

"You're right," T. J. said. "It gets pretty hot."

The king waited.

T. J. fingered a leaping dolphin in the carving of the chair arm. He wanted to walk over and look out at the water, get his bearings. He gazed up toward the clerestory windows. "Your Excellency"—clearing his throat—"is that the proper form of address?"

"It is satisfactory."

"You see, there are a couple of things that crossed my mind, in coming here, I mean; of course, being an American, you can't resist the chance to meet a person of royalty, since we don't have those."

This wasn't going well. "The main thing, as your assistant may have mentioned, I'm performing some research here. Pollution control. River water." He was babbling, but the king seemed to be listening. "Trying to get some idea," T. J. said, "how to persuade the population to commit to the effort."

The king nodded with true sympathy. Maybe the man had cabin fever from the curfew like everyone else and was glad for someone new to talk to. "Last night," T. J. said, surprising himself, "I saw something happen out on the river." He paused to collect his thoughts; he hadn't meant to launch straight into it.

The king's eyes narrowed. "What is it you have seen?"

"Men rolling a body wrapped in a bloody sheet off the side of a boat."

"You are certain this is what you saw?"

"I was less than fifty feet away. Then, this morning, the news of the women being killed." The body—he couldn't believe he hadn't thought of this before—was likely one of them.

"And what is it you are wanting from me?" The king's tone was carefully mild.

At one end of the room, a computer monitor was blipping green in the corner of the screen. It seemed so out of place there on that ornate mahogany desk. T. J. felt a tightening in his throat, feared for a second he might cry. "I'm sorry." He shook his head. "I don't know."

Only a few miles from where he'd sat doing paperwork every day, the V.C. had flayed a couple of men they'd caught in one of their jungle traps, left them skinless and alive, staked to the ground.

He glanced at the guard nearest him. For a moment, the man impassively met his eyes.

"It is perhaps just as well that you have no wish," the king said. "There is in fact very little I can do."

The silence resumed.

T. J. could hear the banging of a pipe deep inside the walls.

A minute clicked on the big wall clock.

Over the desk were framed photographs: the maharajah with visiting dignitaries; the maharajah giving out a tennis trophy; diplomas in Gothic script that he couldn't read from where he sat; an old photograph of a man in a jeweled headdress, long striped coat, and pointed slippers with pom-poms.

"I shouldn't have taken your time like this," T. J. said in apology. "If you could have someone walk me out to the front gate, that would be a great help."

"No."

T. J. blinked, startled by the tone of command.

"I will not permit you to risk yourself. You must stay here the night."

It was only a manner of speaking, surely; he wasn't being held prisoner.

"A little while ago outside," the king said, "pranksters were exploding firecrackers with extra powder added. It is better that you are escorted to your hotel in the morning." He inclined his head with a gracious smile. "And we must have a chance to converse further, once you have rested and recovered from your exertions." He reached over to the desk, picked up a phone, and began speaking in Hindi.

T. J., half dizzy with the sense of burden lifted, looked up into the high vault of the ceiling. A night in the palace at the king's invitation—and here he was in filthy sweat-stained clothes, unshaven. The maharajah continued to make arrangements for him; he wished he could call and tell Jane and the girls.

CHAPTER THIRTY-NINE

FOOTSTEPS—THE sheet is twisted and balled underneath me; I need to cover myself.

A rap at the door. Not Ramesh: he would bellow for me.

"What is it?" My voice sounds sickly. I've slept again. The room is full of reflected sunset, yellow-amber light. My lips and the lining of my mouth are coated with slime.

"May I come in?"

It's Marie; I could have guessed from her halting step. "You will think better of it if you do."

The door jerks open as if she'd expected it to be jammed; I watch from the corner of my eye. She's coming in here to lift her eyebrows and stare in horror at my degradation.

I hear her muffled retch. I let my eyes close; I didn't call her to come and breathe my stinking air.

From the sound of her motions, she has gone to stand at the window. I am not well covered, I know it, with only this dirty rag of sheet. I open my eyes to see that she stands where I thought, with her back to me.

"I'm collecting myself," she says.

"And wanting a gulp of clean air, I would imagine." The ceiling of this room is gray-white, no matter the time of day, like a bleached clamshell. Ganga does not deposit shells on this concrete shore. In winter I would walk for miles along the edge of the ocean, collecting the odd broken bit of shell.

"Have you been lying in here all this time?" she says, her voice muffled and distant from my thoughts.

My eyes close again. "I don't know what you are asking." Before me, the cold surf breaks; I hear the sharp salt-air cry of a sea gull. The ocean was so clean. I should have stayed there, found a place for myself.

"I would never have knocked, but I heard you cry out. I thought all this while that you'd gone with Ramesh"—her voice shakes—"to the authorities."

"What?" My head rises off the pillow. "What did you say?"

"I thought you'd gone to look for T. J. and Jill."

"Ramesh is on the street?"

"All I know is what the man on the next rooftop called out to me; I had a hard time understanding him. I'm the only one here—or I thought I was—for the past two days. I told myself you were surely out trying to help. I didn't know what to do, except worry. The others are gone."

CHAPTER FORTY

THE PALACE guest room had a 1950s modern look, a lot of recessed fluorescent lighting, a rimless mirror over a long, low dressing table. He took a look at himself, from his filthy sneakers to the sunburned top of his head. His hair was rumpled at odd angles. He looked like a homeless drunk.

He put the thought of homelessness out of his mind.

The bathroom, though, was a work of art, all marble; the tub, sitting up on legs, big as a tomb. He'd get in there and soak, come out a new man.

He heard a soft rustle in the room behind him. By the time he was at the door, whoever it was was gone. On the nightstand had been left a tray of soaps and towels, a shaving brush and straight razor. He picked up a square of cream-colored cotton the size of a hand towel, unfolded it. It fell out into pants and a shirt, a pair of *kurta* pajamas that might be big enough.

The vellum card dropped to the floor: "His Excellency will join you at your meal at 7 p.m."

Good—he had an hour for a bath. The soaps smelled like an opium den; he'd set his watch alarm so he wouldn't drift off.

• • •

The king sat at the head of the table, hands folded, a tall, sweating glass of water before him.

The red-turbaned men who stood along the wall had brought food only to T. J. Eating with all these people watching, he felt as if he were onstage, which was particularly uncomfortable, since he was ravenous and he was the only one eating. Plus, he was sitting here in these thin pajamas; they were amazingly cool and comfortable.

The main dish was creamed spinach; self-conscious, he took up another mouthful with the heavy-crested silver fork, and gulped down a swallow of the bottled water that had been cracked open in his presence as if it were champagne.

"The food is over-spiced?" The king raised his hand in summons. "I will call for something else."

"No, no—it's fine. It's delicious."

The servant who'd stepped forward withdrew at a glance.

Maybe the king had eaten earlier in his private quarters with his family. Or maybe they all lived somewhere else and this was just his office. The long polished table had a boardroom look.

T. J. tore a piece of bread in half, broke off a smaller piece. The man was not turning out to be a talker.

"It's very kind of you to have me here," T. J. said again. "You figure there was real risk in my walking home to my hotel?"

"In truth, it was in part because of my interest. You had gone to such extreme, slipping past my guards in order to express your concern for the trouble we are having."

T. J. took another of the breads; this one was stuffed with a potato mixture and maybe chives.

"It interested me," the king said, "what you did. Yet you had nothing to ask, and you offered nothing."

"I was a little confused from the heat, and dehydrated. Now I'm feeling much more myself again. In fact, just now while I was having a bath, I gave some thought to the difficulty here—"

The king, smiling, touched his lips with two fingers; he was wearing a ruby ring, the stone like a glass of red wine held before a fire.

"I must inform you once again, Mr. Clayton, of how very little I can do. I am a man in a ceremonial position. Since 1972, by government decree, the princes of India have had no official title, privilege, or power. It was a change that had been coming for a long time. We were de-recognized, that is the word. In my conscience I cannot argue with it."

"I see what you're saying. But I watched how you were greeted at that gathering. People literally made way for you. They bowed."

"It is true. In Benares, the people have not de-recognized me." He took a sip of his water, the first time he'd touched it. "They expect me to do things no man can do."

"I have heard, though, that in your position you're considered a son of Shiva on earth. Surely Congress could not vote to take that away from you."

"They could try." His eyes were bright. "So far they have not done. And if they did, it might relieve me of a difficult circumstance. It would be easier to raise the dead than to bring about a reliable peace. Muslims and Hindus have conquered and reconquered each other here for centuries. Unspeakable crimes have been done—each savage act followed by a more savage revenge, as if raising the level of violence would somehow put an emphatic end to the fight. It can start with so little, a word of insult." He shook his head. "When exhaustion comes, that is when there will be peace again. And then it may hold for some years."

"But how is the police effort organized? Are you in on that? I was thinking—"

"Mr. Clayton, if you are so bent on doing something, I suggest that you pray." He pushed back his chair, got to his feet.

T. J. stood, napkin in hand. "But hang on a second." He couldn't stop himself: "If all the Hindus of each—"

"I retire now, Mr. Clayton," the king said from the doorway. "I bid you good night."

CHAPTER FORTY-ONE

MY HEAD spins at the shock of sitting up. The wall seems to loom closer.

Marie has sunk her claw into my arm. "Let go of me." The pillow smells like sleep, the sheets oily and soft as skin.

"Natraja, don't lie down." She has taken her hand away.

"These are my private quarters—"

"Drink this."

My breath roars inside the glass. The water slops on my face, drips. I remember when I would stir my glass of milk with a straw until a hole opened in the surface like an underwater tornado. I pictured myself descending into the swirling white.

"They have killed Ramesh, Marie."

"You don't know that. Put this on."

It's so much work to tie a sari; I hold it around me. "There's nothing now that can do any good."

"You need to go up to the roof, talk to the man next door. You'll be able to understand what he's saying."

"That man thinks I am possessed. He forbids his wife to speak to me." Marie searches the floor for my sandals.

"Natraja, there's a mess under this bed. Dear God . . ."

She has had to fend for herself, it occurs to me, since yesterday morning. "Were you frightened?" I say.

"What?"

"At being alone. Did you find enough to eat?"

"No. Yes." She is fitting a sandal onto my foot. "I live alone, you know, in Cincinnati. I was out on the roof for sunrise."

"You took my place."

"That's right," she said defiantly. "I sat in your chair." She gets to her feet with some difficulty. I have let her dress me.

"This is not the right way to wrap a sari."

She ignores me.

"I need to wash."

"Yes, you do."

"I need to go to the toilet."

"Natraja, hold on to the wall or we're both going to topple."

Upright, a hand on her shoulder . . . Dizziness comes over me again, my legs weak as cushions, and it has only been two days.

I want to lie down. "Marie, it's night soon. Look outside." She has interrupted my drift into sleep; I should have been left alone.

"After you've cleaned up," she says, "we're going to go downstairs and sit at the table; make a list of people who can help, the family that owns the inn, whoever else you can think of. We'll get a message to them, hire Sankar, the newspaperman, or anybody with a pass."

"Was there a break today in curfew?"

"I don't think so."

"If this is true, after so many days, conditions must be very bad."

Outside my room, the hall looks long. Marie, steering, balances herself against me; I keep a hand at the wall. Perhaps there simply will be no word. When I have strength again, I will go to the bazaar, find Jawahar, and kill him myself. Marie is right, I must not lie here.

There's a clatter in the stairwell. Here's Jill, when it should be Ramesh.

"There you are!" Marie's voice is full of angry joy. "Where have you been?"

"Out walking, as usual, most of the day."

"But last night?"

"I'm sorry I couldn't send word," Jill says. She has stopped near the door to the privy. As we come closer, I can see the dark lumps of insect bites on her face and legs.

"Where were you?" I say. She looks at me oddly; my sari is not tied.

"On the river. The time slipped by, and I was caught out after dark; I couldn't get back here."

"Where on earth did you sleep?" Marie, speaking with that motherly tone of concern, though still I am certain she never liked Jill.

"On the roof of a houseboat."

Then there is more to this. I understand: she was not alone in this adventure. "And you have killed Ramesh by what you have done," I say. "He has gone out to search for you."

Marie lifts a hand as if to slap me.

"Who was the boy?" I hiss at Jill, who stares, white-faced.

"Ramesh is dead?" Her voice is tiny and thin.

"No, he is not." I'm surprised Marie didn't speak sooner. "We don't know where he is or," she says, throwing a hard look at me, "why he left."

"What about T.J.?" Jill's voice is shaky.

"We'd assumed," Marie says, "that the two of you were together."

Jill shakes her head. "No. But when did Ramesh leave? Did he say anything?"

"Stop!" I say. "I will not listen to more of this." Jill stands, blocking my way to my bathroom. It pleases me to see her dry-mouthed in fright at what she has done. "You," I say to her, "stop asking these questions, repeating yourself all day long. I am tired of you."

She retreats a step.

"Enough." Marie grabs the meat of my arm. "Natraja, shut your mouth. Jill, go downstairs."

Jill scrambles toward the stairwell.

Marie has pushed me through the doorway into the bathroom. The door clicks shut behind me, before me the stinking shit hole, a footledge on either side. The room is barely larger than I am. They have transferred me to a smaller cell.

Marie thinks she can keep that girl away from me. She will have to leave here. She can go again to the river to sleep. I should have told her days ago she would have to leave. She killed him for an hour of pleasure. The boys along the river are seductive, like snakes. They will do anything if you pay them. T. J. must have refused her.

A hand against each wall, bracing myself, I can reach both sides. The room leans. It's my dizziness again. I feel the box I'm in rotating slowly, as if from its center, like the Tilt-a-Whirl ride at the carnival in front of Sears.

Reggie had tried to leave me.

"We need to quit this, Stelle," he said as soon as he came in. Not even hello. He stood in front of where I lay waiting on the feed sacks.

I clambered to my feet. "What's wrong?"

I could feel the heat coming off him in the dark of the shed even though he was a foot or more away. He didn't answer.

"I don't believe you," I said.

"Girl, you don't know."

I put my hand on his neck, right where the knots of hair began. He didn't shrug me off.

I stepped closer so our bodies were touching. I put my face against his shirt. Reggie was tall. I could feel him tense.

I let my hands slide down his sides.

He took hold of my wrists and pushed me away.

"Okay," I said. "If that's what you want."

He reached to pull the door open. I could see a slice of his face in full light. He was thirteen but younger-looking, his face smooth as a Hershey bar. He looked sullen.

"Reggie?"

Whatever he heard in my voice made him push the door shut.

I found him in the dark, bare arm and T-shirt sleeve. I took one step and put my face against the ridge of his collarbone.

We lay down on the dirt, just behind the door. Before I could see at all again, I'd taken his shirt off him and undone his shorts. All the time, I felt like he was half pulling away from me, like undertow, but he was right there.

We didn't listen for anyone outside. We didn't slow down.

I was lying under him. I had both legs around him, and no underpants. We had never done this, we had always played, with just our hands, and it had always been slow.

I held on to him with both arms and both legs until he made his grunting sound, but this time it came from all the way down in his feet. He still had on his big high-top tennis shoes, his legs fallen heavy and still as if he'd gone to sleep.

I felt the trickle from him and me drip down onto the hard dirt.

Neither one of us spoke; we stood up and dressed quickly, pushed the door ajar to get some light, and scraped over the spot in the dirt that had a few drops of blood.

We left the same way we always had: one went, and then minutes later, the other.

We continued to meet at that same place, sometimes every day for a week, for the remaining seven months. There was no more talk about breaking up.

CHAPTER FORTY-TWO

T. J. PULLED the sheet up over his shoulder; it still was night.

Behind him, the door latch rattled, clicked open. He raised his head. In his sleep, he must have heard someone. Then the shadow of a man in white stepped one foot into the room.

"Sahib, sahib." The voice a penetrating whisper. "You are wake now." The man dropped away into the darkness of the hall and was gone.

It was time for the river bath. His eyes scanned the ceiling, then each of its corners, deeper shadowed. He hadn't actually said he was going to do this: it still was so dark you wouldn't see what was floating. The water was full of disease. And after all, the king was not his king; and if he wanted to pray, he could do it without going to the river.

His dream came over him again. He was blind; people standing just out of reach jeered at him. His eyes popped open. On the far wall of the room, the round mirror held a dark reflection of furniture and shadows. He imagined it as a circle of well water, black and mossy, full of his own wavery, hopeful face as it would be if he mustered the energy to go over there.

He sat up, feet on the cold stone tile. He felt hung-over; his scalp was sunburned. The hike to the palace—no food or water, all day in the sun; he hadn't minded at the time. He'd have to get up and at least go put a foot in, he decided.

Stepping into the *kurta* pajamas he'd worn last night, he was ready in a minute.

A sharp knock: the wake-up man had come back to lead him.

The palace halls, dimly lit, threw him into the mood of the dream. He was lost in a dark labyrinth, at the mercy of the mapmaker. Ahead of him, the servant hurried on slippered feet. The hush felt soft around him. Occasionally, they passed a guard in the shadows of an alcove. One of them, narrow-faced, looked like the soldier he'd slipped past at the front gate, seeming to follow him now with hostile eyes.

The route was long, winding back on itself, descending flight after flight of stairs, wide and slow-sloping. They walked down corridors lined with columns, ghostly in the light of the few wall sconces.

Finally the man in front of him opened a carved door in the wall of a basement hall. They stepped out onto a promontory just inches above the level of the river.

Cool air hit his face, sifted through the weave of his *kurta.* The water riffled steadily against the edge of the concrete.

Gray light had spread out over the water. It was wider here, more than a mile to the other side. Just to the right, the pontoon bridge he'd crossed lay flat as a snake along the surface.

From the near distance, he could hear a few muffled voices—other bathers, no doubt, but he didn't see anyone. This really was a fort rising straight up out of the water, the concrete shelf shielded by tall columns, a small Shiva *linga* at the rear. The alcove felt saturated with old ceremonies; he could imagine human sacrifice, like the Mayans: cut out the heart and let the body slide into the river.

The servant had disappeared, leaving a fat towel, another pair of pajamas.

If this were the Nagacochee, he'd already be in, swimming. It was a little surprising he hadn't waded in once since he'd been in Varanasi. The water at his feet was murky. For all he knew, there might be a twenty foot drop-off, though he could see what might be a submerged step.

He reached one foot in, the hem of his pajama leg trailing in the dark water.

He stepped in with the other foot, standing on the slippery underwater ledge. Cold water seeped up his pant legs.

He pulled off his shirt, threw it aside, felt his way down another step and another until he was waist-deep. He waded farther out and found he was walking on a level platform; farther still, and he was standing out in the river, water pouring around his middle. Behind him, the palace wall rose abruptly skyward.

Down and across on the other side, the entire city lay stretched out before him. He sank until the bottom half of his face was submerged and he was looking from the level of the water. Mouth tight shut, he waved his arms to hold himself in place. At a distance, the water looked dark blue, the haze blue; the bland predawn light was getting stronger.

Sunrise wasn't far off, though the palace blocked his view of the sun; instead he'd see the light spread over the city.

He treaded water, eyes tracing the great bulk of the mosque and the spires of temples that were like one of Sally's fairy castles, wet beach sand dripped carefully into towers. She'd stopped making them, though, now that he thought about it; next summer, Elizabeth would be his only drip-castle girl.

The clanging of temple bells was softened by the distance. From here the city looked peaceful.

The edges of buildings were catching glints of yellow, almost as if they were outlined. The haze was holding light; the wide stretch of water shone.

He could hear voices rising from far down the bank. These were people like Ramesh, who would break curfew, risking their lives for this moment. At this distance, he could see only movement and spots of color.

Wait—it was happening. Done.

In a one-two motion, sunrise had started and finished: the whole city was dusted with gold. The sun was up, he could picture it: a yellow ball, bloodshot, hovering over the horizon that was hidden from his view. And in front of him, everything looked newly painted. He hung motionless, spraddle-legged, like a frog.

The sound of the bathers—chanting, singing, calling out their prayers. He had heard it a dozen times, even these curfew mornings. But now it had a different feel. It flowed, not that the voices had melted together—you still could faintly hear individual strains—but they became one constant hum. A river of voices coming toward him, like the jabber of relatives waiting for your arrival: grandparents, aunts, cousins, eager and embarrassing.

He wanted to call to them but his voice would never travel that far. He paddled idly in the direction of the city. The current almost carried him. The loose pants floated out around his legs. He took a few long overarm strokes. It felt so good.

Floating—he was over his head now—he reached down and untied the drawstring on his pants. The billow of light cloth showed muddy green for a moment below him, was gone. He made a good strong kick with nothing to bind him, and rocketed through the water, bare-assed, sleek as a porpoise. He felt wild-headed with elation.

In seconds, the bridge pontoons were rising up in front of him. The current pulled him—he was underneath the boards, sailing between two floating drums, the sound of the water echoing in the huge rusted cans that met over his head.

Out into the sun on the other side, he leveled out and swam hard, as if he were in a race, twelve years old, crossing the Nagacochee, Billy Simons in the corner of his eye. He was pulling ahead of Billy, cutting through the water like a ripping tool.

He swam until his lungs burned.

He slowed, drifting out near the center, his heart knocking from the effort. Now he could see the risen sun.

He wallowed onto his back. Behind him . . . It couldn't be. He brought himself upright, treading water. He couldn't have come this far. The palace was so far upstream it looked like a child's play castle—the turrets, the fortress walls. He could see it shrinking as he watched, the bridge hardly visible. The current just hadn't seemed that strong.

He set himself toward the palace, kicking hard. He swam in earnest, faceup, face under, slinging one arm, then the other, reaching with each stroke far as he could. He swam at an angle, across the current, the way you do in a riptide.

He counted his strokes: twenty-two . . . twenty-six . . . thirty. . . . He pictured the view from above: the curve of the city, the wide, sparkling plain of the river, a swimmer cutting across more than a mile of empty water. He knew better than to have done a thing like this.

He rolled onto his back to rest. All he needed was a few seconds. He made a couple of lazy swings at a backstroke, then flipped onto his stomach again.

The palace was no closer. The patch of trees on the far bank seemed hardly to have receded. He hadn't even passed the last tree. The current was carrying him backward toward the city, eating up all the progress he had made.

He was out of shape.

The obvious fallback was to give up, let himself be washed downstream to the center of the city. He smiled to himself. His coming ashore—if he could even get himself there—would become local mythology: 220-pound tourist, white as a peeled egg, rising out of the Ganges with his dick hanging out.

He dropped his head and blew out a stream of bubbles. He'd already swallowed enough infected water to kill him. Letting himself go limp, he floated facedown like a dead body, his spine pulled into an arc by the weight of the rest of him.

He pushed his head up for air, then sank again. The water was cool on his face, his eyelids. Jane liked to sit out in the canvas recliner, shades on, thinking about nothing.

He felt completely free. Drifting with the current as he was, the water around him hardly seemed to exist. There was no pull against him. Unless he slung out an arm or leg, he had no sensation of anything but coolness.

Did Jane feel like this, sitting out in the yard?

He was so used to trying to pry out her every thought, making sure all was well between them. It was hard work, and it got him nowhere. So maybe he'd ease off for a while.

After a few weeks, she'd be chasing him. He smiled like a Cheshire cat. It was a master stroke. She was going to be surprised.

He made a few overarm pulls.

Up ahead, the city was close now, the hum of voices louder.

He lifted the weight of his shoulders out of the water, rushing forward in a rolling dive. He came up swimming, the current lifting him, carrying him, buck naked, past the first bathing *ghats* into the holy city.

CHAPTER FORTY-THREE

HERE IS THE angle of the lane. I sense it more than see it, though it must be dawn by now. The Joshis' doorway, I know, is a sharp left on the other side. There, across Bojpur Gali. My chest heaves with panting—all this way I've run.

Ramesh may be here, protected by Bhushan and his family. If not, they will know, with all their power and properties, how best to find him. It may be he has run from me. For this I cannot fault him. My rooftop neighbor hurled it across at me last night: a man would be safer on the streets than in my house.

The carved leaves curl and twist in the stone doorjamb. My hand rises to retrace them.

The door swings open moments after I have rung. Sastri—so old!—mutters, *"Namaste,"* as I hoist myself into the foyer. I have not seen him in surely ten years or more. I see no sign in his eyes, hooded as a hound's, that he knows why I am here.

"Bhushan," I say; he at least will talk with me. Sastri, silent, motions me to follow.

We pass down a corridor, through a room piled with a waist-high tangle of silk saris, through another, where two cross-legged men confer over fabric; a boy sleeps at the edge of the heap as if it were a haystack.

Because of curfew, there are only three men when there should be twenty or forty.

Prabha hurries us through the showrooms of the house toward the office.

We step through the doorway, and there is Bhushan, cross-legged on a cushion, his onionskin invoices before him.

My eyes, for one second, fall shut.

He has a mustache, curled. His sly eyes beneath his heavy brows, now graying, are the same.

Rising, he smiles and frowns at once. That way he has of holding his head and shoulders still feels more familiar to me than my shoes.

"Madame Natraja." His voice, its mellow warmth, is like another great door swinging open.

"Bhushan." He has grown an ample girth, though nothing like mine.

He motions that we will sit on the cushions, sends Prabha off for the hot cups of tea.

"I am here on an urgent matter."

"I know this, else you would not have come. Never do you come to our house. It is a grief I have become accustomed to." He is wearing a pale silk *kurta,* the fabric so rich it seems to be a thick liquid that is pouring slowly, heavy cream. I must hold to this lazy pace he has set or he will tell me nothing.

"We each," I say, "have one or two such griefs, isn't it so?"

He laughs. He did not suffer long for me; it is I who toy with the memory. He quickly found another, a wife, and it was a love match, I have been told. "I am frightened, Bhushan. Ramesh has disappeared."

His eyebrows draw together. This, now that I think of it, is a serious matter for the family, since, as owners of the inn, they employ Ramesh.

"When has it happened?"

"He has been gone two nights, leaving a message with a neighbor that he had an errand to attend."

Bhushan shakes his head slowly. "You are thinking he plays some part in the current trouble?"

"Surely not. I am certain, though, that he knows who is involved."

"He is bold. I have known him since I was a boy." He pats and smoothes the soles of his bare feet, a hand on each foot. My impatience boils in me. As soon as he has gathered himself, though, he will move like a shark, I know. Yet I want him to share my fright. "The Muslims are like this," he says in his lecturer tone. "They will choose as victim only the most virtuous of men."

The Hindu killers are no better, I want to tell him.

"I have come to you for help," I say, "knowing both your great influence and how long you have cared for this man."

"And for you as well," he says.

My face flushes hot with pride and shame.

He rests his hands on his knees, staring at the cushioned floor. A sound floats in to us, the laughter of women in some other part of the house.

"We need not assume the worst," he says finally. "He is likely meditating on the riverbank all night, something like this."

"It is the police I fear, Bhushan. He has an enemy."

I see the face of Jawahar before me, as he stood in the market, his loutish, taunting grin; my head is full of sharp pain. Ramesh is gone. I am again in this house, disfigured for all to see. "Bhushan, it was my fault."

He looks at me oddly. It hurts my eyes to see the light on the glossy cloth of his shirt.

"It cannot be," he is saying. "You are upset."

"Of course I am upset."

The light behind my eyelids pulses.

"Here is tea, Madame Natraja. Sastri has come."

The smell of boiled tea has filled the room. I fear I will retch.

"Please, take," Bhushan is saying. "Take some tea and you will feel better."

"We must find Ramesh—"

"We will do everything." He sips his tea; all the while, time is passing, as it has done these days I have lain in my bed.

The room is quiet, only the sips and sounds of swallowing.

I push myself to my feet; the tea tilts and sloshes in the cup.

"I must go. I will walk the riverbank and ask everyone I see."

"That is not the way, my old friend." He rises to stand.

"Silence will not bring him home, Bhushan, I know that much. You are fortunate you can rest here at this time of great trouble, your life rich and easy, your children and grandchildren filling your house; you do not know what it is to suffer."

"Do I not?" He is amused.

The two of us stand barefoot on the soft floor cover. He looks long at my eyes, avoiding even a second glance at my body. "I am glad you have come," he says. "When next I see your Ramesh, I will pay tribute to him for bringing you out of your hiding."

CHAPTER FORTY-FOUR

YAWNING, STILL dopey with sleep, Jill stepped out of the close stairwell into the bright heat of the roof. She grabbed the arm of a chair, dragged it across the concrete to where Marie sat looking out.

"There you are," Marie said. "You missed a fine sunrise."

Jill flopped down in the seat. "Any word?"

"No word. T.J. is surely on some misadventure and will reappear the same way you have."

"I'm worried about Ramesh."

"Natraja went out before dawn to try to get help."

In front of Jill, the river shone like a smooth sheet of metal. Half a dozen or more of the houseboats were anchored a little distance from the bank. There still was a straggle of bathers, a woman onshore repacking her plastic shopping basket of toiletries, stepping wet feet into her sandals.

Jill tilted her face up; the sun felt good. It wasn't too terribly hot yet. She could go back to sleep sitting right here.

"What am I seeing?" Marie leaned forward out of her chair, steadying herself against the guard wall.

Upstream a few hundred yards, Jill could make out the head of a swimmer far out in the river, a dark speck against the blast of sun; he was shouting, apparently to two boys who stood closest on the shore.

She got to her feet, reaching to balance Marie by her elbow.

The man was coming in like a sailboat, at a diagonal with the current.

"Can you tell whether—"

"Not yet," Jill said.

The water was carrying the man quickly downstream toward them. She hadn't seen anyone swim far out in the river. The two little boys—street kids, probably, spending curfew on the riverbank—ran along the edge, keeping pace, one trailing a kite just behind his shoulder. She watched the smaller boy, leaping as he ran.

"It's T.J.!" Marie cried out. "I do believe he is coming out of the water without his trunks."

On the next *ghat* upstream—he'd nearly hit the mark—he was hauling himself up the steps from the water, big pink belly gleaming in the sun, the stripe of pink hanging in the triangle of shadow below.

"Jesus, Mary, and Joseph," Marie murmured.

Jill turned toward the stairway door—to get him a bedsheet, at least, and leave it downstairs at the door—but then hesitated, to see what was going to happen. The little boys were doubling up with laughter, jumping from foot to foot.

"He doesn't seem to be in any hurry," Marie said.

T. J. was sauntering along the bank toward the house, his same swaggering walk, as if he did this every morning.

Jill took one more step toward the stairwell.

There he was, picking his way barefoot, making no attempt to cover himself. The boys, bare-chested and in shorts, bounded along beside him, alternately mimicking his swagger and pretending to hide their own crotches with their hands. Marie was laughing along with them.

With a ceremonial flourish, the boy carrying the kite held it out to T. J.

He took it, a flimsy, bright purple thing the size of notebook paper. The boy pantomimed how he should hold it in front of himself.

T. J. stood completely naked, turning the little kite over in his hands.

All the remaining bathers had caught sight of him by now and stared unabashedly. T. J., busy with the kite, didn't seem to notice. He looked so fleshy and comfortable, big as a beached whale out there in the blazing sun.

He lifted the kite overhead, and the boy with the string started to run. The kite was in the air, darting left, right, left again, then came to rest high and near motionless out over the river.

She heard T. J.'s triumphant laugh, felt a rush of affection that forced the breath out of her. "T.J.," she yelled, waving both arms.

CHAPTER FORTY-FIVE

MY WEIGHT drags at my bones with every step. I should have listened to Bhushan. The block of the *ghat* gives off a smothering heat. I am sick with thirst and tired of trudging.

Ganga is no better than a ditch, undrinkable and filthy. Nor has this holy river helped me find Ramesh, though I beg and pray with every step.

Up ahead, another ragged child squats.

"Boy, you there, you have seen an old man out here this day or yesterday?"

His gamin face tilts up at me, teasing me that he may have knowledge; his face and bony legs are goat-like. He goes on about a man nothing like Ramesh, ignoring the particulars I give him.

"Twenty rupee, madame," he says when I step away in disgust. "Madame, I will search."

I hand him the money, as I have done with stray boys all day. "Saraswati," I say, "if you discover word of this man Ramesh."

I push on. Have I been doing wrong by giving his name? All day, I hadn't thought about it: the risk of attention. My mind has grown hazy. It's the lack of water. This city has no end, the distant railroad bridge no closer than it was an hour ago.

My mouth is bitter. When I try to spit, nothing comes.

The sound of my footsteps rings out against the buildings at the top of the *ghat.*

Here is the wall that divides this *ghat* from the next. I can again lift my foot that high, a half meter. I'm caught, my sandal.

The pavement comes at me—concrete full of dirty craters—jars my chin. Ground in: the brown dust of dung, the smell of dung. Dirt sticks to the walls of my mouth.

Blood oozes inside my lip.

I maneuver a hand to my face. The fat on my back shifts downhill, and the weight of it tips me.

My hand flies out just in time, plants firm on the lower step, buttressing my body.

I lie lengthwise along the step. Yet so much of my weight hangs over the edge.

If my arm lets go, I will roll, tumbling off each concrete ledge to the next in a gathering momentum. By the final drop into the river, I will be battered senseless.

Already the base of my palm is numb.

"Help!" The soft echo hoots at me.

I call louder, gripping the concrete with my whole front. Birds I hear, tiny bits of clatter from far-distant households.

I count the edges of eleven steps between me and the water. My tongue wets my lips with a bit of the blood from my mouth.

CHAPTER FORTY-SIX

TOO MUCH water," Marie said from the chair T. J. had pulled into the kitchen for her. She missed her cane. The broom handle had been worse than nothing, slipping and sliding at the first bit of pressure. "That looks like pancake batter."

T. J. tossed another handful of ground bean flour onto the board. He and Jill were trying to make bread out of what they had dug out of the sacks in the pantry. Neither of them, barefoot in their shorts and T-shirts, knew any more about cooking than how to spread a sandwich.

"Maybe it will be like *matzoh,*" Jill said. A pot of water simmered on the stove, sterilizing.

"The dough needs to be stiff and elastic," she said. Neither one of them was easy to teach, each of them like a train on its own track. "So it springs up."

The bread didn't matter anyway, Marie reminded herself; they weren't going to starve to death. It wouldn't hurt to fast a day, might clear people's minds.

"If something is stiff," Jill said, "it isn't elastic." She was watching T. J.'s hands as he forced in more flour.

"What we're making," he said, "is a big dog biscuit."

"All right, help me up from here," Marie said.

There were no arms on the chair he'd dragged into the kitchen, and without her good cane, her hip was much worse.

"No need to get up, Miss Marie. We're fixing a surprise."

"Well, go right ahead, then." She settled herself again, relieved at not having to do anything. Natraja had been gone all day, though, and that was worrying. Soon it would be dusk. "I think it's time we notified the police."

T. J. and Jill looked around at her.

"The police?" T. J. seemed taken aback.

"They did get me back here after the bomb. I don't know why we haven't gotten a missing-person message to them already. The man who brings the newspapers could carry it."

"Natraja left the house this morning," Jill said. "She isn't missing."

"But Ramesh is."

"Marie, let's hold off a little on that." T. J. kept kneading his ball of dough. "We don't know what we'd be setting in motion."

Jill had gone already to measuring out the ground lentils, if that was what they had decided it was, for makeshift *dal.* She added a little more and a little more into the cup. She was excruciatingly meticulous, crouched so her gaze was level with the rim of the cup. She smoothed across the top with her finger, brushing the extra grains onto the cutting board. She hesitated, then emptied the cup into the trash.

Realizing that Marie was watching her, Jill flushed. "I got some dirt in it."

"Dirt?"

"I touched it, the flour." She forced a bright smile, then faced back to the counter. It appeared, from the jerky motion of her elbows, that she was hurriedly measuring out more.

Again, Jill spun around. My Lord, she was tossing out the second cup.

It was peculiar, even for Jill.

T. J., oblivious, was slapping and kneading the dough. She tried to think. The room was full of weak dishwater light coming in from the one high window that opened onto the *gali.* You couldn't see out. It was a particular child Jill reminded her of, some relative. Michael's cousin's son Ladd, that's who it was. One afternoon she'd been at their house in Akron when he'd come in after school, an eighth- or ninth-grader, quiet, a good student. She'd noticed him searching for a place to put down his knapsack where it couldn't trip anyone or fall on them. Increasingly agitated, he had moved it from the top of the fridge to various spots along a wall. He'd gone upstairs to his room, finally, still clutching the pack to his chest.

A spoon—Jill's—dropped clanking to the floor.

Hooking one hand under the edge of the chair seat, Marie scooped it up. Badly as she was aching, she wouldn't have thought she could do that today.

Jill snatched it, threw it into the sink.

T. J. glanced over at her. "What are you doing?"

She faced the corner of the kitchen, away from either of them. "Nothing." Then: "Cooking." Her voice was flat. T. J. stepped away from the bread, wiping his hands on his pants.

"Jill?" Marie said.

No answer.

Pushing wouldn't do any good; it wasn't any of her business, anyway. She closed her eyes. She wanted to go home, just sit and be old.

"Jill," she said; the reddish dark behind her eyelids felt snug and restful. "It's okay to touch the ingredients when you're cooking." When she looked again, the two in front of her seemed fixed in the same gray light. "You have to get your hands into making bread; you won't poison anyone."

"Thanks"—Jill was sarcastic—"for letting me know."

She was asking for real trouble if she was going to talk like that. Now she had gone to straightening the perfect row of spice pots, placing them against the wall, lined up just so.

"It's a shame to see you suffer, that's all."

"You don't see me suffering."

T. J. kept his eyes on Jill.

Marie pushed her now: "I know it's none of my business, but I've seen this before—worrying too much. There are drugs now—"

The spice bottles knocked louder against the countertop. To get out of the tiny kitchen, Jill would have to squeeze past her chair.

"Sure," Jill said in the same biting tone. "Don't worry. Lighten up. Take it easy."

The weight of the house seemed to hang overhead, making Marie's neck hurt more. Jill could keep her problems. She was no doubt used to them; she'd been just as anxious before the violence had begun.

"Drugs," Jill said, "are for people who wash their hands until the skin comes off."

"There are all kinds of variations. The people who wash like that are scared of *getting* germs. But you seem to be worried about *giving* germs, or somehow accidentally hurting other people."

The pan of steaming water on the burner rocked on its dented bottom.

"A lot of times," Marie said, "the problem doesn't even show."

The house was still except for the rocking of the pot and the water's urgent boil.

"A person may be simply preoccupied," Marie said, unable to give it up, "or obsessed, I guess, with the fear of causing harm. Worrying about Ramesh—you might be having more trouble with it than usual."

Jill banged down a bottle, and it slipped. Marie watched it plummet to the concrete. The glass broke into big pieces, emptying crumbled leaves onto the wet floor.

A perfume of jasmine rose off the sodden tea. Jill ignored the mess at her feet. "The night on the houseboat"—her voice sounded squeezed, choked with disappointment—"I thought the river had fixed things."

CHAPTER FORTY-SEVEN

BALANCED ON the cusp of a step, I smell the river, like the water poured from a flower vase that has sat until stems and leaves have rotted. The smell of fat seems also to come off the water. The air feels greasy, though the burning *ghat* is far upriver behind me. When my eyelids get heavier, I can see the globules of fat floating on the air, humming like bugs.

Minutes have passed, I think: five, ten, I don't know. The arm that holds me propped has locked shut; water slopping past seems so close I sway with it: the way it lifts, sinks, lifts, so quickly, the little waves. The surface is brown, opaque, like the lake near Neavis. There the mud embankments were slick from the dragging stomach of the water monster that ate little children who weren't supposed to swim there.

Later at night, when Reggie and I swam, I never saw any monsters; I sat many days there after he was gone, hidden in the weeds at the top of the bank. . . .

I may have slept for a moment.

Perhaps I only dreamed I called for help, lying out here like one left to die, like that great corpse of a water buffalo that remained two days in the sun, in view from my roof, before a team of men dragged it into the water to finish its rotting.

The shadows of ripples make faces on the surface.

For years, I did not look at Vic, never for more than a second. I knew his footstep, took to the laundromat the sheets he slept on with my mother.

There—the water has smoothed, reflecting only the sky.

I wonder if behind me on the rooftops there is someone who sits watching, only just now come up into the air. I try again: "Help"—a cry that hardly carries as far as the water.

The water ripples again—faces slip and slide against each other . . . Reggie, and Vic, and Vic again, the hard set of his mouth. . . .

Pushing with my stiffened arm, I manage to swing a leg down to brace myself. My foot hits the step below, holds. Quickly now—swing the other leg beside it.

It's done. My feet are beneath me.

In this position, I am properly arranged, lying faceup at the angle of one ascending the stairs, head toward the top step, feet toward the river—same as the silk-wrapped corpses. I will rest a moment.

It is almost too late: five of two on the clock in front of homeroom. The cafeteria will be closing. I need food I can carry with me, a square of sheet cake with butter icing or a cinnamon bun. My head hurts behind my eyes.

They all know: "Her colored boyfriend . . ." They cut their eyes around when I walk by. "Did you hear? Dogs found him. . . ." I stare at the floorboards, full of dust in the seams and narrow, half the width of my foot.

The edge of the *ghat* step has a small bay in it, scooped out with wear; it fits my neck like a pillory.

Near the tall fan at the corner of the lunchroom, a few girls huddle at a table. Their heads bob down at the sight of me. It's Donna: "Well, it was her own father that did it. You won't catch me setting my foot in that house."

Vic? No . . .

It couldn't be true.

The colored woman who's sweeping casts an eye toward them, then trains her cold gaze on me.

When I left this morning for school, he was still asleep, same as always. I can't think it—racing up the cafeteria stairs—two steps, three, at a time.

The cafeteria odor comes up from the river: waxy beans and the steam-table trays of pea-and-macaroni casserole.

From the balcony, I will scream down at them. Instead I lunge for the door. If I stop, I'll fall, I might get sick, crawling on my hands and knees in front of them.

The hall between classrooms is dark.

Donna has stayed at my house dozens of times, hundreds of times, since kindergarten, everybody knows it. We played dress-up, wearing Mama's slips for evening gowns; the boas flung around our necks were Vic's Sunday ties.

CHAPTER FORTY-EIGHT

PROSTRATE ON the tile of the temple courtyard, Ramesh prayed to the Kala Bhairava before him. He felt the gaze of the god on his bare pate, a slight pressure like the knit cap he'd worn after shaving for his cousin's mourning.

Verses of praise marched through his mind for the thousandth time these two days.

> You are able to bear everything. Because of this bearing, you will be known as Bhairava. Because you appear as Death itself, you shall be Kalaraja, King of Death. . . .

The muscles in his neck burned as he lifted himself, inched forward again. Vigilant prayer was all he could do now. There, ahead of him, in the shadows of the central sanctum floated the god's half-hidden face. So many hours since sleep . . . Before him the veiled image swam: blank, wide-set eyes gleaming silver. He pressed thumb and forefinger into the cords of his neck. The mouth and body of the image were ever hid beneath the drape, coyly wrapped and seductive as some Muslim wife out in the market, her spangled sandals peeking from beneath the *burquah.* The god's eyes shone.

"You, Bhairava, are given the name of Papabhakshana, the Sin-Eater," he repeated, once more rousing the priest's boy, who lounged at the edge of the courtyard.

So close to the deity, he could almost see the hard figure beneath the thin red cloth: swollen belly, sharp-pointed trident.

> O Kalaraja, you will always be governor of the city of liberation, most excellent of all places. . . .

Words of the Puranas wove together with his own.

> Bhairava, destroy our sin. You who have committed murder and atoned by wandering the world with skull for begging bowl, I beg you, devour the bloodshed and evil that oppresses our city. Look with unwavering stare on each vile thought and act. Fill your mouth with these horrors and dissolve them in the acid of your entrails.

His mind drew back from the import of the words that came next, of the anguish he asked for Natraja to endure.

> Give, Kala Bhairava, the blessing of your punishment: pain of all the lifetimes gathered into one splinter of a second, distilled to agony that scalds the spirit clean. . . .

CHAPTER FORTY-NINE

I MUST get up. My hand stings where it has pushed so long against the concrete. I dreamed again: Ramesh hurrying down the steps of the *ghat,* bringing me a half-pint of milk in a waxy red carton, a straw in the spout, nice cold milk.

Vic was good to take me, people said over and over. Six months old, I never would have known if they hadn't told me later, except he looks so different from Mama and me, both of us fair and lanky; he's short, stubby, brown; even the whites of his eyes are tea color. He doesn't like it when the men call him Bulldog, says it belittles him.

Mama says he is a man of rectitude. Mama did not know what happened. She could not let herself know, and went nearly deaf instead.

The sky has a gold look to it, the light coming from behind me. My joints are stiff—if I put it off longer, I won't be able to get up.

The current eddies trash against the paving. A green plastic detergent bottle, the label washed away, bobs like a mechanical toy.

I don't know who got Mama pregnant with me. It wasn't anybody in Neavis. I once heard that he was a soldier passing through; he got on the bus and never knew I existed. I don't think she cared anything much about him.

"Vic" was what I called him, never Daddy. I don't know who decided that.

The house will be completely in the dark by now if they haven't taken down some of the oaks. Lynnette says Vic's given up his metalworking in the shed, messes at a computer, now, at a table in my old room, staring at the monitor hour after hour. I can't picture him old, or sitting for long. It was only a few months after what happened that Mama announced she was pregnant with Lynnette. Vic must have decided I was lost and talked her into trying again.

When I was little, two or three, maybe, I would stand on the tops of his wide feet, him holding me by the wrists; he'd take little steps, and I would walk with him.

On my way out of the school, past the clusters of kids, I overheard more in bits and pieces: "You think she let a colored boy do it to her? . . . his head torn near off . . . four of them . . . her daddy wasn't even drunk. . . ." I lay in my bed that night, stiff, dry. I hadn't seen Vic in the day and a half since they'd found Reggie's body. Lying there, with the bedroom window open, I heard when the truck pulled in—one o'clock in the morning, him getting in from work. The dead bolt on the back door clicked: his scuffling footstep inside, in the kitchen. Mama had gone to bed early, the door to their room closed. I got up, walked, dazed, in my nightgown to the doorway of the kitchen. He cast a glance in my direction. "Get a robe on, Missy." He quickly looked again toward the glass of buttermilk he was pouring.

I stayed where I was.

He crossed to the refrigerator, the door opening made its kissing noise.

When he saw I was still there looking at him, his eyes went hard, his lifted chin jutted. I felt the walls of the room bend. His eye darted to the cloth draped on the edge of the sink, the water faucet, the anger on his face altering into shock. I saw plainly in that instant of his stare: he was there again in his mind, with Reggie.

Vic stepped down from the cab of the truck.

Murphy and Doole had the boy out there, waiting. So this was the one—rabbity-looking colored boy, gawking from one of them to the other. Vic leaned over and felt of the dirt—clay crusted from the heat—breaking around his feet. He sniffed it: hot cornstalk and the whiff of soda ash. He hadn't smelled that smell nor even stepped into a field once since the bank took the farm.

The boy stood shifting and twisting every which way. Nobody had spoke a word. Doole leaned on the fender, grinning at the boy; Murphy sat on the tailgate, faced away. He'd have spared Murphy seeing this, but he said better he were here.

It had to be taken care of. He passed a finger across the stubble beneath his lower lip, wiping the sweat.

"Boy."

"Yes, sir?" His voice sounded breathy, girlish.

"You know who I am?"

The boy's chest was pumping—skinny, looked like chicken-wire cage.

"Yes, sir," he said, pressing those lips together like he was trying to hide them. Big gangling hands . . . It made him sick to think about. A hot wave came over him again.

"I wouldn't be a man," Vic said, "if I looked the other way."

The boy kept his eyes cast to the ground. Doole had ambled around to the kid's flank, wheezing his gassy laugh, letting him know he was cut off.

"Would I?" The boy was going to have to pay attention, do his part in this.

He stood there, panting.

"Answer when you're spoken to. I wouldn't be any kind of a man, would I?"

The kid rolled his eye whites, imploring toward Murphy, who sat rigid on the gate of the truck, staring at the ground.

Vic stepped closer until the boy's mule face hung above him. He wished he'd brought a bridle and bit. "A man will do," he said, "the thing that is necessary to protect his family."

"Yes, sir." The boy cast him a wild glance to see if begging, sniveling would help. He wished she could see this, know what the boy was made of.

"Get on your hands and knees."

He cast one whimpering look toward Murphy's back, dropped to the ground, fingers wrapping around a clod of dirt.

"Look at the yellow bottoms of them feet," Doole said from the other side. "Murphy, looka here. Boy, you know the soles of your feet are almost white?"

"Enough, Doole. Don't say nothing more." Vic felt the sweat running off his forehead.

The kid was making snuffling noises, hunched like a possum. This was what had dared to touch her.

A hot rush of acid came up from his stomach. A running step forward, and he swung. His foot, dead weight at the end of his leg, came up under the boy's face, the impact wrenching at his joints. Withdrawing, he felt a lacing hook on his boot rip loose from where it had snagged in flesh. Blood was pouring.

He spit acid out onto the dirt. His head felt light; behind him, the boy howled like a dog. Couple more, and they could get out of here.

He took out a handkerchief, wiped his lips. "Don't think I like doing this," he said over his shoulder. The boy would still be able to work. He'd just be wearing a warning was all.

A thud behind. He spun around as Doole's boot came down. A squeak came out the boy's throat, and a whoosh of air. Murphy, a wail starting out of him, staggered forward. Doole stood over the boy, talking at him. He lay rolled over, eyes open, his body bucking. Looked like—Dear Jesus—Doole had kicked the side of his head in.

A shout rang out his own mouth, spreading over the field, piercing, until he thought he was hearing the mill whistle. He stepped across cornhills. "Doole, get away from there." He shouldn't have brought Doole. The boy writhing, brain broke open—

Murphy—he'd got to his feet off the gate of the truck—came weaving toward Doole. Doole threw a punch that smacked loud against Murphy's face. Murphy went down, lay still.

"He'll be all right," Doole said with a glance toward Murphy, sprawled, with his mouth lolled open. At the edge of the woods, the peepers had started up whirring. The boy's body lay in a furrow running with blood, staring straight up, fish-eyed. Vic had made sure himself not to get the eyes. . . .

I couldn't look at him any more. Holding to the door frame, I felt my mind drop down and down, a wild sound buzzing in my chest. It was him. I'd seen it clear in how he looked.

Here came his face, close, straining at me. "Now, baby—"

"Don't touch me."

I smelled him, sweat and cigarettes.

"You shush," he said.

I pushed him. He stumbled back.

His boots were brand-new. The light in the room rose brighter until it was coming from inside my head.

I grabbed at the drawer pull in reach of my hand. The drawer stuck, rattled.

"Stop that—you'll wake your mama."

The drawer slid open, blades and cooking forks banging against the end.

He stepped close behind me. "Estelle." His voice went tender; it shook. "You've got to be careful of yourself, baby, mind what you do and say. You don't want to break your mama's heart."

Lying on the steps of the *ghat,* I feel the dull edges of the concrete press into me, across my calves and at my hips. The next morning, Vic had taken his place at the kitchen table, set to eating his fried eggs that were hard at the edges, sopping the yellow with loaf bread. There was no glimmer that we had stood in the room the night before. If Mama was acting any different, handing me the plates to carry to the table, it was that she was sweeter than ever, like she was nursing Vic and me, both of us home, sick with a bug.

Twenty-seven years—Not once, waking or sleeping, have I let myself see it in my mind.

Now the whole horizon fills with the table in that kitchen: my eyes cast down on the dots and swirls of the Formica, the see-through saltshaker with dingy grains of rice. From the transistor on the counter, the announcer gives prices per bushel; trucks bang past out front on the road. The dishrag smell of the plastic tablecloth, the fry pan soaking in the sink—all of it snaking into my brain, coming and coming. Vic's voice: "You remember this morning to get more of these apricot preserves and, while you're at the store, some borax soap, Twenty Mule Team." It was two men from the sheriff's department who carried him out of the swamp, not even bothering to cover him. The son of one of them said at school his face was crushed beyond recognition.